9/28

Carpool
Diem

Carpool Diem

Nancy Star

NEW YORK   BOSTON

Copyright © 2008 by Nancy Star

All rights reserved. Except as permitted under the U.S. Copyright Act of 1976, no part of this publication may be reproduced, distributed, or transmitted in any form or by any means, or stored in a database or retrieval system, without the prior written permission of the publisher.

5 Spot
Hachette Book Group USA
237 Park Avenue
New York, NY 10017

Visit our Web site at www.5-spot.com.

5 Spot is an imprint of Grand Central Publishing. The 5 Spot name and logo is a trademark of Hachette Book Group USA, Inc.

Printed in the United States of America

First Edition: March 2008
10 9 8 7 6 5 4 3 2 1

Library of Congress Cataloging-in-Publication Data
Star, Nancy.
    Carpool diem / Nancy Star. — 1st ed.
       p. cm.
    Summary: "A tale of a professional mom who loses her job and finds herself caught up in the kiddie soccer craze"—Provided by the publisher.
    ISBN-13: 978-0-446-58182-0
    ISBN-10: 0-446-58182-8
  1. Working mothers—Fiction.   2. Unemployed—Fiction.
  3. Family—Fiction.   4. Soccer for children—Fiction.   I. Title.
    PS3569.T3355C37 2008
    813'.54—dc22   2007018769

for the home team:
larry,
elisabeth, and isabelle

one

By now, Annie had figured it out. With her laptop strap and large purse slung over opposite shoulders, two bags of take-out food dangling from her right wrist, and her small black roly bag held in place by her left foot, she could stay balanced enough to get her key into the lock and open the door with one hand.

It would have been easier if Hildy, the babysitter, would remember, even once, to unlock the door at seven forty-five, which was when Annie got home every Friday night. But she couldn't really blame Hildy. Hildy had a lot to do, plus it was probably not a good idea to leave the front door unlocked, even for a few minutes, even in a neighborhood like theirs, which felt safe.

"Charlotte?" Annie called out as she stepped into the house. "I'm home."

She parked her small suitcase in the hall, collapsed the handle, and brought the take-out bags to the kitchen.

"Hildy? Charlotte? I'm home," Annie called again.

She put the bags of food on the counter for Hildy to put

on platters and reclaimed her roly bag, which she lugged up to her bedroom.

Tim had been traveling this week too, and although he'd promised to be the first one home, when she quickly surveyed the room she saw no suitcase on the floor, no cell phone on the night table, no shoes at the bedside, and no body in the bed. His plane must have been delayed.

Annie stripped off her gray linen suit and slipped on a plain T-shirt and jeans that were beginning to feel snug. She unzipped her suitcase, took out her small bag of toiletries, put them in the bathroom cabinet, and dumped the rest of the wrinkled contents of her Monday-through-Friday life into the hamper. She was back downstairs in less than seven minutes. Her quick change from work clothes to home clothes was getting faster every week.

She peeked into the kitchen to say hello to Hildy, but Hildy still wasn't there. She called down to the basement for Charlotte, but Charlotte didn't answer either.

Maybe they were out in the back. It was, she noticed for the first time, a beautiful night.

She unpacked the food herself. Hildy deserved a break too. Like Annie, she'd had a jam-packed week. Day camp was starting soon, and Annie had delegated a long list of chores, including shopping for T-shirts, bathing suits, swim goggles, new towels, and bug spray.

There probably wouldn't actually be any bugs at the camp, which was located not in the woods but inside a small, air-conditioned school. Still, Annie liked Charlotte to be prepared, even for an unlikely swarm of mosquitoes, just in case.

Annie scooped all the books, mail, flyers, newspaper wrappers, rubber bands, pencils, magazine subscription inserts, a sock, three hair elastics, and a pile of what she hoped were unused tissues off the dining room table. She threw out the tissues, stuck the elastics in her pocket, tucked the sock in a nearby sneaker, and quickly alphabetized the paperwork for filing.

The distressed wood file cabinets she'd ordered online had turned out to be less attractive than she'd expected, but that was okay. She had lined them up against the dining room wall anyway, next to the box of hanging folders, which was under the box of labels she'd given Hildy along with detailed instructions for how to help Charlotte get organized by filing away her work every night.

The folders and labels were still in their shrink-wrapped casing. Hildy hadn't yet found time to explain the system to Charlotte, but Annie understood that. There weren't enough hours in the day for either of them to get everything done.

After the table was cleared, Annie gave it a quick blow to disperse the dust. Dusting was not one of Hildy's jobs.

She opened the drawer where the place mats were stored and was glad to see that today they were where they belonged. She pulled out four hard mats decorated with old photographs of cityscapes. But as she carried them to the table her right thumb hit a sticky spot on a San Francisco trolley car. A quick survey turned up another sticky patch at the base of the St. Louis Arch, as well as a thick splotch on the Liberty Bell.

Was it pancake syrup? Jam? Project glue? It didn't matter. She brought them to the kitchen, wiped them with a damp paper towel, and set them on the counter to dry.

The set of striped cloth place mats she picked next weren't completely clean either, but at least the stains weren't tacky.

She opened the back door and called out, "Hello?"

She put the place mats on the dining room table, covered the stains with the dinner plates and made a mental note to add stain removal to Hildy's next To Do list.

"Dinner's here," she called as she dealt out napkins, forks, knives (did they need spoons? Yes), and spoons. She filled the water glasses and then went to the foot of the stairs.

"Charlotte?" she called. "Anybody home?"

Charlotte pounded down the stairs. She was twelve, tall for her age, and string-bean lean, but she walked like a giant, heavy footed no matter the mood or time of day.

She gave her mother a perfunctory hug. "I must have fallen asleep while I was doing my homework."

"Did you get a chance to read that article I emailed you about how important it is to get a good night's sleep?" Annie asked.

"I only read the first ten reasons," Charlotte admitted. "But thanks for sending it. Did you see Dad? He's in here." She led her mother to the living room.

Annie didn't know how she had missed the suitcase on the floor, the shoes next to the suitcase, the newspaper next to the shoes, a trail leading to the prone body on the sofa. Tim lay with his phone in his hand, his eyes closed, his iPod plugged into his ears. His mouth was slightly open, and he was snoring. She touched him gently. He jumped.

"Was I sleeping?" Tim gave Annie, and then Charlotte, a hug. "I didn't mean to be sleeping."

"I have an article about why it's important to get a good night's sleep," Charlotte said. "Do you want me to get it?"

"Nope," Tim said. "I want you to stay right here and tell me, how was my favorite twelve-year-old's day?"

"Good," Charlotte said.

"Just good?" Tim asked.

Charlotte knew her father's routine. "Super good."

"If everybody's super good," Annie said, "why don't we sit down and have a nice dinner?"

Annie had come up with the idea of a Friday night family feast sometime during her third month of working all week in her client's Connecticut office. It was only one of several strategies for helping the family cope with a situation none of them liked.

It wasn't exactly going as she imagined it. Tim had missed the last three dinners because of out-of-town business trips with delayed return flights. Still, Annie persisted, stopping each week on her way home from work, searching for the perfect food to make everyone feel better.

"Where's Hildy?" Annie asked.

"Hildy?" the three of them called together, another routine.

Hildy raced down from the third floor. "I didn't know you were all home. I was upstairs folding laundry. When did you get in?"

For a second, Annie thought of reminding Hildy that she came home at the exact same time every Friday night. If traffic was light, she'd stop and take care of some errands on the way to get a head start on Saturday. Either way, she was always on time.

And shouldn't Hildy have known Tim was home? Wasn't she supposed to be paying attention to who was going in and out of the house?

She let it go. Hildy was busy folding laundry. How could Annie complain?

"I just got in," Annie said. "Did the flowers come?"

That was another detail Annie organized to make the weekend feel festive. She ordered flowers—even had them delivered so Hildy wouldn't have one more thing to do.

Hildy looked around, blank faced. "I don't know."

Annie went to the kitchen and opened the side door. "There they are." She brought in a large bouquet of yellow tulips and purple irises wrapped in clear plastic. "The greens are just a little wilted," she said. "Nothing some cool water and a crumbled aspirin can't cure."

Tim, Charlotte, and Hildy sat down at the table. Annie took care of the flowers. Everyone was chatting happily, so she let them be as she hurried back and forth from the kitchen to the dining room, bringing in the food. Finally, she sat down. "There. Done." She glanced at her watch. Not bad. "Dig in," she said. "Fried chicken," she added proudly. That was Charlotte's favorite.

But Charlotte didn't look very happy. Could someone's favorite food change in a week?

"Today was Family Food Day at school," Hildy explained. "Layla's mother brought in fried chicken for everyone at lunch."

"What's Family Food Day?" Annie asked.

"It's where you bring in food from your culture to share," Charlotte explained. "We did it for the unit on Ellis Island."

"Was there a flyer?" Annie didn't remember seeing one. "I would have made something."

"Don't worry," Hildy said. "I took care of it."

"She made pork butt," Charlotte told her parents, and then covered her mouth to contain her giggling.

"I thought that might go over big with sixth graders," Hildy said.

"It did," Charlotte said.

"The teacher didn't look pleased," Hildy admitted.

"She wasn't," Charlotte confirmed.

"I wish I'd known about Family Food Day," Annie said.

Everyone quieted. Tim got up and went into the kitchen. He returned with a glass of amber liquid, which he immediately downed.

"I'm really not that hungry," Charlotte said.

"You did eat a big lunch," Hildy reminded her.

"That's fine." Annie tried not to look disappointed. "You don't have to eat if you're not hungry."

Charlotte turned to Hildy. "When you're finished, do you want to kick around a ball with me?"

"I'm done," Hildy said. "Sorry," she said to Annie. "I guess I ate too much pork butt at Family Food Day too."

Charlotte laughed and then stopped herself. "May we be excused to go outside and kick around a ball?"

This was supposed to be their special dinner. Annie had planned it that way.

"Sure," Tim said. "Go ahead."

"I can only play for a few minutes," Hildy told Charlotte as she followed her.

The back door opened, and slammed shut.

"I don't know if I can do this anymore," Annie said, once they were alone.

"How long until Proxo's period of transition is over?" Tim asked.

"Three more months," Annie said.

"We can make it," Tim said. "Three months is only ninety days away."

"There it goes," Annie said. She pointed to her eye. "See?"

Tim peered at her.

"Look at my left eye," Annie said. "Can't you see? It's twitching right now. I can feel it."

Tim shifted his body closer and studied Annie's eye, not for the first time.

"I can't see anything," he said. "I'm sorry."

Annie's eye had been twitching for months, and almost as annoying as the twitch itself was that no one else could ever see it. She blinked hard. Sometimes that made it stop. It worked.

She took a deep breath. "Okay. I can do it. Three months isn't forever."

"We just have to take one day at a time," Tim said. "Come on. Why don't we go outside and watch Charlotte kick around a ball?"

"Since when does Charlotte kick balls anyway?" Annie asked as she got up and started scraping, stacking, and clearing the dishes.

"Leave it," Tim said. "I'll take care of it later."

Annie didn't like to leave things for later, but Tim took her by the hand and pulled her along with him.

Outside, the light was dim. They couldn't see much—just the vague outline of Hildy crouched at the far end of the yard and a moving shadow they knew was Charlotte.

Charlotte's foot connected with the ball with a loud boom.

"Great one," Hildy called. "Try it with your other foot."

Another boom. The ball thundered across the yard.

Hildy caught the ball and walked over to Tim and Annie.

"I told my brothers she has a perfect kick with both feet but they don't believe me," she said. "You want to take over?" She tossed Annie the ball. "I have to go to class."

Annie fumbled the catch. The ball dropped to the ground and rolled away, into the dark. Annie crouched down, trying to feel where it had landed.

"That's okay," Charlotte said. "I don't feel like playing anymore."

Hildy gave Charlotte a quick hug and went in to collect her things.

The Fleming family stood, awkward in their own backyard.

"I have an idea," Annie said. "What about a board game?"

"I have homework," Charlotte said. She disappeared into the house.

"Homework on a Friday night?" Annie asked Tim.

He shrugged. "Come on. I'll play with you."

Fifteen minutes later the Scrabble board was set up on the kitchen table. Annie had organized her letters according to points. Tim took a more haphazard approach, putting each one on the wooden bench in the order in which it had been picked.

When Charlotte came down to the kitchen to get dessert she found her parents sitting perfectly still before a blank Scrabble board.

She ran back upstairs and got the article—"Thirty-Seven Reasons Why a Good Night's Sleep Is Important"—and put it on top of the blank board so her parents could read it when they woke up.

two

POWER POINTERS—*June 15th!!!*
News of the Day

Attention all members of this year's legend-worthy team, The Power: Once again the time has come to tackle this year's Travel Team Tryouts!

As we all know, being a member of the Power is an honor. But honors do not come with guarantees!! All girls fortunate enough to have played with me this year must now ask themselves: Am I good enough to earn my spot again? Am I really?

Tryout Day Reminder: True competitors treat tryout days as if they were game days. To that end, there should be no late-night doughnuts, no sleepover get-togethers, and no cell phone calls, texting, or computer chatting after dark. Watching videos of soccer games is, of course, permitted, provided it does not interfere with going to bed at a reasonable, by which I mean early, hour.

Remember: A good performance on the field comes from one thing and one thing only: good training and hard work.

Special Notice for Talented Play at our last Tryout-Practice Skills Session goes to Shelby. Shelby's shot on goal in the third second of scrimmage was stunning! Parker told me even he could not have stopped that ball!

I assume Parker was joking! If not, Parker is fired and Shelby, you are my new head trainer!

Second Special Notice for Talented Play goes to Dinah. It is difficult to be aggressive when scrimmaging against one's own teammates. It is harder still when an injury to a teammate is the result. Bravo, Dinah, that this fear did not stop you!!! As for Heather King, we are so happy to hear that your nose is healing nicely! Please accept our wishes for a full and speedy recovery!!

Aggressive Play Reminder: I know young athletes tend to think that when a ref shows them a yellow card it is a warning to be feared. I urge you instead to view the yellow card as a form of tribute to aggressive play! The next time a ref shows you a yellow card, accept it as the compliment it really is!!!

Good News Department: Our valiant goalkeeper, Bobbi, has told me that the intermittent pain in her left knee will not stop her from playing in our final tournament!!! This is exactly the kind of commitment that has allowed our team to reach its current elite level of competition!!

Reminder: All players' families must call me immediately regarding attendance at the upcoming Binghamton Father's Day tourney. This is the last tournament open to all of this year's Power players! All subsequent tournaments, including the July Fourth tournament in Virginia (bring plenty of sunscreen as the Closing Ceremony is also a Beach Barbecue!), will be open to next year's Power players only!!!

Remember: Though tournaments are entirely optional, as stated in the Mountain Ridge Soccer Board handbook, I view them as a vital way to glue our team spirit together. I encourage any player who must miss a tournament to speak to me immediately regarding less demanding alternatives to the Power!

Notification of next year's team selection will begin on the 25th of June. Players who are moved down to the B team, the Asteroids, will receive a call from the B coach, Gerri Picker. But do not despair! A is only one letter away from B! Any player who is moved down from our Elite team to the B team will have the opportunity, over the next season, to work hard and climb back up if she so desires!!!

Good Luck to One and All from Winslow West!!!

three

Annie was well prepared. She was a change specialist, after all. She was an expert at spinning events so
that even unexpected, unwelcome changes could be
perceived as good. She knew how to organize information
on the spot, how to modulate tone to keep listeners engaged,
how to make eye contact to seduce the willing, and how to
use body language to soften the opposed. For the earnest,
she relied on an impressive reserve of numbers and facts.

For this morning's hastily convened meeting, she'd managed to get all the necessary players to attend, and promised
them she'd have them in and out in less than twenty minutes.
But the meeting was running long. And it wasn't going well.

She concentrated on Bingham Biblow. It was Biblow who
had hired her, mentored her, and given her the Proxo engagement in the first place. He was also the one who kept promising the infuriatingly elusive carrot of partnership.

Biblow was listening, which was good, but he was also
avoiding her eyes, which was bad. He swiveled restlessly, back
and forth, back and forth, in his sleek leather chair. Annie
shifted eye contact to Crawford.

Crawford, the CEO of PC&B, had never been her champion, but he was known to be fair. Except Crawford was avoiding eye contact now too, staring instead into his lap.

Annie could tell from the position of his head that he was scrolling through his email on his BlackBerry, the twitch of his shoulders giving away each time he typed a reply.

That left her two choices for eye contact: Roxanne Lacombe, the firm's youngest and most ambitious partner, and Paul Pederson, the company founder.

Pederson's presence at the meeting was particularly worrisome. The spindly founder spent most of his workdays at the golf course now, trying to improve his stroke and handicap before he had one and got one. She hadn't invited him to the meeting, and while she knew his unexpected attendance meant something, she hadn't yet figured out what.

She pushed on. "I assure you I will stay with Proxo as long as necessary. And I will actively help you search for a replacement for that engagement before I move on to another. But I have to move on to another."

Biblow stopped swaying. He looked up and reshaped his doughy face into an approximation of concern. "You sound very upset. Would you like some water?"

Before Annie could say no, he cut her off.

"Phyllis," he called out to his antique secretary. "We need more water here."

Crawford looked up from his BlackBerry and shook his head as if to clear his brain. "Annie, the word on you has always been that you're a team player. But I have to ask—is the word wrong?"

Roxanne leaned forward in her chair and spoke in a voice

just above a whisper. "Remind us again why you don't see your Proxo engagement as the opportunity it is."

Annie took a deep breath. She was surprised to hear it come out loud and shaky.

Pederson, sitting next to her, heard it too and recoiled in his chair. He turned to Roxanne. "Is she going to cry?"

Roxanne patted Pederson's veiny hand. "No. Annie's too smart to cry. Aren't you, Annie?"

She was. Annie willed herself to reabsorb any liquid in her eyes that might be mistaken for tears.

Phyllis, Biblow's secretary, sped into the room, set a second pitcher on the table, and quickly left. The ice cubes collided, ringing like tiny bells.

"Can someone get those damn cubes to stop," Biblow snapped.

Roxanne got up and started refilling everyone's water glass.

Annie covered her glass with her hand. "No, thank you," she said, to regain control.

Roxanne sat back down. "Face it. Proxo loves you. And like all lovers, they want more of you. How is that a bad thing?"

"I love the Proxo people too," Annie said firmly.

"We don't think you do," Biblow said. "Because love means commitment. And it sounds to us like you're waffling in the commitment department."

Annie straightened her navy skirt and pulled at the sleeves of her crisp white shirt. That was her uniform, navy or gray suit and white shirt. Limiting the colors in her closet allowed her to cut a full minute from getting ready for the day. It was the same reason she kept her wheat-colored hair cut short. It dried quickly and on its own—more time saved. Everyone knew this about her. Annie was an expert at compressing, compartmentalizing, and commitment. What exactly was going on here?

"Proxo is in its transitional stage," Roxanne said. "You, of all people, know transitions don't last forever."

"They're short-term," Pederson added, in case Annie didn't get it.

Annie stuck to her script. "That's true. But as I've already explained, this morning Proxo asked me to extend my current level of engagement for the next three years."

"Proxo actually said they want you to commit to living in Connecticut five days a week for three more years?" Roxanne asked.

Annie nodded, feeling—finally—understood.

"Wow," Roxanne said. "That is an exquisitely beautiful number of billable hours."

"It's not reasonable," Annie said.

"We are prepared to put together a very attractive relocation package for you," Biblow said. "We understand you have a situation."

"I don't have a situation," Annie said. "I have a family."

"We all have families," Crawford reminded her.

Annie did not think the lives of Crawford, Biblow, or Pederson's country club wives or poised, hard-drinking children had much in common with her family life. As for Roxanne, Annie had heard she had cats. Annie had also heard that after the cats died, Roxanne liked them even more.

"With all due respect," Annie said, "we can't move from New Jersey. My husband's business is based in New Jersey." Tim's work troubles flashed into her brain. Things at Hot Holidays were not going well. But this was not the time to think about it. She pushed Tim and his brother's travel business out of her head. "And my daughter, Charlotte, is almost halfway through middle school. It would be a terrible time to uproot her."

"Let's try to stay on point, shall we?" Roxanne asked.

Annie did a quick analysis. They might try manipulation and intimidation, but they weren't really going to risk losing her. For one thing, whom could they find who would work harder than she did?

"Here's the point," Annie said. "I can't live in Connecticut for three more years. So I need a new engagement. I'm sure we can all agree that it would be best for Proxo if we made the change quickly, by the end of the summer."

"Or?" Roxanne asked.

"Pardon?" Annie replied.

"Are you giving us an ultimatum?" Crawford asked.

"No," Annie said.

"Good," Biblow said. "Because Proxo is a very big client. It's like Roxanne said. They love you to death. We love them to death. You get where I'm going?"

What Annie got was that she was feeling absolutely no love in this room.

"Let me make this perfectly clear," Biblow said. "Resigning from the Proxo engagement means resigning from the firm. Is that what you want?"

Often, when Annie was ragged from overwork, or sick of sleeping on a bad hotel bed, or worried that Charlotte might have grown so much in a day that Annie wouldn't recognize her anymore, she let herself wonder what it would be like if she were independently wealthy, or had won the lottery, or if Tim earned enough money for her to afford to quit. But she wasn't, and hadn't, and Tim didn't, so there was no point in indulging those thoughts.

"All I'm saying is that I cannot move to Connecticut for three more years." Annie kept her voice steady and calm. "But I am completely confident we can find a mutually agreeable solution."

"I'm sorry it has to end this way," said Biblow. He stretched out his hand, and then, thinking better of it, let it rest on the table. The light reflected off his manicured fingernails. "On behalf of the entire PC&B family, we wish you a world of luck. God bless."

Biblow got up and left. Crawford and then Pederson followed.

Roxanne went to the phone at the back of the room and made a quick call.

"Human Resources wants me to escort you down," Roxanne said, after she hung up. It was clear this was not an offer.

Annie and Roxanne walked together down the long hall. At the end of the hall the HR manager waited. He led Annie into his office and showed her where to sit. Annie struggled to process what was happening.

The HR Manager took charge. "You have resigned," he said in a slow clear voice. He slid a thick exit manual across the desk.

"I did not resign," Annie said. She stood up. "Is that what you think? Is that what they think? Because I thought I was fired. If they think I resigned we can clear this up right now."

"Why don't you sit down," the HR manager said. "Please."

"Okay." Annie sat down. "I didn't resign," she said again.

"Right. Let me ask you this. Did you refuse to continue to work on the Proxo engagement?"

"I didn't use the word *refuse*," Annie said. "What I did was explain that I cannot move my family right now. So I have to move off of Proxo to another account."

The HR manager leaned closer. "Annie. Face it. Refusing to work for Proxo means you've resigned."

"It does?"

He nodded and pushed the exit manual closer to her. "I need you to read through this," he said, tapping the thick book. "But take your time."

Annie opened the manual and skimmed over the words, but she couldn't take anything in. She turned the pages and closed the book, retaining nothing.

The HR manager showed her where to sign, in four places. Then he escorted her to her office and stood, watching, as she packed up her things.

By the time she got to the elevator, a crowd had formed.

"Is it true?" Phyllis asked. Her face was flushed. Her eyes looked red.

Annie's best friend, Linda, pulled her aside and spoke quietly into Annie's ear. "Just so you know, you walked into a setup. Biblow's been waiting to do this for a while."

"No he hasn't," Annie said. "Biblow likes me."

"Biblow used to like you," Linda whispered, "until you sent that email to HR about Blaine Glass. Remember that email?"

"The one where I recommended Blaine for a diversity workshop?"

Linda nodded.

"Blaine Glass needs help," Annie said. "He offended half the staff on his first day here. Everyone knows that."

"No one would disagree with you," Linda said. "Even Biblow wouldn't disagree with you. However, Biblow's sister is another story."

It clicked. "Blaine Glass is Bingham Biblow's nephew?" Annie asked.

Linda nodded. "Don't worry. He won't last a week in your job."

"Blaine Glass is getting my job?"

"He offered to move to Connecticut permanently," Linda said.

Annie struggled to keep up. How had she misread this so badly?

But she knew how. She'd been stretched too thin. She'd worked too hard. Proxo had sucked the brain cells out of her head.

"They're going to beg you to come back," Linda said. "You'll see."

The elevator doors opened.

"They can't do this to you," the mailroom guy yelled out.

"Why does it always happen to the nice people?" Phyllis wanted to know. "Annie is the only one here who remembers to ask about my grandchildren."

Annie stepped into the elevator.

"Have fun at home," a voice called out.

She turned toward the voice. Blaine Glass leaned against the wall, slowly waving good-bye. The elevator doors closed. Annie rode down to the lobby, numb.

She didn't remember walking to the train, but somehow she got there. She put her box of personal possessions—photographs of Charlotte and Tim—on her lap and held them close, as if they needed to be protected. She looked around.

It was the first time she'd ever taken a morning train home. Who were these people? she wondered. What did they do? What would she do?

For the first time in nearly twenty years, Annie was unemployed and without a plan. She shook off a chill of fear and turned her focus to her future.

four

Winslow West looked up at the crayon blue sky and cursed the perfect picnic temperature of seventy degrees.

It was something few would imagine, how much he hoped for rain on tryout days. When it rained, the halfhearted players stayed home, where they belonged, complaining of stomachaches or sore throats or chills. But on a day like this, dry, clear, with a dazzling sun and that damn blue sky, every child with at least one leg would be dropped off and commanded to play.

Last year, on an equally brilliant day, so many players turned up for tryouts he'd had to form six new teams. One week later, when it rained during practice, all six teams fell apart. And he was the only one who wasn't at all surprised.

His eyes flicked to the woman at the perimeter of the field who was yelling something he couldn't hear at a child he didn't know.

"Who, may I ask, in God's name," Winslow said, "is that?"

Vicki, his wife, followed his gaze.

She shook her head. "What else can we do? We put it in

the flyer. We underlined it. We capitalized it. We bolded it. It says, 'Parents Are Not Permitted to Watch.' What more can we do? I mean, really? What more can we possibly do?"

Vicki, tall and commanding, marched across the field to set things right. Her long red hair flashed like a fiery warning in the sun.

Winslow watched from his post atop the hill. He liked to stand on grassy hills, mounds of dirt, and rock piles, even though his rail-thin, broad-shouldered frame topped well over six feet on flat ground. With his long, straight, enviably thick, jet black hair blowing back in the wind, and beetle brown eyes that he knew how to use as weapons, he could intimidate from a ditch. Still, given a choice, he preferred to tower.

His head trainer, Parker Stone, showed off his bulging biceps as he gave five quick blows on his whistle.

Thirty eleven-year-old girls raced off the field. Thirty twelve-year-olds raced on.

Vicki jogged back, red faced and hot.

"Who are they?" Winslow asked, his eyes carefully scanning the players.

"The mom is Annie Fleming," Vicki reported. "The twelve-year-old is Charlotte."

"Twelve-year-old? Why don't I know her?" Winslow was in charge of all Travel Soccer in Mountain Ridge, but the team he cared about, the one he coached as if his life depended on its success, was a team of talented twelve-year-old girls.

"She's a town-soccer kid," Vicki said. "It's her first time trying out for a travel team."

"Oh." And like that, Winslow's interest disappeared. There was no hope for a town league player that old.

He watched as the fifteen girls who made up his team hustled onto the field in perfect triangular formation, assuming their regular positions. Parker organized the others, four players whom Winslow had enticed to try out from travel teams in other towns, and ten pathetic hopefuls from the B-rated Asteroids. As for Town League Girl, Winslow's eyes had already edited her out. To him, she wasn't even there.

Parker blew his whistle to signal the start. Immediately, a blur of a player raced across the field, the ball connecting to the toe of her cleat as if it were magnetic.

"Shelby is looking very good today," Winslow said.

"That's because her mother upped her allowance to twenty bucks a goal," Vicki reported.

"Marilyn is awful, isn't she?" Winslow said, and smiled. "Do you think I should talk to her about funding my next Soccer-Plex?"

His first Soccer-Plex was being built on the outskirts of town, on land that had been a farm when Winslow was a boy growing up in Mountain Ridge. The grand opening was only a couple of months away. But already he was feeling the itch for more. One wasn't enough. One wasn't enough at all.

Evelyn, the girl he'd been courting from Tyler Park, sent the ball to the far end of the field.

"Look at that kick," Winslow said. "I've got to get her on this team."

Evelyn took his breath away, and it wasn't just because of her perfect-aim foot. Her eyes got him, too. She had the burning eyes of a competitor. The best ones always did.

"I've got the father on board," he said. "But I'm worried about that mother."

"Carpool," Vicki said. "That's all you have to do. They live an hour away and the mother does not want to drive two hours, back and forth, five days a week, to take her daughter to practice."

"Are you offering to pick her up?"

Vicki laughed off that idea. She scanned the field. "See the girl with the tie-dyed headband? She's Evelyn's neighbor. If you put that girl on the team, Evelyn's yours."

Winslow smiled. He knew there was a reason he'd married Vicki. He hadn't even considered the slow girl with the tie-dyed thing on her head.

He studied his list, looking for someone to cut so Evelyn's friend could join the team. His pen stopped at Heather King's name.

"No," Vicki said when she saw where his eyes had landed. "You can't cut the cop's kid. Brian King is why we don't get tickets when we park on the field."

The maddeningly gentle breeze tickled the back of Winslow's neck. "You forget. Heather has a younger brother. As long as Officer King has a young son's athletic career to think about, we're fine."

A ball rocketed past them, inches from the sideline.

"Hello," Winslow said. "Who was that?"

"Charlotte Fleming," Vicki said. "The town league girl."

A second later, with Evelyn bearing down toward her, Charlotte wavered, and backed away.

"Why is that mother still there?" Vicki asked.

Winslow glanced across the field at Town League Girl's mother. Her body language told him the whole story. Arms tightly crossed, face stiff and grim. Nothing but trouble there.

It didn't concern him. He marked a tiny B next to Charlotte Fleming's name and reviewed the list, scanning for weakness. Dinah? No. His daughter was not a possibility.

Vicki watched as Charlotte took back the ball and booted it. "I don't know, Winslow. You might want to take another look at that girl. She's got a really strong left foot."

But Winslow didn't respond. He was thinking about Bobbi, the goalkeeper, and how she got injured in almost every game.

He walked over to Parker. They huddled close for several moments before Parker stepped away and went off to make the necessary changes.

That night, Vicki sat on Dinah's bed brushing her fine red hair and reassuring her that yes, she'd been great at tryouts and no, her father would never cut her from the team.

Winslow sat in his study, eyes closed, planning.

He had to find some free time so he could get some books written. A series would be ideal, with a set of DVDs to follow. There would be speaking engagements, of course, and newspaper articles. But what he really needed was to do the talk show circuit. That was how to make things happen. He could really expand the program if he could get on a few talk shows.

He pictured himself sitting across from Larry King, leaning back in his chair and smiling before answering the question that would be on every interviewer's mind. Because in the end, they all would want to know the same thing: How had he done it? How had he taken a team of inexperienced six-year-old girls and trained them so well that every single one of them went on to medal in the Olympics?

He opened his eyes and stared at the roster, wishing it told a different story. It was even worse than he'd remembered. He'd have to drop at least four of last season's weak links if he wanted a winning team.

He closed his eyes and dreamed of glory.

five

I saw you get the evil eye from Vicki today," the woman said to Annie in the grocery store parking lot. "Are you okay?"

Annie didn't want to admit she had no idea who Vicki was, that she hadn't noticed anyone giving her the evil eye, and other than feeling a little weird that a total stranger was talking to her as if they were next-door neighbors, she was fine.

"You don't know who I am, do you?" the woman said.

Annie smiled and studied the woman's face, hoping for a bolt of recognition. She got nothing. Was she a former Proxo person? There had been so many people coming and going at Proxo, it was hard to keep track of them all.

The woman laughed at her confused look. "I'm Bonnie Gelb," she said. "Your next-door neighbor."

"Oh." Annie said. "Of course. I knew you looked familiar. You're the new people who moved next door."

"Two years ago," Bonnie said. "We'll be in the house two years next month. Can you believe we haven't met? Honestly, I was beginning to wonder if you even existed."

"Well, I do," said Annie. "I most certainly do exist."

"I know Tim, of course," Bonnie went on. "And Charlotte. I love Charlotte. Hi, Charlotte!" She waved.

Charlotte, who was leaning against the car, annoyed at having to make an unscheduled grocery store stop, brightened long enough to say hello to Mrs. Gelb, and then withdrew back into her mood.

"It's tough trying out for travel soccer for the first time at her age," Bonnie confided.

"She's only twelve," Annie said.

"Hildy told me she's very talented at soccer. I love Hildy," Bonnie added. "All the moms on the block love Hildy." She leaned closer so Charlotte wouldn't hear the next.

"Look, I'm sure Winslow won't hold it against you that you stayed to watch at her first tryouts. But if Charlotte comes back tomorrow for second tryouts, you might want to just drop her off and go." Bonnie waved at Charlotte. "Good luck, honey," she called as she got in her car and drove off.

"See?" Annie told Charlotte. "Even going to the grocery store I learned something. I didn't know there were two days of tryouts. Isn't that great? If you didn't play your best today, you get another chance tomorrow."

"I'm not trying out again," Charlotte said.

"Is it because I stayed?" Annie asked. "Because I can call and apologize. I don't mind. It's not a problem. I find dealing with things straight-on is always the best approach."

"It won't make a difference," Charlotte said as they got into the car. "The girls on the A team are better than me. The team isn't even considered an A team anymore. It's a Super A team. I think it's even higher than a Super A. If I get on a team at all, it will be a B team. And that's fine. B is where I belong."

Annie struggled to keep up with the flow of information. The A team was really a Super A or higher. What did that mean? What did Charlotte mean about belonging on B? Did they give letter grades for tryouts?

"You might have gotten an A," Annie said, to be encouraging.

Charlotte shook her head in dismay.

"I did notice that a lot of the girls were wearing the same striped socks," Annie added. "Do you think you got points off for not having the right socks?" She should have networked it. But who was she kidding? She didn't even recognize her next-door neighbor, let alone have a network.

She could have asked her sister-in-law, Trissy. Trissy lived on the other side of town, with Tim's brother, Hank, in a perfect, big house with four perfect, big boys. Some of them used to play soccer. Trissy definitely would have known what to wear.

Except she hated asking Trissy for advice. Trissy was so perfect that some days her very presence made Annie feel like a failure. And now that Tim had joined Hank's company, Annie felt even more awkward. Trissy didn't technically work at Hot Holidays, but Annie suspected nothing happened at the office that Trissy didn't know about first.

No. Going to Trissy for advice was best left to emergency-only situations.

But maybe this was an emergency.

"I should have asked Aunt Trissy where to get those socks," Annie muttered out loud as she pulled into the driveway. They got out of the car and Annie unlocked the front door.

"If I find a pair of those socks for you tonight, would you wear them to tryouts tomorrow?"

"I'm not trying out tomorrow," Charlotte said. "I'm done trying out. And you can't buy those socks. The girls got them because they're on a select team."

"Is there a store for select clothes nearby?"

"You don't know anything," Charlotte grumbled.

Annie couldn't argue with that. She followed her daughter inside. "I should have researched it. I know how these things go. You never want to wear a pink suit to a navy meeting. I wish I'd known about those socks."

"I'm not going to make that team," Charlotte said.

"Charlotte," Annie said. "What happened to your can-do attitude? Did you leave it in the car?"

"That's not funny," Charlotte said, her face grim. She turned and started up the stairs.

"You forgot to take off your cleats," Annie called after her.

But Charlotte was stomping too loud to hear. Annie watched as clumps of dirt were released deep into the cream-colored carpet.

Stomp, stomp. Two steps covered. Stomp, stomp. Four steps covered.

They'd lived in this house for eight years and Annie had never once thought about the carpet color. Whose idea had it been to put in cream-colored carpet? Was it Tim's? Had it been there when they moved in? Why didn't she know?

And when had the house gotten so dingy? It felt like only yesterday that they'd painted the walls eggshell white. When did the walls turn gray? When did that paint start peeling at the molding? When did the ceiling get that network of cracks that was spreading like mold? Why were there dead bugs in the bottom of the light fixtures and cobwebs dangling from the bulbs?

And why was Charlotte continuing her slow stomp up the stairs, leaving behind a climbing trail of dense black dirt dislodged from her cleats? Was she doing it on purpose?

"Why are you walking like that?" Annie yelled and immediately regretted it. It was her first full day home. She didn't want to have a fight on her first day home.

Charlotte stopped. Her soccer uniform was pasted to her back. Her braids were unraveling; tiny bits of Heidi hair were sticking out in all directions. She slowly lifted up her right shoe, then her left shoe, examining the bottoms.

She turned around and said, "They're clean," which was now true. Then she stomped off to her room and slammed the door.

It's okay, Annie told herself. The carpet could be cleaned. The walls could be painted. Striped socks could be bought. She'd get to know Bonnie next door. She'd find a new job. She'd improve her relationship with Charlotte. She'd always done that in making her lists—saved the hardest, the most important, for last.

"Charlotte?" she called up the empty stairs. "Are you hungry? Do you want a snack?"

She got nothing. Annie was at a loss. What was she supposed to do? What was the routine? What did Hildy do? Why wasn't Hildy here?

The phone rang. It was Tim.

"Hey," he said, and she knew by his voice that he wasn't having a very good day either.

"Did Charlotte make the team?" he asked.

"She says she didn't make the good team," Annie told him. "She's very negative. Have you noticed that?"

"Give her a chance," Tim said. "Give yourself a chance. Maybe it's just a gloomy day."

"Is it gloomy where you are? Because it's a beautiful day here," Annie said.

"It's not the end of the world if she doesn't play on the best team."

Annie felt herself stiffen. That didn't sound like Tim.

"Don't you think we should be encouraging Charlotte to be the best she can be?" Annie asked. "And doesn't that mean playing on the best team she can be on? Don't you want the best for Charlotte? Because you used to."

"That's not fair," Tim said. "Of course I do. Look, we're just overwhelmed. That's all."

"What are we overwhelmed about?" Annie asked. "I'm not overwhelmed. I've already written my Plan for the Day for tomorrow and for the day after that. I've put in calls to three headhunters. I've got a long list of former clients I'm going to contact for consulting work, and Linda called me with a great lead. Do I sound overwhelmed?"

"Yes," Tim said.

Annie sat on the steps. "I don't want to be overwhelmed."

"I know," Tim said.

"I'm not an overwhelmed-type person," Annie said.

"I know," Tim agreed.

"Neither are you," she added. "Which is why we've been able to make everything work for all this time. We don't get overwhelmed."

"Maybe everyone gets a little overwhelmed now and then," Tim said.

"We don't," Annie insisted. "We push on. That's what we do. No looking back for us. We work hard, and if that doesn't do it, we work harder. It's who we are."

"I don't know," Tim said.

Annie sat up straighter. Tim always knew. Tim was clear, steady, sure.

"Tim," she said gingerly, because she was about to ask a question to which she really didn't want the answer. "Are you all right?"

The pause that followed told her everything.

"Of course," he said, too late. "I'm fine."

It was unconvincing and would have broken her heart, if she hadn't got distracted by the twitch in her right eye.

"Damn," she said. "It's both eyes now."

"What?" Tim asked.

"The twitch. It's happening in both my eyes. I know," she added. "You can't see anything."

They laughed, and, eager to take advantage of the chance to end on a positive note, they got off the phone.

six

Hildy walked in the house only moments after Annie found the pile of To Do lists on the bottom shelf of the dining room corner cabinet. There were twenty in all, dated, and in sealed envelopes. Annie knew they were To Do lists because she had written them. It was part of her Sunday routine.

The lists included errands, appointments, information about upcoming family events, and suggestions for fun activities. Each one ended with a compliment. She agonized over those, careful to construct her sentences so they sounded heartfelt and sincere.

She typed each list in draft form first, then read it aloud to make sure she liked the way it sounded. The tone needed to be right. After all, she saw Hildy as a partner in her life and felt it was important to do everything she could think of to be sure Hildy felt appreciated.

"If you weren't going to read them, why did you bother to save them?" Annie said, confronting Hildy. "Why didn't you just throw them away?"

Hildy got defensive. "How do you know I didn't read them?"

"They're sealed," Annie said. She tossed them on the dining room table where they scattered softly. "See for yourself. They've never been opened."

"Maybe the moisture in the house made them reseal," Hildy suggested. "It could happen, right? Excuse me, but I have to make dinner for Charlotte."

Annie followed Hildy into the kitchen.

"Did I offend you with one of the lists?" Annie asked. "Were they too long? If you have a problem with them, you can talk to me. Whatever the problem is, it's important that we talk."

Hildy grabbed a pot, filled it with water, and placed it on the stove.

"Look, I'm sorry," Annie said, because no good would come of their fighting.

"That's okay," Hildy said, softening. She pulled out a box of macaroni and cheese from the pantry, ripped off the top and dumped the elbows in the water.

"The water's not boiling yet," Annie pointed out.

"This is how I always make it," Hildy said. "Charlotte doesn't complain, so it must be okay." She walked to the hallway and called up the stairs.

"Charlotte! Our favorite show is on."

Charlotte blasted out of her room and ran down to the kitchen. She hopped onto a stool at the counter, picked up the remote control, and clicked on the TV.

"You guys," Annie said, keeping her tone friendly. "Did you forget it's Wednesday?"

"No," Hildy said.

"Is there something special on today?" Charlotte asked.

"I was talking about the rule," Annie said. "No TV during the week. Wednesday is definitely during the week, right? Or am I crazy?"

"I think maybe crazy," Hildy said.

Charlotte laughed.

"Can I speak with you for a moment in the other room?" Annie said. She did not want to have this conversation in front of Charlotte.

"Okay." Hildy followed her to the front hall.

"First of all, please don't call me crazy in front of Charlotte."

"You asked me," Hildy said. "I just agreed."

Annie decided not to argue the point. "Second of all, I know we've spoken about the TV rule. I'm not that crazy."

"We did," Hildy said. "I remember. It was right before Charlotte started kindergarten. Charlotte's going into seventh grade soon. You didn't mean she shouldn't watch TV all the way to seventh grade, did you? Because that wouldn't be normal."

"When did it become abnormal to have a rule of no TV during the week?" Annie asked. "Lots of families have that rule." She had researched this. She had interviewed everyone at work who had kids. She read dozens of articles on the subject. She knew she was on firm ground.

"Okay. Whatever you say." Hildy marched into the kitchen and turned off the TV.

Charlotte hopped off the stool. "I'm going out back."

Hildy slowly stirred the milky water above the giant lump of macaroni.

"Look," Annie said. "We're getting off on the wrong foot

here. I don't know how long I'm going to be working from home."

"What do you mean?" Hildy asked. "I thought you took the day off."

"No," Annie said. "I'm not working where I was working anymore." She didn't want to have to explain this to Hildy right now. "I'm going to get a new job. But I don't know for sure how long it will take before I do, or even what it will be."

Hildy put the spoon on the counter. "Are you letting me go?"

"Of course not," Annie reassured her. "I just wanted to let you know I may be around for a while."

"What will you be doing?" Hildy asked. "What do you mean by 'a while'?"

"I'm going to make the small room on the third floor into an office. I'll be consulting until I find a new position. Or maybe I'll just stick with consulting. I haven't worked out all the details yet."

"My floor?" Hildy asked.

"Yes," Annie said. "I'll be using the room across from yours. But I won't bother you. You don't have to worry about that."

Hildy turned off the flame under the pasta water, which had never reached a boil. She dumped the blob of macaroni into a colander and slid it back into the pot.

"You'll have complete privacy," Annie added.

Hildy emptied the pouch of powdered cheese into the pot and then splashed in some milk. She broke up the loaf of macaroni with a wooden spoon, gave it a few stirs, and slid half the glutinous mixture into a cereal bowl.

"Charlotte," she called through the screen door. "Dinner."

She put the bowl on the table, along with a napkin and spoon.

Annie stared at her daughter's dinner. In addition to the ignored weekly To Do lists, Annie wrote out menus each week. She spent a lot of time figuring out menus of carefully balanced meals that were easy to prepare. She even included a grocery list.

Nowhere on any list of menus had she written boxed macaroni and cheese.

"Do you want me to get out a vegetable for you?" Annie asked, because none was in sight.

Hildy opened the refrigerator and took out a bag of baby carrots. "I'm fine." She tore open the bag, and put half a dozen carrots on a small glass plate. "See? Vegetables."

"How about if I wash them for you?" Annie offered.

Hildy picked up the bag, pointed to the small print, and read aloud. "Prewashed." She passed the bag to Annie in case Annie didn't believe her.

All Annie saw was the expiration date, which was three weeks ago.

Charlotte came in and sat down. Hildy began cleaning the pot.

"Do you mind if I eat these?" Annie asked Charlotte. She took the plate of expired carrots and started popping them in her mouth.

"Go ahead." Charlotte said. "I don't like vegetables anyway."

Hildy announced, "Done," and put the pot upside down on the counter, suds still clinging to its sides.

"Do you want me to rinse that off for you?" Annie asked.

"No, thank you," Hildy said. "I'm trying to conserve water."

"Hildy is very concerned about the environment," Charlotte boasted.

"I'll see you later," Hildy said. She scooted out of the kitchen. The front door slammed shut.

"Where is she going?" Annie asked.

"She has school Wednesday nights," Charlotte said. "Volleyball."

"Volleyball? I thought she was taking classes to become a teacher."

"Not anymore," Charlotte said.

"But I thought becoming a teacher was her long-term plan," Annie said.

Charlotte could see that a change of subject was needed. "Mom, do you still want to go get socks?"

"Sure," Annie said, relieved that at least Charlotte had changed her mind about that.

"But even if we find the right ones," Charlotte added, "it doesn't mean I'll get on a travel team. And even if I do get on, I still might want to stick with town soccer. I think I like town soccer better."

"Isn't travel soccer better than town soccer?" Annie asked.

"Yes," Charlotte said, without pausing to think about it.

Annie's eye began to twitch again. When had Charlotte stopped eating vegetables and started watching TV during the week? Why didn't she want to play the soccer that was better? Annie had given Hildy a long pep talk about how important it was for Charlotte to develop her passion and drive. She used to have both. Now she didn't seem to have either.

"It was probably stupid for me to try out," Charlotte said. "I think I'm too old for travel soccer."

Too old? Where did that come from? Why did she sound so defeated? Did she learn that from Hildy? Because defeat was not something Annie ever felt. Even now, forced out of her job, she didn't feel defeated. She felt energized. She had something to prove.

Charlotte needed an attitude adjustment, that was clear. And maybe she'd get one if she played the better soccer.

"Come on," Annie said. "Let's go get those socks. And new cleats. And some shirts. And some shorts."

"Okay," Charlotte said, because in the end it really was easier to agree.

Annie stopped at the hall closet to grab a light jacket in case the evening grew cool.

The jacket fell on the floor, where it landed amid a jumble of winter boots, summer sandals, sneakers, dust, and dog hair. Why were the winter boots still in the closet? Hildy was supposed to change over the closets twice a year. And why was there dog hair? They didn't even have a dog. Did Hildy have dogs come to visit? Who else came to visit?

The twitch started up again, worse than ever. Could it be an allergic reaction to all the dust and dog hair in the house? Could Annie be allergic to her life?

She blasted the thought out of her mind and put a smile in her voice.

"Come on, Charlotte," she said. "Let's go get you dressed for the winning team."

seven

They went to three stores but all the striped socks were wrong. The shorts and shirts were all wrong too.

"How can all the shirts be wrong?" Annie asked as they left the last store and headed for the car.

"I don't know," Charlotte said. "But they are."

When they got home, Charlotte headed upstairs to shower. Annie went to the kitchen, where she saw the flashing light of the answering machine.

She played back the message. It was from Tim, calling from his cell phone. The connection was bad. Even after playing it several times, Annie still could make out only a few words. But it was enough to get the idea. His flight was delayed once again.

The rush of disappointment she felt surprised her. She wasn't used to missing Tim. They were accustomed to being apart. They had gotten good at quickly reconnecting. Why now this feeling of unease?

She tried Tim's cell, but the call went into voice mail. She checked the front of the refrigerator where Tim always posted his itinerary, but for some reason this time he'd forgotten to hang it there. She called information for the number of the Atlanta hotel where Tim always stayed.

"I'm sorry, but we have no guest by that name," the hotel receptionist told her.

"Can you check again?" Annie asked. "I'm sure he's there."

"We have several other hotels in the area," the receptionist offered when a second check came up with nothing. "Perhaps you've called the wrong hotel."

Annie tried Tim's Mountain Ridge office instead.

"Hello," came Trissy's voice on the machine. "You have reached Hot Holidays. Our regular office hours—"

She hung up and thought about trying Hank at home. Hank would surely know where Tim was staying. But what if Trissy answered? Trissy would never not know where her husband was. And Annie didn't want to hear the judgment in Trissy's voice when she explained the reason for her call.

Anyway, it wasn't like it was an emergency. She just wanted to know where Tim was, what had happened, and why his plans had changed again.

By the time she went to bed, Annie had left three messages on Tim's voice mail. She no longer just missed him, and she was done being mad. Now she was worried.

Anxious and restless, she dreamed of Tim in hotel lobbies, at airport gates, in dark cafés. Tim sipping martinis, laughing, telling whispered jokes to women with blank faces. One of the women was chasing Tim down an alley when Annie was jolted awake.

Tim's belt buckle banged against the bedroom doorknob a second time. He dropped his suitcase on his foot and tried, unsuccessfully, to stifle a yowl.

Annie sat up.

"I'm sorry," Tim whispered. "I didn't mean to wake you."

Annie looked at the clock. It was two in the morning. "That's okay," she said. "What happened?" She quickly added, "I'm so glad you're home."

"Me too," Tim said. He sat on the bed and exhaled.

Annie smelled it all—hotel soap, Scotch, gasoline-tinged jet air.

He kicked off his shoes. One hit the wall. "Sorry," he said. "Long day. Long, bad day."

"Where were you?" Annie asked.

Tim looked at her oddly, like he didn't understand the question. Then he turned away, took off his suit jacket, tie, and pants, and changed into a T-shirt and shorts.

"I'm going downstairs," he said.

"It's after two," Annie said.

"I know. But I'm not ready to go to bed."

Annie tried to shake off the feeling of discomfort that had settled around her. She wasn't sure she could even explain it. Her dreams would sound ridiculous to Tim. He didn't drink martinis. He didn't tell jokes. She was overtired and at loose ends. But he hadn't answered her question. Where had he been?

She got up and went downstairs, then followed a loud thrumming noise to the basement. Tim was walking fast on their dusty treadmill.

"What are you doing?" she asked.

Again, Tim looked confused by her question.

"You never work out," Annie said.

It was true. Tim had been born fit and remained fit without

expending any effort. He didn't run and had never joined a gym. He could eat whatever he wanted without gaining weight. It had taken Annie several years to stop being annoyed by this. But she accepted it now. It was a fact, like any other. So why the treadmill?

"What's wrong?" she asked.

Tim had started running now. He couldn't hear her over the noise of his pounding feet. "What?"

"What's wrong with you?" she yelled.

Tim studied the treadmill console to try to figure out how to turn it off. He gave up, looked at Annie, and shrugged.

"Tim," she shouted. "Why are you exercising at two fifteen in the morning?"

"What happened?" came a voice from the stairs. It was Charlotte.

"Everything's fine," Annie said. She rushed over to the treadmill and pressed the arrow that slowed it to a stop.

Tim hopped off. "Hey," he said to Charlotte. "How's my favorite girl?"

"Good," Charlotte said.

"Just good?" he asked.

"Super good," Charlotte said. "Why were you shouting?"

"The treadmill was loud, and we couldn't hear each other," Annie explained. "Did we wake you up?"

"I don't know," Charlotte said.

"Come on," Annie said. "Let's all go back to bed."

She took Charlotte by the hand to lead her upstairs. Charlotte stretched out her other hand for her father. They walked together to Charlotte's room, and Charlotte climbed into bed.

Tim tucked in the covers. Annie pulled them out at the bottom so Charlotte could move her feet.

When they got back to their room, Annie turned to Tim. "Since when do you run on the treadmill?"

"Why is that such a big deal?" Tim asked.

"It's not," Annie said. "I'm sorry."

Tim sighed. "It's okay. Actually, you're right. I've been in a funk and I thought running on the treadmill might help me get out of it."

"Did it work?"

"No." Tim sighed again. "I wish I had never changed jobs."

Tim's decision to leave his accounting firm and join Hank at Hot Holidays hadn't been an easy one. Except for the brutally long hours, he had been one of the few people he knew who actually liked his job.

But once Annie got sucked into her all-week workweek in Connecticut, Tim's long hours started to feel like a problem. They both worried that neither of them was around enough anymore.

Hank swooped in as if he'd overheard their pillow talk. He'd been begging Tim to come aboard for years, but now he pushed Tim harder, promising the irresistible combination of shorter hours and better pay.

Finally, Tim gave in. He was happy for about a week. A week was about how long it took him to discover that Hot Holidays was in dismal shape. His job as Chief Financial Officer immediately segued to Director of Dismissal. Now all he did was travel to branch offices and close them down.

It wasn't how he and Annie had planned for it to go.

Tim got into bed and stared at the ceiling. "There are

thirteen employees in the Atlanta office," he said. "I got them all together in the conference room. I brought the doughnuts as usual."

This was a theory Tim had—that bad news went down better with good doughnuts. It wasn't Annie's idea of a business plan. She had suggested a more conventional approach and offered to write him a termination script. Termination terminology was one of her specialties. But Tim liked his doughnut theory. He felt it lent a human touch.

"I'm in the conference room, making small talk, waiting for everyone to settle down. The last one who comes in is the receptionist. She sits across from me. She's about eight and a half months pregnant. A single mom. And she's playing with a letter opener. The letter opener is shaped like a dagger. Basically, it is a dagger. She's just sitting there stabbing her notebook. And I'm thinking, I'm about to tell a pregnant woman holding a weapon that she no longer has a job."

"Did she stab someone?" Annie asked. "Did she stab you?" This would explain everything.

"No," Tim said. "She might have, but I didn't give her a chance. I told everyone I'd stopped by to say they were doing a heck of a job. Which is true. They are. And then I left."

"You didn't close the office down?" Annie heard the harshness in her voice. "I'm sorry," she said. "I know your job is rough right now. But I don't think it would be a good idea for both of us to lose our jobs in the same week."

'I'm not losing my job," Tim said. "My brother's not going to fire me just because I didn't close down the Atlanta office today. I'm going to take care of it. I just don't like it, that's all."

"It's a rough patch," Annie said. "But we'll get through it.

We just have to buckle down. Work hard. Push on. We can make it work. We just have to stick to our plan."

"Can we talk about something else?" Tim said. "I'm really tired of talking about work. What's new here? Anything good? What's good at home?"

Annie tried to think of something good to report. But all she could think about was the woman at the hotel who hadn't been able to find Tim as a guest. Annie had to ask. It was bothering her too much not to ask.

"Tim," she said. "I called the hotel you usually stay at and you weren't there. Where were you?"

Tim didn't answer and then she heard it—the small catch at the back of his throat that told her he had fallen asleep.

Annie lay staring at the ceiling. She was wide awake now. There was no way she was going to sleep. There was no point in even trying.

She got out of bed and crept up to her third-floor office, where at least she could begin tomorrow's Plan for the Day. She would make a new plan for Tim too. He wouldn't have to follow it, but maybe it could be useful as a jumping-off point for discussing his future.

As she got close to Hildy's room, she slowed. She did not like being on the third floor when Hildy was there, even when Hildy was sleeping. She crept on tiptoe, careful to avoid the creaky floorboards that waited for her like traps.

She heard Hildy's TV and glanced at it, just for a moment. But in that moment she saw everything. The dark, blurry movie. Hildy on top of the blanket. A boy on top of Hildy. The boy looked up and met her eyes. Annie saw she had misjudged his age by roughly twenty years.

The man stood, grabbed his pants, and held them in front of him like a shield. "I'm very embarrassed," he said.

Annie willed herself out of her frozen state and turned to Hildy. "Here? In my house? While we're home?"

"I thought you were asleep," Hildy said. "And someone's always home now. What do you want me to do? We were being quiet."

"This is so awkward," the man said. He pulled on his pants and moved toward the stairs. "Believe me," he said as he zipped, "this is not how I imagined we'd meet."

Annie did not want to meet this man or see his naked hairy chest. She closed her eyes and wished she could will him away. She opened her eyes and his hairy chest was still there.

She kept her voice low because she did not want to wake up Charlotte. Her anger came out like a growl. "Get dressed and get out of my house."

"I thought you said it was okay for me to be here," the man said to Hildy.

Hildy threw him his shirt. "What am I supposed to do? Be a nun?"

"I'm sorry," the man said to Annie. "I thought it was okay. I'm Wayne. From next door. Bonnie and I moved in—"

"Two years ago," Annie finished his sentence. "Bonnie told me."

Wayne quickly buttoned his shirt. "I didn't know you and Bonnie had met. I hope you don't feel the need to tell her about this. She and I have an understanding. But, still, because it's here, next door, with Hildy, well, you know."

"What does that mean?" Hildy asked.

Annie noticed Hildy was now packing a small suitcase. Suddenly Annie felt dizzy. She leaned against the wall and concentrated on taking deep breaths.

"Are you okay?" Wayne asked her.

She met his eyes. "You need to leave my house."

"Wayne, can you drive me to my friend Kathleen's?" Hildy asked.

"Right now?" Wayne said.

Hildy shoved her suitcase into his chest, nearly pitching Wayne backward. "Yes."

"Watch it," he barked as he regained his balance.

"Shh," Annie hissed. "Charlotte is sleeping."

Hildy brushed past Annie and Wayne and clomped down the stairs.

Annie followed. "Where are you going?"

Wayne came stomping after them.

"I'm moving out," Hildy said.

"Now? What about Charlotte? Aren't you even going to say good-bye?"

"Do you want me to wake her up?" Hildy snapped.

"No," Annie said.

"Then I'll say good-bye when I come back for the rest of my things. Wayne!" Hildy called as she stormed out of the house.

He followed her out the door, then turned to Annie. "I am really sorry," he said. "I had no idea this wasn't okay. You seem really great. I'm kind of glad we met, even though—"

Annie slammed the door and leaned against it.

"What's going on?"

She looked up and saw Charlotte standing at the top of the stairs.

"Nothing, honey," Annie said. "Just go back to sleep."

Charlotte, too tired to resist, shuffled back to bed.

Annie returned to her bedroom. She hoped the slamming door had awakened Tim so they could talk about what had just happened. But he was dead asleep. Nothing would wake him now.

She climbed into bed, turned on her side and curled up close beside him. They fit together perfectly. She closed her eyes and dove into sleep.

eight

POWER POINTERS—*July 15th!!!*
News of the Day

Welcome, or Welcome Back, to all brand-new as well as all continuing members of this year's Power!!!

A special hello to two of our newest players, Evelyn Murphy and Jolie Blum, who are joining us all the way from Tyler Park!

I am confident our "old" players will make all our "new" players feel right at home!!!

Reminder to All New Players: Please purchase a two-inch three-ring binder for this and all subsequent team dispatches as well as for our team roster, snack schedule, and volunteer sign-up sheet, which is being typed up by our noble team manager, Ken, father of our amazing midfielder, Bailey!!!

I am pleased to announce that Marilyn Brown, mother of Secret Weapon Forward Shelby, has agreed to serve as my special assistant. This is an unofficial yet extremely important position, as all of our returning families know.

Practice Update: Practice will continue to be held on Mondays, Wednesdays, and Fridays throughout the summer, from eight forty-five to twelve fifteen and four forty-five to six thirty, irregardless of the weather!

Remember, no Power player has ever melted because of rain!!!

Please note the following allowable excuses for missing practice:

One: Death

Two: Official Power Team Tourney

Note: As soon as the Winslow West Mountain Ridge Soccer-Plex officially opens, we will begin ball skills sessions every Tuesday and Thursday, from nine fifteen to twelve fifteen and two fifteen to four forty-five. These sessions are recommended for all players who wish to improve their skills. This includes everyone except Bobbi, who will attend the special Soccer-Plex Goalkeeper School as soon as her right ankle and left knee heal.

Important Note for New Players: Please do not schedule any activities for Saturdays as Saturday Scrimmages will begin shortly!!!!

Final Note on Practice Times: The Power training program alone is not sufficient to take us to the next level. We will only reach the next level if every player on the team continues to train on her own, during her free time, each and every day!!! Believe me when I say that I can tell within the first twelve seconds of practice who has been working hard and who has not.

Note: Any player who does not want to improve her conditioning by participating in our high-level training, should see me as soon as possible for alternatives to the Power!!!

If you have any questions, please do not hesitate to call Ken, Marilyn, or myself!

Note to New Parents: For obvious reasons, I am not available on game weekends for discussions of any sort on any subject!!!

Good Luck to One and All from Winslow West!!

nine

Winslow stood on what would soon be the dead center of the field of his Soccer-Plex, and inhaled the promising scent of wood shavings, newly poured concrete, epoxy, and paint.

Soon, deliciously, the air would fill up with other smells: artificial turf, sweat, french fries, young dreams.

"Winslow?" Tony, the electrician, called him back to the present. "Do you have a minute to walk through the control room?"

"Of course," Winslow said, but only because Tony was someone he liked. The control room didn't interest Winslow. He'd already given that responsibility to Parker. It would be Parker who would keep an eye on the pressure of the control room blowers. Winslow had other pressures to think about.

Like the pressure on the team, which he needed to keep up high—very, very high. If he let it slacken for even one day, he knew precisely what would happen. The top players would leave.

It was something people didn't understand. The parents at the top had the loyalty of a flea, always looking for the next dog to suck dry. Lose the top and the middle followed. And what did that leave him but the dregs.

It happened every day. Teams collapsed in less time than it took to blow a whistle. And he would not let that happen to him.

For a moment he pictured Shelby in the red jersey of his rival team, and he let out a groan.

"You okay?" Tony asked as he stopped at the control room door.

"What?" Winslow asked. "Yes. Yes, I'm fine." He smiled.

"Okay. Here we go." Tony entered the security code into an alarm pad on the wall.

"Does Parker have that code?" Winslow asked.

"Yup," Tony said. "I gave it to him yesterday. You have it, he has it, and I have it. If I were you, I'd leave it at that."

Tony opened the door and led Winslow inside. The door slammed shut behind them with a tight seal.

Winslow felt the hum of the giant blowers. His body vibrated with their power. He loved the blowers, this room, the Soccer-Plex, his life. He opened his nostrils and breathed in the charged air.

"Your two main fans are over there," Tony yelled to be heard over the noise.

Winslow nodded. He checked his watch. How long was this going to take? He ought to be in his office, calling that coach from Holder. For the third time in a week he'd heard boasts that the Holder coach had taken his team to a new level. Now, all of sudden, the Holder Crush was the team everyone said smelled like a state cup win. Of course that couldn't be true. Winslow wouldn't let that be true.

Tony's voice droned on. "And those blowers over there are your auxiliaries."

"You did go through all this with Parker, didn't you?" Winslow wanted to make sure it wasn't necessary for him to pay attention.

Tony nodded. "He knows the system backward and forward."

"Good," Winslow said.

Tony flipped a lever, and the noise level increased to a roar. "These little babies are what's going to let you sleep at night," Tony shouted.

Winslow smiled and nodded and tuned out Tony's voice. Thanksgiving was the other thing he needed to attend to. If he made the calls today he might actually pull off hosting the first-ever Winslow West Thanksgiving Soccer-Plex Tournament.

"Automatic backup," Tony shouted.

This had gone on long enough. Winslow mouthed, "Can't hear you," and pointed to his ear. Tony nodded that he understood. They headed to the door and stepped back out onto the field. The silence felt heavy, as if it had snowed while they were gone.

"Those fans are beautiful, aren't they?" Tony asked.

"Beautiful," Winslow agreed. He glanced across the concrete subfloor and was disheartened to see the plumber waiting for him.

"Winslow," the plumber called. He jogged over. "How's it going?"

"Very well, Roy. Very, very well. How's the plumbing coming?"

"I'm ready to lay the pipe to the first stall," Roy said. "But I don't like how the concrete was poured. And you know as well as me, if you don't get those things right from the get-go they screw you later on. I had the same problem over at the tennis bubble near the parkway."

Winslow couldn't fathom why people insisted on giving him so many unnecessary details. He asked the only question that mattered. "Will you be able to finish on time?"

"Definitely," Roy said. "The only thing is someone told me you might be bringing your team in here to practice soon, which worries me because there are certain solvents I don't want to use if there are going to be kids around."

"You tell me how long you need me to keep the girls out and that's exactly what I'll do," Winslow said.

"Actually, I was thinking maybe you could bring the team in during the day," Roy said. "And I could work with the solvents at night."

Winslow liked that—Roy coming in when he wasn't around. "You don't mind?"

"Hey—I got a kid too. And Nadine, she's dying to get in here and onto the field. To me, this isn't a job. It's personal. Just like with you."

Time to disengage. "Yes."

"Speaking of which," said Roy. "I hate to bother you, but I'm a little concerned. About Nadine and all."

Winslow didn't respond, but that didn't make a difference.

"If she stays on that Asteroids team," Roy said, "I think she's going to start losing interest in the game. Don't get me wrong. Gerri Picker's nice and all. But she's more like a baby-sitter than a coach. And the team has a lot of players who spend a lot of time on the field fixing their hair, if you know what I mean."

"There are different levels of commitment on every team," Winslow said.

"I know," Roy said. "It's just that Nadine is one of those really committed players. She knows it's all about working hard. I tell her all the time. You work hard, you'll move up to the Power. And she is. She's working really hard."

"Working hard is its own reward, isn't it?" Winslow asked. He glanced around, looking for an escape route. Where was Parker? Where was anyone?

"The thing is," Roy went on, "we haven't been notified about the teams yet. I understand first dibs on the Power go to the girls who've been playing with you since they were little."

"That's true," Winslow said. He didn't share that there were only two of those left.

"I don't want to put you on the spot," Roy said. "I just thought maybe you could give me an idea. You know, let me know what direction your thinking is going."

"We're in the final stages of planning now," Winslow said.

"So does she have a chance?" Roy asked.

Winslow thought about Dick, the other plumber who'd bid on the job. Dick was more expensive, but clearly Winslow had made an error in not offering the job to Dick.

"Here's what I think, Roy. I think people don't really understand what my girls do. I think people don't get that my girls practice with me at least four hours every day. Then they go home and get in another hundred touches on the ball. Because it all comes down to that, doesn't it? Touches on the ball?"

"Nadine is sleeping with the ball," said Roy.

"I'm sure she is," Winslow said.

"What I was thinking," Roy said, "is maybe you could let Nadine train with you over the winter, if she doesn't make the team. Because I know if she trains with you, you'll see in a minute how good she is."

What Winslow saw was Tony coming out of the fan room.

"Pardon me, Roy, but if I don't meet with Tony about the inflation levels, I'm afraid the whole bubble might come down on our heads."

"Nadine is tough," Roy called after him as Winslow strode across the field to where Tony was packing up his tools. "She'll never let you down."

"Roy giving you a hard time?" Tony asked.

Winslow smiled. "Nothing I can't handle." He gave his back to Roy and engaged Tony in a lengthy discussion about Tony's new summer house in Port Pleasant. When he was absolutely sure Roy had left, he turned.

He should have waited longer.

Roy jogged over. "What do you think about the winter training idea? Of course, I'll pay. I'll pay extra if you want me to."

"Why don't we talk tomorrow?" Winslow said. He tapped his watch. "I promised the Holder coach I'd get back to him at exactly five o'clock. It would be bad form to keep him waiting, don't you think?"

"Sure," Roy said. "No problem. Sure."

Roy watched Winslow walk away, and smiled. He'd done it. Nadine was in. Because no way would Winslow have asked if they could talk tomorrow if she wasn't in. No way.

ten

It came together more quickly than Annie could have hoped. Her friend Linda gave her the name of an acquaintance who had the magic combination of deep pockets, lots of work, and not enough bodies to get the work done.

"Promise me this," Linda said. "When Sondra asks you your rate, think of the highest number you can imagine, and double it. Zaxtec is desperate. Keep that in the front of your brain. Desperate."

"I don't think I can double it," Annie said.

"You're right," Linda said. "You should triple it. You're worth it, and they'll pay. I'm telling you Annie, if you don't triple that number I'm going to come out to New Jersey and find you."

"That's not much of a threat," Annie said. "Besides, you've always made it very clear that you come from a long line of New Yorkers who don't believe in crossing the Hudson River."

"I'm willing to cross it once," Linda said. "Maybe. If you get this project."

Annie made the call. Sondra, the client, asked for her rate. Annie thought of an unthinkable number, and doubled it.

"Wow!" Sondra said. "Great!"

Annie immediately knew she had undervalued herself by a lot. But that was okay. This was her first client, and the first was always the hardest to get.

She quickly reorganized herself so she could get to Zaxtec for the early morning meeting. Tim was happy to help out by pushing back his return trip to Atlanta so he could get Charlotte off to camp. Getting out of the house had been easy for Annie. She simply left before anyone else was awake. As it turned out, she was grateful for an excuse to leave early. The night before, they had finally told Charlotte what happened with Hildy. Not surprisingly, it hadn't gone well.

They had put off telling Charlotte all week because they had both believed Hildy would be back any day to explain why she had left and to say goodbye. But when Hildy finally did return for the rest of her things, Charlotte was at camp and neither Annie nor Tim was home.

Charlotte found the loving note Hildy left for her on the kitchen table. But even after reading it, she couldn't believe her babysitter was gone for good. Finally, Annie took her up to Hildy's room so she could see for herself.

Charlotte scanned the empty closet, the bare shelves, and the naked bed.

"I'm so sorry," Annie said. "I know you two were very close."

"That's okay," Charlotte told her. "I'm kind of old to have a babysitter."

Annie was surprised by Charlotte's stoic response. But later that night as she passed Charlotte's closed bedroom door she heard the sound of quiet crying. Her daughter wasn't as tough as she pretended to be.

Annie knocked gently and let herself in. Charlotte lay in bed, her eyes closed, her eyelashes damp with tears she hadn't had time to wipe away.

"Charlotte?" Annie said.

Charlotte squeezed her eyes tighter, as if that would fool her mother into thinking she was fast asleep.

Annie leaned over and gently kissed Charlotte's head. When Charlotte recoiled slightly, Annie understood immediately that her daughter had decided Hildy's departure was entirely her mother's fault.

It was good that Tim would be the one to wake her up today. Because Hildy-departure-management could not be her problem right now. Now she was racing across Park Avenue, in record-breaking heat, to meet her very first consulting company client.

As she crossed the street she felt the macadam melting, but she didn't care. The bottoms of her pumps stuck slightly each time she took a step, but it didn't slow her down.

She was working for herself. No Crawford, Bingham, or Roxanne Lacombe. No puffed-up Blaine Glass or petering-out Pederson. No more nights in musty hotel rooms. No more debilitating waves of mother guilt. Now that she worked for herself, finally, her hard work would pay off.

She arrived at the Zaxtec midtown office smiling and feeling great. She was a perfect eight minutes early. It was a perfect day.

The receptionist cheerfully escorted her to a small conference room and promised that Sondra would join her in a minute.

The room was cool, just the right temperature for storing

potatoes or wine. Annie noticed the thermostat across from her, locked in a wall-mounted Lucite box, like a museum display. The digital numbers stared back at her: sixty-eight degrees. It felt good, refreshing. Annie breathed in deeply, letting the brisk air energize her.

She waited a long while before checking her watch. She had nowhere else to be but here. When she glanced at it, briefly, fifteen minutes had passed. That was okay. She looked again after twenty minutes. Then, half an hour.

After forty-five minutes, the digital thermostat reported a temperature of sixty-four degrees. The steel frame of the conference room chair was so cold Annie's leg began to feel like it was burning. Soon her hands went numb. She was wiggling her fingers in the air to see if that would revive them when a woman burst into the room.

"Hi. I'm Sondra. Hello to you too," she added, returning what she thought was Annie's jiggling finger wave.

Annie flung out her numb hand, hoping it would obey her brain's instructions to give something resembling a firm shake. But Sondra had already turned her back to close the door. Annie quickly let her numb arm flop down to her side.

"Meetings," Sondra said, and shook her head.

Annie didn't know if this referred to why she was late, or to what they were about to do. Either way, it didn't matter. She smiled and looked sympathetic.

She recognized Sondra's type immediately. Young, ambitious, pretty, smart. She had dimples when she smiled, and she knew how to use them. She had lots of ideas she thought were better than anyone else's, and she knew how to use them too.

Sondra leaned toward Annie. "I hear you're totally wonderful," she said. "In fact I hear you're the best change management specialist in town. Which is perfect for us, because at Zaxtec our culture is all about being the best."

"That's great to know," Annie said.

"We are going to make things happen here for both of us," Sondra said.

Annie couldn't believe her good fortune. They were soul mates already.

Sondra flipped opened a thick folder. Her BlackBerry vibrated. She scanned it for emails.

"Finally," she said after reading the first one. "Hah!" she said after reading the next. "Shit," she said after reading the third.

She looked up at Annie and smiled. "Where were we?"

Annie pointed to the folder.

"Right. Let's talk about the Context for Change outline."

Then another email came, and one after that, and a third and a fourth. The fourth one really troubled her. Sondra excused herself after reading it so she could put out a fire that—she promised, really—would only take a minute.

But the fire was followed by several more flare-ups, a few blazes, and a downright conflagration. Sondra was up and down and in and out so often she began to sweat, even in the refrigerated conference room where Annie struggled not to show that she was shivering.

"Just another day in the wars," she told Annie, when she finally returned. Her BlackBerry vibrated again. She sat down and closed the folder. "Why don't I have my assistant make copies of everything in here," she said. "You can read it at home and we can do this over the phone."

"Perfect," Annie said.

Sondra yelled for Mimi, her assistant, who came racing in. Mimi was tiny, with a deer-in-the-headlights look that at first made her appear to be somewhere around Charlotte's age. But as Mimi hovered, listening to Sondra's instructions, Annie saw the lines on her forehead deepen, the fallen jowls hang lower, and the gray roots of her blonde highlighted hair emerge more fully under the stark office light.

"Copy every single thing in here for Annie to take home," Sondra said. "And do it TASAP. All right?"

"Done," Mimi said. She took the folder and ran with it.

Sondra leaned forward. "If I don't tell her to do everything twice as soon as possible she gets nothing done at all."

Annie nodded sympathetically, because that's what seemed called for.

"Here's what I want," Sondra said as she worked the keyboard of her BlackBerry, answering emails. "Start with the Context for Change outline. If we're all on the same screen with that, we'll immediately move ahead to Brochure. If that goes well we'll do Transcripts, Video Link, Leadership Alignment Script, Executive Tool Deck, Presentation Deck, Elevator Speech, and Buzz Management Kit."

"The usual," Annie said as she jotted down notes. "Time frame?"

"I need it yesterday but I can give you until next week if yesterday is a problem."

"Having it done yesterday isn't a problem at all," Annie replied.

Sondra let a loud chuckle escape in a puff of air. "I think I'm going to love you."

"Mimi?" she called out. "Mimi? Do you have the folder yet?" She turned back to Annie. "If you have any questions, Mimi has my numbers. Cell, home, country house, and email. I'm always on email," she added in case Annie hadn't noticed.

Someone zipped past the doorway.

"Oh my God," Sondra said. "Mimi, is that Ralph? I think that was Ralph."

"Who's Ralph?" Annie asked.

"Just my boss, the CEO's son, and a jerk, all rolled into one," Sondra said.

"Ralph," she called. "Wait up, Ralph." She smiled and took off down the hall.

Annie felt elated. She had a crazy client, but she didn't have a Ralph.

She made the train with minutes to spare. Once home, she jumped in the car and arrived at the end of the day camp carpool line just as it began to inch forward.

Charlotte slid into the backseat wearing a damp bathing suit with a towel wrapped around her waist. Her face was flushed with fun.

"Hi, sweetie," Annie said. "How was your day?"

Charlotte stared in the rearview mirror.

"Is everything okay?" Annie asked.

Charlotte pressed her lips together.

"Did something bad happen at camp?" Annie asked.

Charlotte shook her head. She unzipped her backpack and foraged for a piece of paper and a pen. She scribbled a note and passed it up to Annie.

Annie read it. "I don't understand. Why aren't you going to talk to me anymore?"

Charlotte wrote another note and passed it up.

"I didn't fire Hildy," Annie said. "She quit. Remember?"

"You should get a cat," Charlotte said after a moment. "My friend Peter said after his mother fired his babysitter he didn't talk to her for a year, so she got a cat. For company."

"I didn't fire Hildy," Annie said again. "You do understand the difference between quitting and being fired, right? I know from personal experience the difference isn't always that clear."

"I can't answer because I'm not talking," Charlotte said.

They rode home in silence, and since Tim was working late, they ate in silence too. The silence continued all the way through to dessert, cookies and milk, which Charlotte allowed Annie to serve her.

Finally, after draining her glass Charlotte said, "Are we getting a new babysitter or not?" She sounded as if they'd been arguing about it for hours.

"How about if we try without one?" Annie asked, thinking this would be a welcome suggestion. "I'm going to be working from home and I think it will be fine just as it is. What do you think?"

Charlotte made a zipping gesture along her mouth.

"Do you want me to get a new babysitter?" Annie asked.

"Not talking," Charlotte reminded her. She heaved a world-weary sigh and went outside to kick around a ball.

"Do you want me to catch for you?" Annie called.

"Not speaking," Charlotte called back.

"Okay," Annie said.

She could do this. She could make this work. She could fully focus on Charlotte. She could find a way to figure it out. She had to. Because somehow, without meaning to, she'd made quite a mess of it.

It was just a matter of coming up with a plan. Maybe a cat was the way. Maybe Charlotte had brought up the idea of a cat because she really wanted one. A cat might be just the thing to help soften whatever it was that had come between them. Annie made a mental note to add, Discuss Strategy for Identifying a Perfect Cat at the bottom of today's Plan for the Day.

It was going to be okay. She was absolutely sure of it. She could make this work.

eleven

Annie opened the front screen door. It groaned and snapped shut behind her. It was impossible that Charlotte hadn't heard the door, but she was good at pretending. Annie sat beside her on the front steps.

Back in the day, before Proxo wore her down and Blaine Glass pushed her out, Annie had been pretty good at changing the mood of a meeting. She would use whatever was available—a piece of gossip, a pointed personal question, a joke she'd heard over lunch—whatever she had. Now she had nothing.

She glanced at the sky. The sun was setting. Clouds were streaked with wide stripes of reds and yellows.

"Have you ever seen such a beautiful sunset?" she asked.

Charlotte slid three inches away. "Ow," she said as the step scratched the underside of her thigh.

"Are you okay?" Annie asked.

Charlotte shrugged, the edict against speaking still in effect.

Annie tried to content herself with just being there, just sitting. Her neighbors—on one side, the Gelbs, and on the other, the people she now thought of as the ones who didn't sleep with her babysitter—were all closed up against the night. All was quiet, except for the loud hum of air-conditioning. The sidewalks were empty too, everyone tucked away from the summer's humid air.

Across the street Annie saw the blue light of a TV, and what looked like people sitting together on a couch. She knew nothing about them, but it seemed from afar that they were happy.

A firefly darted in front of her, then another, both of them flickering as they made slow loops in the air, drunken pilots of their own bodies.

"I haven't seen fireflies in years," Annie said. "I thought they were extinct."

Even in the dark she could see the whites of Charlotte's eyes as they rolled in disgust. At least she's listening, Annie thought.

"When I was your age we used to catch them," Annie persisted. "We'd collect them in jars, and stare at them, just waiting for them to light up."

"Putting them in a jar is mean," Charlotte said, forgetting herself.

"What was really mean was my next-door neighbor Neal, who crushed fireflies on the sidewalk to get his sneakers to light up."

"There's no difference between putting fireflies in a jar and stepping on them," Charlotte said. "Either way, the fire-flies don't like it, and they end up dead."

"I guess you're right," Annie said. She checked her watch.

"Dad's not as late as you used to be," Charlotte said as if reading her mind. "When you came home at all."

Annie sighed. She had actually thought it was all under control.

"I was thinking about your idea to get a cat," Annie said. "I think it's a great idea. Why don't we do some research? We can go online and look at different kinds of cats. You can pick the one you like best."

"The cat idea was for you," Charlotte said.

A car coasted down the hill and stopped in front of their house.

Charlotte and Annie both stood up, happy to be rescued from their conversation.

A woman got out of the car. "Howdy," she said as she walked over to greet them. "Are you the Charlotte Fleming family?"

"I'm Annie Fleming, Charlotte's mother," Annie said.

"I'm Gerri Picker and I'm here with a socca-pology." She extended her large hand to Annie and gave her a crushing shake.

"Normally, I'm a prompt-aholic," Gerri said. "But they're killing me with paperwork this year. And there is nothing I can do about it."

"Pardon me?" Annie said.

"I know. You were expecting me to call in June," Gerri said. "And here I am at the end of July. We should be practicing by now, I know. But it's been a socca-nightmare. I didn't get the team roster until today. Rosterless! Can you believe it? Can you forgive me?"

She seemed to be directing this to Charlotte.

Charlotte said, "Sure."

"I'm sorry," Annie said. "I don't understand."

"She's the soccer lady, Mom," Charlotte said.

Gerri laughed. "That's me. The soccer lady. Manager extraordinaire of the Asteroids of Mountain Ridge. And we might as well get this over with up front. No, it's not."

"Not what?" Annie asked.

"Not Winslow West's team," Charlotte whispered to her mother.

"What's Winslow West's team?" Annie asked.

"Ha!" Gerri laughed. "That's a good one."

"She's not kidding," Charlotte said. "She really doesn't know."

"Oh," Gerri said. "Okay. Easy to explain. Winslow West's team is the Power. That's a seven-day-a-week, twenty-four-hour-a-day, Olympic-hopeful, cultlike, famous socca-legend team. I coach the Asteroids, my daughter, Meredith's team. It's the B team, and we're famous too, but only for not being the Power. We practice twice a week. We have been known to lose. And sometimes we actually have fun."

"Charlotte," Annie said. "You made it! You got picked for a really great travel soccer team!"

"I don't think sarcasm is called for," Gerri said.

"She's not being sarcastic," Charlotte explained. "She doesn't know how it works."

"It's simple," Gerri said. "The super talented players get picked for Winslow's team. His team used to be considered the A team. But now they've moved up."

"What does that mean?" Annie asked.

"The soccer league has a rating system," Gerri explained. "Usually the best team is the A team, and the second best is the B team."

"What do you mean, usually?" Annie asked.

"Well, in this case we have the Power, which is considered a Super A team, which is borderline elite, which means they only play other Super A and borderline elite teams. Unlike the Asteroids, which is a B team, which only plays other B teams, which is why I'm thinking of moving us down to C."

"There's a C?" Annie asked.

"I know," Gerri said. "Most of my parents don't like that idea. They seem to think C is worse than Rec, which we all know Winslow loves to spell out loud, with a *W.*"

"Pardon me?" Annie said.

"That's the town league," Charlotte explained. "It's the Rec League that I was in. Only, Winslow West calls it the W-R-E-C-K 'Wreck' team."

"I tell my parents all the time, *B* does not stand for *bad,*" Gerri said. "Now I have to convince them *C* does not stand for *crappy.*"

"I'm fine with B or C," Charlotte said.

"I knew you were going to be my favorite new player," Gerri said. "I'm fine with B or C too."

Annie didn't understand a lot of what Gerri had said. But she knew she was not fine with B or C. How could Charlotte be fine with that? *C* wasn't an okay letter for anything. If she was fine with a C team, would she be fine with a C grade?

What about a C job? Or a C life? And what if times got tough and she slid down to an F? Would she be okay with an F life? Annie did not want Charlotte to fail life.

Gerri gave Charlotte an affectionate pat on the head. "I love your attitude. I love your whole family's attitude. You cannot imagine how many people are unhappy when I come to see them. And I don't bother trying to change their minds. Because the last thing I need is more unhappy girls on my team."

"Do you have a lot of unhappy girls on your team now?" Annie asked.

"Mom," Charlotte said.

"That's okay," Gerri said with a smile. "I have two less than I used to because, thank God, the Hinmans decided to switch Abigail to cross country, even though she's slower than mud. And the Jacksons just put Hillary in year-round hockey. Like hockey's going to be any better. I mean, seriously. Have you ever tried to have a conversation with a hockey mom?"

"No," Annie admitted.

"Listen," Gerri said. "I know what you're thinking. I've heard Charlotte is a socca-rific player, and you probably want to know how come she got stuck with me. But I'm telling you, with a little coaching Charlotte will be able to fast-track it to the Power. Unless—who knows—maybe she'll actually enjoy playing on my team."

"I will," Charlotte said. She turned to her mother. "Can I join the team? Please?"

It was the first time Charlotte had displayed any excitement in a long while. How could Annie say no?

"Of course," she said.

Maybe this was it. Maybe this was what she'd been looking for. The way to fix things. She turned to Gerri. "What do
I do?"

Gerri handed over several sheets of paper. "First, get these
three forms notarized." It was getting dark. She took a flashlight out of her purse and shined it on her clipboard. "Actually
it's four forms, counting the Good Sportsmanship ditto."

"Now, this one is important." She handed Annie another
paper. "For this one you'll need a two-by-two photograph of
Charlotte taken within the past twenty-four hours. And here's
your snack schedule. You have to sign off on that. There's a
little booklet about nutrition there too. But don't be intimidated by it. Just think fruit and you'll be fine."

"Here are the medical release forms." Gerri handed her
those. "You have to get your pediatrician to sign them immediately. Plus I need a notarized copy of Charlotte's birth certificate, so they know she's not a ringer. You can get all this
back to me by three tomorrow, right?"

"I'll try," Annie said. "But I do work."

Gerri laughed. It was a loud contagious laugh that made
Annie laugh too.

"Oh," Gerri said, fanning herself with her hand as she
calmed down. "That's a good one. I work. Like who doesn't?
"Okay," she said, abruptly turning serious. "This is really
important." She handed more sheets of paper to Annie. "Both
you and Charlotte have to sign these. These are new. They're
all about field marshal duty. Because safety is our new number one priority. Still with me?"

Annie nodded.

"Our first game is Sunday. Which is soon, I know, but

that's how Winslow scheduled us. However, if I don't get all these forms with the photo and the medical releases to South Oakdale by the end of the day tomorrow, Charlotte can't play."

Annie looked at her watch. It was nine o'clock. She was pretty sure the passport photo place was closed. And she had a good idea the pediatrician wouldn't think this qualified as an after-hours emergency.

"I know it's last minute," Gerri said. "But what can I say. The soccer board makes the Motor Vehicle Department seem flexible." She turned to Charlotte. "I am so happy you're going to be one of my girls."

"Me too," Charlotte said.

"Off to the next socca-victim. Five more stops and I'm done." She got into her Navigator, beeped twice, started to pull away, then remembered something and backed up. Her window rolled slowly down. "I forgot the most important thing. We're having a parents' meeting tomorrow night. Eight o'clock at my house, 27 Sunset Drive. It's a potluck. Bring a pasta for eight and you'll be fine. Bye."

Gerri drove off and Annie went through the list in her head. Pasta. Photo. Pediatrician. Fruit snacks. B team. C team.

She struggled with that last part, the letters, but then it clicked. Charlotte was just beginning her travel soccer career and the B team was the entry level position. Of course she'd have to start at the bottom. There was no shame in that. But if she worked hard she'd move up. Gerri said so.

"Congratulations," Annie said.

"For what?" Charlotte asked.

"For making the team."

"It's not hard to get on that team," Charlotte said.

"I'm sure that's not true," Annie said. "It's an accomplishment. You should be proud of yourself. Now all you have to do is to give it your best so you can move up to the next letter."

"You're upset it's B, aren't you?" Charlotte picked at her sneaker laces. The sneakers were new but the laces were already shredded.

"No," Annie said. "*B* is for *beginning.* You're a beginner, that's all."

Charlotte got up and went inside the house.

Annie wondered why it was so hard to get it right.

She was still thinking about that when another car pulled up. This time it was Tim.

"Hey," she said when he got out of the car.

"Hey," he said and sat beside her.

Annie thought he didn't look right. "Bad day?" she asked. "Hank give you a hard time about Atlanta?"

"Hank wasn't in today," Tim said. "He's away on some island somewhere."

"On vacation?"

"No," Tim said. "There's some new property he wants to buy. It's a total mistake but he really wants it. And you know how Hank is when he really wants something."

Annie nodded. She knew they were both thinking about the same thing—how much Hank had wanted Tim, and how hard he'd worked to get him. She put her arm around her husband and gave him a squeeze. She leaned her head on his shoulder. He leaned his head on hers.

He smelled so good, so clean, so damp. She sat up straight. "Did you just take a shower?"

"Yes," Tim said. "I joined a gym. Isn't that great?"

"Why would you join a gym?" Annie asked.

"What's wrong with joining a gym?"

"Look," Annie said. "Something is definitely going on. I don't know what it is but it would be better if you would just tell me now."

"Okay. I'll tell you. It's true. I admit it. I joined a gym."

"I'm a change specialist," Annie reminded Tim. "I know how to recognize change. And last time I checked, you were not a gym person."

Tim said nothing. He stared at the ground.

"If you don't want to tell me because you think it's not a good time for my life to completely fall apart, that's true," Annie said. "But if there's something going on with you that I need to know about, it would be much better if you tell me now so I can deal with it." She gripped the underside of the step and waited for the brick to drop on her head.

"What are you talking about?" Tim asked.

The front door opened and slammed.

"Hi, Dad," Charlotte said. She gave her father a tight hug.

"Hey," Tim said. "How's my favorite girl?"

"Good," Charlotte said.

"Just good?" he asked.

"Super good," Charlotte said.

"Got any super good news?" Tim said. "I could really use some super good news today."

"Not really," Charlotte said.

"Yes you do," Annie said. "What about your soccer news? That's pretty great."

"I got on a travel team today," Charlotte said. "But it's just the B team. And they might move down to C."

"Why don't you tell Dad how the coach said she heard you're a great player and you might be fast-tracked to the A+ team," Annie said.

"There is no A+ team," Charlotte said. She turned to her father. "Can you explain it to Mom? She still doesn't understand."

"I'm not that good at explaining things to Mom," Tim said. His voice was flat. "I'm going to go change."

Tim went inside. The door banged shut behind him.

"He's just in a bad mood," Annie said. "It has nothing to do with your getting a B on the team."

"I didn't think it did," Charlotte said. She got up and went to the backyard.

Annie went in the house. Above her she could hear Tim's footsteps. They perfectly matched the angry rhythm of the thump, thump, thump of Charlotte's soccer ball hitting the back of the house in the pitch-black night.

twelve

nnie woke early, and was surprised to see Tim was already up and out of bed. She found him in the basement, running on the treadmill, his iPod plugged into his ears, his T-shirt colored with sweat. He smiled when he saw her. She turned and marched back up to the kitchen.

She couldn't think of a single person who would understand that the sight of her husband on the treadmill disturbed her. To her it was the same as if he'd suddenly come home with a tattoo, or taken up painting or prayer.

"Good morning," Tim said when he joined her a few minutes later. He wiped his neck with a towel. "That was tough."

Of all the people who wouldn't understand, Tim was at the top of the list.

He opened the refrigerator, stared at the offerings, and reached for a yogurt.

"Yogurt?" Annie said. "You never eat yogurt."

"I'm trying to be more health-conscious. Nothing wrong with that, right?"

Annie did not respond. She took a bowl out of the cupboard. This was not a good time for her to wonder why

Tim would suddenly decide to reinvent himself. She yanked open a packet of instant oatmeal and added water. She had a daughter to reconnect with. She put the bowl in the microwave and set the timer for five seconds less than the directions suggested. She had a business to create. She pressed start and tapped her foot. She had a pediatrician's appointment to make and a birth certificate to get notarized and a nutrition booklet to digest, for God's sake.

Tim was fine. Her marriage was fine. It had to be fine. Tim had decided to be healthy. So what? That was a good thing. A new, healthy Tim. That was all it was. She didn't have time for it to be anything else.

She stopped the microwave before the timer sounded. The oatmeal was watery and thin. She tried to eat it but gave up.

"I have to get some work done," she told Tim as she put her bowl in the dishwasher. "I'll be down in time to take Charlotte to camp." She left the room quickly, looking away from Tim's puzzled face. Stay focused, she told herself. Be organized. Stick to the Plan for the Day.

She had roughed out today's plan on the train coming home from the meeting with Sondra. But that was before Gerri Picker had stopped by. Now the plan had to be completely revised.

She'd fill out the soccer forms first thing. That shouldn't take long, even if there were over a dozen. If she could find her camera, she could take a digital photo of Charlotte before they left for camp. She could stop and get a two-by-two copy printed somewhere on her way to the pediatrician. She could read the nutrition booklet while she waited for the nurse to fill out the medical form. Maybe the nurse would have an idea of where to go to get Charlotte's birth certificate notarized. If she was really lucky, maybe the nurse would turn out to be a notary public.

She could easily get the soccer stuff done by noon, put it all in an envelope and leave it outside her door for Gerri to pick up, as requested. It wasn't how she'd originally planned to spend her morning. She still wasn't sure how much time she'd really need to review the Zaxtec folder. But at least she'd have the afternoon for work. At least she had a plan.

When she returned to the kitchen, her plan fell completely apart.

"Are you coming to my swim show?" Charlotte asked.

Tim stopped reading the newspaper. "When is it?"

"Nine," Charlotte said.

"Nine when?" Tim asked.

"Today," Charlotte said.

"I'm so sorry," Tim said. "I can't. I have to fly back to Atlanta today."

"That's okay," Charlotte said. "Mom, you don't have to come, either. It's kind of stupid. And it's not like you haven't seen me swim."

"Are you kidding?" Annie said. "I'm not missing your swim show. That's the beauty of being a consultant. I can work all morning and take the afternoon off for your show."

"My show is in the morning," Charlotte said.

"Okay," Annie said. "Just as good. I'll do it the other way around."

When the car service pulled up to take Tim to the airport, Annie glanced at the refrigerator door and saw, once again, there was no itinerary posted.

She ran outside. "Tim," she called as he got into the car. "Where are you staying in Atlanta?"

But he had already closed the car door and didn't hear the question.

She turned and found Charlotte staring at her.

"What's wrong?" Charlotte asked.

"Nothing," Annie said. "Everything is great. I was just going to make French toast. Want some?"

Charlotte nodded.

Annie made a hurried breakfast, which Charlotte ate slowly, as if they had nowhere to go. When Charlotte finished eating and looked up, Annie had the camera lens pointed at her. "Smile," Annie said, and snapped. "It's for your soccer playing card." She checked to see how the photo had turned out. "Look." She showed it to Charlotte. "How adorable is that?"

Charlotte studied the photograph. "It's supposed to be just my shoulders and head. And I'm supposed to be in uniform. And I'm not supposed to look adorable."

They were already going to be late. What was the harm in being even later? Charlotte changed into the uniform Gerri had dropped off. She carefully tied back her hair and then took her position, standing against an empty wall.

"Just from here to here," Charlotte said gesturing from her shoulders to the top of her head.

"I understand," Annie said. "Okay. Smile."

Charlotte narrowed her eyes and tried to look fierce.

Annie snapped the picture. Charlotte circled round to see the results.

"Is this one okay?" Annie asked.

"It has to be. We're late."

"I can take another one," Annie said. "It will only take a second."

"We have to go," Charlotte said. The photo session was over.

Camp was thirty minutes away, but there was an accident on the road, and traffic was backed up. They arrived over an hour late.

"You're lucky," Magda, the camp director, told them when they rushed into the building. "We're running behind."

"Great," Annie said. "What time does Charlotte's group swim?"

"Less than an hour," the director told her.

As Annie waited on a chair in the parents' lounge, she heard Magda say, "less than an hour" to every parent who walked in, no matter the age of the child.

Finally, the swim show began. The head counselor blew her whistle, and Group I, made up of the youngest campers, jumped into the pool. All, that is, except for one small boy who refused.

The head counselor blew her whistle again and ordered Group I out of the pool. She then joined five other counselors, the camp director, and the boy's mother in a tight circle around the boy. After twenty minutes of trying to coax the boy into the pool, they agreed to give up.

The Group I swimmers were ordered back into the pool where they demonstrated fifteen minutes of diving, backfloat, sidestroke and treading water. The counselor blew her whistle twice, and on cue the children lifted themselves out of the pool and took a bow. The little boy who refused to swim suddenly conquered his fear and jumped in.

For the next fifteen minutes, six counselors and his mother stood above where the boy clutched the side of the pool and tried to coax him out. Finally one of the counselors jumped in and, playing rescue, removed him.

The swim show limped on. Group II swimmers lined up and jumped in next. Within a minute a girl in the pool screamed that she'd been stung by a bee. Several mothers near Annie began to murmur about the girl's bee allergy.

The nurse rushed over with an EpiPen. An ambulance was called. Only after the oxygen mask was placed on the little girl's face did another girl admit, through tears, that she was the bee—she had pinched the girl on the foot, as a joke.

In all—Annie timed it—it was two hours before Charlotte's age group was called. The girls dove in together, perfectly synchronized. Then one of the girls vomited. Some synchronized vomiting followed.

The swim show was canceled. The pool would have to be drained. Nauseated campers glommed onto their mothers, begging to be taken home. Annie watched, dumbfounded, as, one after another, the mothers around her caved.

"Can I please go home with you?" Charlotte asked. "Just this once? Everyone else is."

It looked like a fire drill as mothers and their charges hurried to their cars in a perfect line. Finally, it was just Charlotte, Annie, and one other child, who sat by herself, looking like an orphan used to being overlooked for adoption.

"Please," Charlotte said. "Everyone in my age group is gone."

"Not everyone," Annie whispered, looking at the waif.

"That's the camp director's daughter," Charlotte whispered.

"She's the one who threw up first. She threw up yesterday too."

Annie signed Charlotte out of camp. On the way home they stopped at a diner for lunch. Charlotte was starving and ordered a cheeseburger, french fries, and a milk shake. The minute they got in the car she leaned over the side and threw it all up.

By the time they got home, Charlotte was weak and sleepy. Annie helped her get settled on the couch in the family room in front of the TV, a garbage pail beside her.

"I have to run to the doctor to drop off that soccer medical form, and then I have to go get your birth certificate notarized or you won't be able to play."

"Okay," Charlotte said.

Annie felt terrible leaving her home. "Do you want to come along?"

Charlotte leaned closer to the garbage pail. "No thanks," she said. "Do we have any soda?"

"I'll stop at the store on the way back," Annie promised. "Call me if you start to feel worse."

With her cell phone clutched tight, Annie rushed out and drove too fast to the pediatrician.

"Can you fill out this form out while I wait?" she asked. "My daughter is home sick. By any chance are you a notary public?"

The nurse blinked as if Annie were speaking a foreign language. "I am a nurse," she said. "A busy nurse with a full waiting room of sick children." She gestured toward the sniffling coughers in case Annie hadn't noticed.

"I'm sorry," Annie said. "And I'm sorry the form is so last

minute. But Charlotte can't play soccer if I don't get this to the soccer people today. Would you like me to come back after I get her birth certificate notarized? Is there anyone here who could notarize this?"

"Does this look like a bank?" the nurse asked. She picked up a folder and called the next young patient's name.

Annie went to three banks before she found one with a notary public. She stopped off at the grocery store next, and bought a six-pack of ginger ale, a box of bendable straws, Tylenol, bread, jam, JELL-O, pudding, and broth. By the time she got back to the doctor's office it was even more crowded.

"Here," the nurse said, holding the form out for her.

Annie was sure the only reason the nurse had filled the form out so quickly was to get rid of her. But Annie didn't care. She was just happy it was done.

When she got back home, Charlotte was running a slight fever. Annie gave her Tylenol and a glass of ice chips.

"I have to go back out and get the photo for your playing card," she said. "Will you be okay if I leave you for a few more minutes?"

"Uh-huh," Charlotte said.

Annie drove to the photo store and waited on a long line, only to find out that the picture she'd taken that morning had been inadvertently deleted. She raced back home to take another one. Charlotte was sleeping. Annie thought about waking her, but changed her mind and took the picture as she was.

The crowd at the photo store was gone, and somehow Annie got the manager to agree to Photoshop Charlotte's eyes so they looked wide open.

This time when she got home, Charlotte was awake.

"Could you keep me company for a while?" she asked.

"Of course," Annie said. "I just have to leave this package outside for Gerri."

She jammed what she hoped were all the soccer forms in a large envelope, left a message for Gerri on her cell phone as instructed, and left the package outside.

She settled in on the couch beside Charlotte, to keep her company. Within minutes they were both asleep.

When Annie woke startled, for no reason, at five o'clock, Charlotte's head felt a little cooler. She carefully extricated herself, put a blanket over her daughter, and tiptoed out of the room.

She retrieved her BlackBerry from her bag and found twenty-one emails from Sondra.

She ran up to her office to call. Mimi put Annie right through.

"Thank God," Sondra said. "Where were you? Did you turn off your BlackBerry so you could get stuff done? That's what I should do. I tell myself that every day. But I never do. You are so disciplined."

"Actually," Annie said, about to explain, but Sondra cut her off.

"This is nothing to worry about, but you need to know that Legal says you can't start work until you sign our confidentiality agreement. You did get it, didn't you?"

Annie quickly switched into her email and scrolled down. There it was. "Yes," Annie said.

"Did you get a chance to read it yet?" Sondra asked. "You didn't give it to a lawyer, did you? It's boilerplate. Totally standard. I'm sure all your clients have the same one."

"Standard," Annie said, hoping she was right. "I'll sign it as soon as I read it."

"You don't even have to read it," Sondra said. "Trust me. It's fine. Honestly. Would I lie?"

Annie got off the phone and attempted a careful reading of the agreement, but the document was written in dense legalese. There were entire paragraphs she couldn't understand.

Getting a lawyer had been on their To Do list for years, but she and Tim hadn't gotten to it yet. So she called her friend, Sylvie, in-house counsel at PC&B. Too bad Sylvie was away on vacation.

Reluctantly, she moved on to her only other choice, Trissy. Her sister-in-law had been a lawyer for years. And Trissy loved—in fact she told people she lived for—doing legal favors for her friends.

"Email it to me and I'll read it right now," Trissy offered, after Annie explained the situation.

Trissy called back in fifteen minutes. "Looks great. Nothing out of the ordinary that I can see. I'm comfortable with it. I think you're good to go."

"Thanks," Annie said. "I guess I better get to work. Which means I guess I'm not going to the Asteroid parents meeting tonight."

"Why not?" Trissy asked.

"I've got too much to do."

"That's not okay," Trissy said. "You can't miss the first meeting. You can miss a meeting later in the season, maybe. But the first meeting? No. Believe me, you don't want to get off on the wrong foot with that group. Can't you do your work tomorrow, or when you get home from the meeting tonight?"

"I could," Annie explained. "But Tim's in Atlanta and Charlotte's sick. I can't leave Charlotte home alone sick to go to a soccer meeting."

"I thought Tim was home," Trissy said. "I thought I saw him. Or was that yesterday? It doesn't matter. Here's the important thing. This is not just a soccer meeting. It's the soccer kickoff meeting. And soccer teams don't understand sick. They interpret sick to mean lack of commitment. Believe me, for Charlotte's sake, you have to go. You don't want her to be shunned, do you?"

"Of course not," Annie said.

"Tell you what. I'll come over and watch her," Trissy offered. "My kids are all scattered around town anyway. I'm just sitting here by myself. I might as well do something useful."

Annie gave mild resistance but not for long. After all, she didn't want Charlotte to be shunned.

By the time she got back downstairs, Charlotte was awake and hungry. "I feel a lot better. Can I go to camp tomorrow?"

"Yes," Annie said.

"Can I go to the soccer meeting tonight?" she asked.

"Aunt Trissy's already on her way over to stay with you."

"Can you keep me company till she gets here?" Charlotte asked.

"Sure," Annie said. "I just have to do one more thing."

She ran up to her office, printed out the confidentiality agreement, signed it, and faxed it to Sondra. She emailed Sondra that it was on its way and then logged off of everything.

By the time she got back downstairs Trissy was sitting in her spot on the couch. "What are you bringing for the potluck?" Trissy asked.

Annie decided not to admit she'd forgotten all about it. "I have to run," she said instead, and grabbed her coat. She was already late. Now she had to stop at the grocery store to buy something that looked lovingly homemade so Charlotte wouldn't be shunned.

thirteen

I t was late to shop for dinner. The prepared food section of the store had been picked over and stripped. All that remained were four individually wrapped portions of vegetarian lasagna.

Annie bought them, and a large aluminum foil tin to put them in. Using the trunk of her car as a counter, she transferred the four large rectangles of food into the tin, and tried to spread out the cheese on top so it looked like it was of one piece. But the cheese was cold and immovable, so she quickly covered it with foil, and hoped no one would know it was hers.

Mountain Ridge was not well lit at night. Annie cruised slowly, looking for addresses, wondering why so few people put them where they could be seen. Luckily, a dozen parked cars served as a signpost that she had arrived at the right block. Finding the house was easy. It was the one that was completely lit up. Through the large picture window in the living room, Annie could see people, heads tilted, talking, laughing—a spirited meeting in progress.

She walked in through the open front door, ducked into

the dining room, where she deposited her dinner contribution on an empty table, and found a seat in the living room where the meeting was under way.

It wasn't until the first subcommittee member gave her report on the lunchtime enrichment program that Annie began to suspect she'd made a mistake. She leaned over to the blonde, pleasant-looking woman to her right.

"Excuse me. What meeting is this?"

The woman looked puzzled at the question. "South Mountain Elementary School PTA Board Summer Kickoff."

Another woman began her committee report, updating the group on the fund-raising efforts for the speaker system in the auditorium.

Annie stood up. Everyone looked at her. The woman stopped speaking.

"Sorry," Annie said. She took her cell phone out of her purse and held it up. "Emergency at home. I'm so sorry. I have to go."

"Who was that?" she heard someone ask as she left.

By the time she found Gerri Picker's house, she was nearly an hour late.

"Don't sweat it," Gerri said when she came to the door. "At least you didn't completely blow us off." She stuck her head outside and looked around. "Where's the rest of your family?"

"Tim's out of town," Annie explained. "And Charlotte's sick."

"You could have brought her," Gerri said. "We're not that uptight."

Annie apologized for leaving Charlotte at home. She followed closely behind as Gerri cruised quickly through her formal living room, decorated in a Washington-once-lived-here style, and a dining room where the long table was completely covered with empty casseroles.

"I forgot my lasagna," Annie said. "I went to the wrong house first," she explained.

Gerri didn't care. "We're done eating anyway. Unless you have dessert."

"No," Annie said. "Sorry."

"It's okay," Gerri said. "We'll deal." She continued on to a large open kitchen and family room. At the far end was a furniture showroom's worth of couches arranged in a square. Annie followed Gerri to where the group sat.

Gerri clapped her hands to get everyone's attention. "Hold on, people. Before you massacre each other, say hello to Charlotte Fleming's mom, Annie."

A few people nodded. One smiled. Everyone but Annie wore a name tag. Annie took a seat.

"We were just discussing the Power," Gerri explained. "A few people are still hoping their kids will be moved up to that team."

"Does that happen?" Annie asked. "Do kids get moved around after they're sorted?"

"Not often," Gerri said. "But I thought it would be helpful to go over the roster, talk about the standings, and make a plan for the future."

Perfect, Annie thought. She loved to plan for the future, and standings, whatever they were, sounded important.

"How can there be standings?" asked a man whose name tag read "Chip." "The season hasn't officially started."

"Look it," Gerri said. "I'm just telling you what I know. And I know that three Power players are at risk of being dropped from the team."

"Why are they at risk of that?" Annie whispered to the woman next to her. But the woman seemed not to hear her.

"Who exactly are we talking about?" Chip took a notebook out of his pocket and got his pen ready.

Gerri leaned forward in her chair. "This cannot leave the room."

Everyone else leaned forward, so Annie leaned forward too.

"I'm not saying these three spots will be available for any of our girls," Gerri said. "All I'm saying is three players on Winslow's team, Rose, Gwen, and Bobbi, are going to get booted off."

Several people scribbled down the information.

"Why Bobbi?" asked a woman, name tag Pat, as she tapped notes into a palm pilot. "Bobbi is the Power's only goalie. They need a goalie. Why would he get rid of her?"

"I can't go into details," said Gerri. "But I can guarantee my intelligence is correct. Those three players are going by the end of the season."

"I don't understand," Annie said. "Going where?"

"Let's just hope they're not coming here," Pat snapped. "Especially Bobbi. She was so mean during tryouts. She made Winnie cry."

"Maybe we'll get lucky and they'll all move out of town," Chip said.

Annie started to laugh, but apparently Chip wasn't kidding.

"You think that's funny?" he snapped. "A person moves here because they hear the soccer is top notch, they end up on a nothing team, and you're laughing?"

"This is not a nothing team," Gerri protested.

"I'm just saying," said Chip.

"Let's stay on point," said the woman next to Annie, name tag Mona.

"Right." Gerri checked her clipboard. "Next item is our flight. As you all know we've been flighted by the soccer board as a B team, but after careful consideration I have requested that they move us down to C."

"Why would you do that?" asked a woman, name tag Peggy Ann.

"If we want a better record," Gerri said, "we have to play teams that are on our level. Face it, moving down is the only way we're ever going to win."

"Is there a morgue flight?" asked name tag Lloyd. "Because I think the only way we're going to win is if we play a team of dead people."

Annie noticed several people on one side of the room were rolling their eyes. Several on the other side scowled back. There were factions.

"Speaking of the morgue," Chip muttered.

A man walked into the room, tall, big, and awkward, avoiding eye contact as he lumbered to the sofa.

"Can I sit here?" he asked in the general direction of the nearest couch.

"You won't fit there, Roy," Chip said. "And you're just not cute enough to sit on my lap."

Roy didn't smile.

"You can bring in the piano bench from the parlor," Gerri suggested.

Roy left to get the bench. When he came back he squeezed the bench into the small space next to the couch where Annie sat. His girth made the bench look flimsy, as if it were constructed out of matchsticks, ready to break under him.

"Moving along," Gerri said. "I want to go over some new rules for parent conduct." She looked at Peggy Ann. "This season there is to be no coaching from the sidelines."

"I never coach," Peggy Ann said. "I encourage."

"*Attack* is not an encouragement word," Gerri said. "Neither is *kick, kill,* or *eat them*."

"I don't know why we suddenly need so many rules," said Mona. "The team is doing fine."

"You think we're doing fine?" Peggy Ann asked. "Last year the only game we won was against a team one step up from cripples."

"Could you please not use the word *cripples*," Mona said.

"Don't tell me what words I can use," Peggy Ann snapped back. "It's a free country and if I want to say *cripples,* I will. Okay? Cripples."

Lloyd stood up. "For the record, I would like to say you're making me embarrassed to be on this team."

"Really?" a woman said from the other side of the room. "Then quit. It's not like your daughter is making a contribution on the field."

Annie could sort the factions out now. Four people on one side of the room were shouting. Four people on the other side were shouting back. The rest looked on with the dull gaze of the resigned. This wasn't the first time a meeting had degenerated into a shouting match.

"Come on," a voice called from the hall. "They're fighting again." A herd of girls tumbled into the room to watch.

"Out," Gerri ordered. "Back to the basement. Now."

The girls immediately retreated.

"Next on my list," Gerri said loudly to get everyone's attention, "is winter training. I've been working with Winslow to get us a slot in the new Soccer-Plex as soon as it opens. The girls need to keep up their training through the off-season."

"Got those toilets flushing yet, Roy?" Chip asked. He turned to Annie and winked. "Roy here is personally putting in all the toilets in the Soccer-Plex."

Annie heard a noise—Roy grinding his teeth.

"So if your daughter complains that her little deposits aren't disappearing fast enough," Chip went on, "this is the man to call. Right, Roy?"

More laughter.

Roy stared into his lap.

"Can we have a show of hands?" Gerri said. "Who wants to participate in indoor winter training?"

Annie saw hands go up all around the room, so she raised hers too.

Gerri glanced around, writing down names. "Not you, Roy?"

"We have other plans," Roy said.

"Ooh," Chip said. "Other plans." He wiggled his fingers in the air.

Again Annie heard the sound of gnashing teeth.

Gerri checked her clipboard. "Great. All that's left is sign-up for the volunteer positions."

Almost at once, everyone stood. There was a loud chorus of "Got to go." Children's names were shouted in urgent voices. Annie was carried along in the crush of escaping families.

"Wait up," Gerri called, clutching her clipboard as she followed them outside. "Okay. We can have sign-up at the next meeting. Don't forget our first game is Sunday, Cunningham Park, at noon."

Car doors opened, and slammed.

"Remember to check your snack schedules," she called.

More car doors slammed.

"Oh—and I need someone to volunteer to stay with the girls at the field after practice on Tuesdays because I can't. Can anyone help out on that?"

A chorus of car starters answered her.

There was a lot Annie didn't understand, but one thing she knew was how to step up and help out. "I can," she volunteered.

"Super-ific," Gerri said as she ran over to Annie's car. "Thank you so much." She leaned into the open window. "It's not a big deal. All you have to do is stay on the field until all the girls are picked up. Because we can't leave them unattended in the park."

"I understand," Annie said. That sounded simple enough.

"Most of the parents come on time," Gerri added. "Except for Peggy Ann and Mona and Chip. Actually my advice on that is just carpool with them. I don't mean that they'll ever take your kid to practice or anything. But if you take their kids home every week, at least you know you'll get home at a decent hour. If that sounds okay. If you don't mind."

"I don't mind at all," Annie said. "It sounds great."

"What job did you sign up for?" Trissy asked when Annie got home.

"I'm supervising pickup at the park after Tuesday practice," Annie said, "which apparently means driving a bunch of kids home every week."

"The old one-way carpool," Trissy said. "Not bad for a beginner. You could have done much worse."

"Thanks," Annie said.

"I mean it," Trissy said. "I never thought I'd see the day, but you're turning out to be a natural born soccer mom. I guess you were just a late bloomer, that's all."

Normally, this was exactly the kind of comment that would make Annie bristle. But now she saw that in her own odd way Trissy meant it as a compliment.

Could it be, Annie wondered, that she had actually cracked the code?

She said good night to her sister-in-law and smiled. Maybe this was it. Maybe she had finally figured out how to work out her life at home.

fourteen

I t felt like only minutes between the time Annie went to sleep and the time her alarm went off, at six o'clock.

She forced herself out of bed. Today, there was no time for the Snooze button, no time for a leisurely rise to consciousness. Today, she had to stay on course. Because now she knew it only took a day to fall behind. And Annie was not a fall-behind kind of person. She did not believe in the shortcut, the catch-up, or the work-around. She believed in dedication, concentration, and hard work.

A faint voice in her brain sent the question: Are you sure you don't need to hire a babysitter?

Yes, she told herself. She could do this. It was simply a matter of staying on course.

She brewed a pot of extra-strong coffee and chugged two mugs fast. Clearly, one cup a morning was not going to be adequate. This was what she had to do—tweak her work-from-home strategy to rev up her focus. All systems had to be on full blast.

First decision: Getting up at six was a luxury she could no longer afford. Tomorrow she'd get up at five.

She poured a third cup of coffee and took it with her up to her office where she sat down to write up her Plan for the Day. Today it was beautifully simple, with a short and clear mission: Read through the Zaxtec folder and formulate a complete and comprehensive response with recommended course of action and timetable.

She turned off her phone and her BlackBerry, and closed her office door. She had exactly half an hour before she had to get Charlotte up for camp—just enough time to get started. After the camp drop-off she would come home and work straight through until today's plan was done.

Her desk was orderly. Her mind was clear. She took the folder out of its envelope. A flicker of worry passed through her brain like an electrical current, but she didn't stop to wonder why. The flood of dread came a moment later when she opened the folder. She saw it before she understood it. A single piece of paper lay inside, the cover sheet to a long document that had not been included.

Mimi had messed up.

Annie picked up her BlackBerry, turned it on, and scrolled through the dozen emails from Sondra. The early ones were offers of encouragement and support, but they quickly turned anxious until they reached a crescendo of panic.

"ARE YOU THERE?" the last one read. "OR ARE YOU DEAD?"

Annie called all the numbers Mimi had given her for Sondra, but Sondra wasn't anywhere. So Annie called the last number Mimi had given her, which was Mimi's number at home.

"The folder is empty," Annie told her.

"Oh God," Mimi said. "Oh God. Oh no. Okay. You can't tell Sondra. I beg of you. I'll fix it. I'll get everything to you this morning. I'm leaving for the office right now. I'll call you back as soon as I get there."

The phone rang only moments later.

"That was quick," Annie said.

"Pardon me?"

It wasn't Mimi. "I'm sorry," Annie said. "Who is this?"

"Nurse Pike," said the voice. "From camp. I'm calling to tell you camp is canceled today due to an outbreak of lice. We will reopen on Monday if everyone cooperates."

"Lice?" Annie didn't know anything about lice.

"We've had four reports of cases in your daughter's age group. You'll need to treat immediately."

Annie had no idea what she was supposed to do for lice. Her body began to itch all over. "Should I take her to the doctor?" she asked.

"Haven't you ever checked your daughter for lice before?" Nurse Pike sounded incredulous. "We ask all parents to check for lice before they send their children to camp. This is exactly how outbreaks begin."

"Of course I've checked her," Annie said. "I just haven't checked her lately. And I wanted to make sure the procedure hadn't changed."

"Well, it hasn't." Nurse Pike was brisk. "You check her head, but even if you see nothing, if she complains of being itchy you get lice shampoo and you treat. Then you comb and you launder. And by launder I mean clothes, bedding, stuffed animals, hats, scarves, coats—yours, hers, everyone's."

"Mine?" Annie asked. That didn't seem fair.

"Are you telling me in the past you haven't laundered your own clothes after you've treated for lice?" Nurse Pike asked.

"I would never tell you that," Annie said.

"Good. Because I want to be sure you understand. I will check every child before I let any of them back into camp. So there's no point in shirking. You might as well get the job done right the first time."

"I always get the job done right the first time," she told Nurse Pike.

She heard a toilet flushing. Charlotte was up. Moments later, Annie found her in the kitchen. With sleep still stuck in the corner of her eyes, Charlotte was busy digging her fingers into the back of her scalp. Suddenly, Annie was itchy there too.

"The camp nurse called to say you might have lice," Annie said. "But don't worry. Having lice isn't as bad as it sounds."

"I know," Charlotte said.

"I have to run out to the drugstore. But I'll be right back, and we'll take care of everything. So don't worry."

"I'm not worried," Charlotte insisted.

Annie quickly drove to the nearest drugstore to get the necessary supplies, but the clerk told her they'd sold out the night before. The news was the same at the four other drugstores in town. By the time she found what she needed, in a tiny pharmacy two towns away, her own scalp was itching so badly she could barely think.

She came back home with two family-size kits of lice shampoo and handed one to Charlotte. "First, you wash your hair with regular shampoo. Then you put this on."

"I know how to do it," Charlotte said. "Every year since

I've been in kindergarten somebody has had lice. Is this why you went to the drugstore? Because we have lots of lice shampoo in the closet." She went upstairs to treat herself. When she was done, it was Annie's turn.

Five hours later, Annie took out the last load of laundry from the dryer. "Done," she said as she removed all the stuffed animals Charlotte still kept carefully arranged at the foot of her bed. Annie was halfway through a losing battle to refluff the menagerie of bears, dogs, cats, and monkeys when she realized Mimi had never called back.

She found her BlackBerry and quickly counted Sondra's emails. This time there were thirty. They all said the same thing. "I'm here. Where are you? I'm here. Where are you?"

Mimi picked up on the first ring.

"The package still hasn't come," Annie told her.

"Oh my God," Mimi said. "This is bad."

"What happened?" Annie asked.

"I meant to send it. Oh my God. She's going to kill me. Oh my God. You cannot tell her."

"Where is it?" Annie asked.

"On my desk," she whispered. "Oh my God. She's going to freak."

"Why don't you just send it to me in an email?" Annie asked.

"I can't do that," Mimi said. "Sondra says our email is not secure. I could fax it, though. People can't hack into a fax, can they?"

"I need to speak to Sondra," Annie said.

"She's not here," Mimi told her. "I'll let her know you called. And I'll fax everything over right now."

Annie put down the phone and turned to find Charlotte standing there, scratching her head.

"It still itches," she said.

They went to the bathroom, where the light was best, so Annie could check Charlotte's hair with the fine-toothed comb that came in the kit. But Charlotte's blonde hair was perfect camouflage for lice. And repeated visits to a Web site's enlarged pictures of the ricelike eggs did nothing to make detection any easier.

"It itches a lot," Charlotte said.

Annie skimmed the Web site and read, *Sometimes the first treatment doesn't work.* They both retreated. Annie did another three loads of laundry.

When she was done, she checked the fax machine, but nothing had come.

"I'm tracking it," Mimi said when she called her.

"I thought you were faxing it," Annie said. She didn't feel good about this.

"I was going to," Mimi said. "But Sondra wants you to have the original documents. So I sent it same-day service. It's going to be okay."

"I've never heard of same-day service," Annie said.

"It costs a fortune but I'm going to offer to pay for it myself. So we're good here. Don't worry. The package will arrive before nine tonight."

Mimi called again at six fifteen. "It's coming tomorrow morning with a nine o'clock guarantee."

After dinner, Annie and Charlotte treated for a third time. They had just finished, fingertips completely wrinkled, heads exuding a strong chemical smell, when the phone rang.

"Welcome to the disaster called my life," Sondra said. "This is it. We are dead. We are cremated. We are dust."

"What's wrong?" Annie asked.

"You know, I really thought Mimi would have known enough to take the pages over to you herself. Why would that be a hard thing to do? She hails a cab, rides out, hands you an envelope, and rides back. If she had done that you'd be finished by now. But she didn't do that. And you haven't started, have you?"

"It's not a problem," Annie reassured her. "I can pull together the Context for Change outline as soon as the pages arrive. And Mimi said it's guaranteed for nine o'clock tomorrow morning."

"That's not going to happen," Sondra said. "Because when Mimi sent the package overnight she neglected to check off the Saturday delivery box. Which means the earliest you can get the package is Monday morning at nine o'clock, which is exactly the time Ralph is going to walk into the conference room expecting to see the presentation."

"We can make this work," Annie said. "If Mimi takes a taxi over now, I can still get it done in time."

"Did I mention Mimi doesn't work here anymore?"

"Is there anyone else you can send?"

"I could come," Sondra said, "if I had nothing better to do than to ride out to your house. Unfortunately Mimi sent you the originals. Did I mention Mimi doesn't work here anymore?"

Annie didn't know what to say.

"There is only one way this is going to work," Sondra said. "You and I have to hole up in my office on Sunday and piece this thing together from scratch."

Annie quickly went over the weekend in her head. Tim was flying in Saturday morning, so that could work. But Sunday was Charlotte's first soccer game, and she didn't want to miss it.

"You know," Annie said. "I don't think we should put this off. Why don't we do it tomorrow?"

"Because I'm running a conference tomorrow," Sondra said. "'Change, Diversity, and Failure.' Want to come?"

"What about tomorrow night?" Annie suggested.

"Sunday is when I can do it," Sondra said.

Annie checked her calendar. The soccer game started at noon. She didn't want to, but she could do both.

"I can be at your office at three," she said.

"That only gives us eighteen hours."

"Don't you think eighteen hours is enough?" Annie asked.

"I hate working on Sundays," Sondra said. "I am allergic to working on Sundays. It is a nearly unbearable thought."

"What about two forty-five?" Annie suggested.

"I should have Mimi killed," Sondra said. "I don't think there's a jury in the country that would convict me if I had Mimi killed."

"Sunday at two forty?" Annie asked.

"Two thirty," Sondra said, to get her way.

"Great," Annie said, and hung up the phone before Sondra's murderous thoughts could turn toward her.

fifteen

harlotte woke her the next morning. "Mom? Mom?"

Annie looked at the clock and jumped out bed. "How did it get to be eight?" She grabbed her robe. "I was supposed to get up at five. You better hurry. You're going to be late for camp."

"It's Saturday," Charlotte said.

"Oh." Annie fell back into bed.

"Is the doctor open on Saturday?" Charlotte asked. "Because if he is I think I should go. My scalp really hurts."

The earliest appointment Annie could get was for twelve. The waiting room was packed when they arrived.

"How are you?" the nurse asked Charlotte when they checked in.

"I'm okay," Charlotte said.

"How's Hildy?" the nurse asked.

"Will there be a long wait?" Annie interrupted.

The nurse glared.

"I'm her mother," Annie said. "I've been here before," she added.

"Then you know we can't predict the wait," the nurse said and slid the glass panel between them closed.

Annie and Charlotte took the last remaining seats, next to a set of six-year-old twins whose wet coughs sprayed into the air with the regularity of a plug-in room freshener. Several million germs later, the nurse called Charlotte's name.

"It's a chemical burn," the doctor said after a perfunctory look. He turned to Annie. "How many times did you apply the lice shampoo? Did you read the directions first?" He narrowed his eyes awaiting her answer.

Annie didn't have time to be scolded. "What do we do now?"

"The damage is done," the doctor said. "You just have to let it heal. Keep out of the sun for a while," he told Charlotte. "Don't shampoo for three days and don't go swimming for a week."

"If I can't swim and I can't be in the sun, what am I going to do at camp?" Charlotte asked.

"No sun, no pool," the doctor said, "Sounds to me like no camp."

"What about my soccer game tomorrow?" Charlotte asked.

"If it's sunny, I guess they'll have to play without you," the doctor said.

Annie's eye began to twitch. "Can you see my eye twitching?" she asked the doctor. "It's twitching right now. It's so annoying. Do you think it's just stress, or do you think it could be something more serious?"

The doctor just stared.

"You probably can't see it. No one can ever see it."

"I'm a pediatrician," he said. He turned away and opened

Charlotte's chart, then started his entry in his compressed secret handwriting.

Annie thought she saw the word *mother* entered on the chart. But doctors didn't write comments about mothers, did they?

"Stay away from those lice, okay?" he told Charlotte.

Charlotte nodded, and he left the room.

Annie was sure that in the past he'd always stopped to shake her hand when he was done. But maybe she just remembered wrong.

On the way home, Annie and Charlotte listened for a weather report. When the weatherman announced Sunday's forecast was for a mostly cloudy day, Annie cheered.

But when they got home, Annie's cheery mood vanished. Tim had left a phone message saying that he had to stay in Atlanta until Monday.

She didn't want to call Trissy, but she needed someone to watch Charlotte on Sunday night.

"I have a favor to ask," she said. "Actually it's two favors."

"Yes to both," Trissy immediately told her.

It was exactly why people didn't hate her. She might be an irritating perfectionist, but Trissy would drop everything to help a friend.

"Can Charlotte sleep at your house tomorrow night? I have to work late and Tim is away until Monday."

"Of course. It's my pleasure," Trissy said. "Next?"

"Tim forgot to leave his itinerary and I don't know where he's staying in Atlanta. Could you ask Hank if he knows?"

"Hank is away too," Trissy said. "Are you sure Tim is in Atlanta?"

"Yes," Annie said. "Why?"

"Never mind," Trissy said. "Tell Charlotte I can't wait to see her. What's her favorite dessert? I'm going to bake tonight. Is she a cupcake girl or does she prefer brownies?"

Annie had no idea. "Cupcakes?" she said.

"That's what I would have guessed too," Trissy said.

By the time Annie went up to bed, Tim still hadn't called. But when she woke up the next morning her phone was beeping with a text message Tim had left sometime after twelve.

Is everything okay at home?

Yes, Annie wrote back. *Call me,* she added and pressed Send.

She made Charlotte a quick breakfast and then got dressed. But when it was time to leave for the game, Charlotte took one look at her and stopped short.

"You can't go like that," she said.

Annie was wearing her favorite navy suit. Underneath the jacket was a simple white shell. She had on pantyhose and conservative black heels. There was absolutely nothing objectionable. That was the point.

"Why not?" she asked.

"No one wears a suit to a soccer game."

"I have a meeting right after your game. I'm going to drop you off at Aunt Trissy's and go straight into the city. I told you all this, remember?"

"Can't you change into your suit at Aunt Trissy's?" Charlotte asked.

"I'm going to be running late as it is," Annie said. "Don't worry. It's a great suit. No one could dislike this suit."

Charlotte rode in moody silence all the way to Cunningham Park.

Annie pulled into the lot. Why was there only one other
car? "This must not be the right field."

"We're just too early," Charlotte said. "That's all."

"Are you sure?" Annie asked. "Do you think the game
could be at Grainer's field, where practice is held?"

"No," Charlotte said. "I think it's here. I think we should
just wait awhile and see if anyone else shows up."

"How about if we drive over to Grainer's field and take
a peek to make sure no one's there?" Annie said. "You don't
want to be late for your first game, do you?"

"No," Charlotte admitted.

They found a game at Grainer's field, but the players were
teenage boys. They checked out the high school next. The
football team was warming up on the grass, and the cross-
country runners were doing stretches on the track. At the
South Mountain School, the Kinder-kickers were setting up
orange cones. At the field next to Trissy's house, a man was
trying to train a Welsh springer spaniel to retrieve a stick.

After forty-five minutes of driving back and forth around
town, Annie returned to their original destination.

"They're here," Charlotte said as she got out the car. "We're
so late. The ref is already checking playing cards."

Annie saw that the Asteroids were lined up in a perfect
row while a man went from one to the next looking from
card to face, checking for imposters.

"I'm so sorry," Annie said. "Now you won't get to start."

"Why not?" Charlotte asked.

"I read that on one of the sheets I signed. If you're late to a game you don't get to be in the first group that plays. I'm really sorry."

"It's okay," Charlotte said. "It doesn't matter if I don't start."

"But it's not fair. It's not your fault that we're late," Annie said. "It's my fault. Gerri shouldn't penalize you for my error. I'll explain what happened." She started onto the field.

"Mom," Charlotte said. "You can't go out there. You're wearing a suit." To be sure there was no further discussion, Charlotte ran, head bent into the wind, to join her teammates.

Annie backed off and walked over to where a group of parents stood on the sideline. She recognized some of them from Gerri's house, but they looked different now. Everyone was dressed alike. They wore green jackets with gold lettering that read "Asteroid Parent" on the back. They sat on green chairs and drank from identical green coffee mugs.

Annie hadn't known the parents had uniforms too.

The ref blew his whistle to start the game.

Annie didn't understand much of what went on, but she did note that Charlotte had started, and that she seemed to be in the front of the pack as the girls moved up and down the field.

Most of the parents stood up when the play began. Several moved their feet as if they were playing too.

"Stay with it," a parent yelled.

"Stay with it," Annie echoed, happy to try out the new language of parental cheers.

"Go wide," a man screamed.

"Go wide," Annie yelled. It felt really good to yell.

"Go Asteroids," someone shouted.

"Asteroids are the best," she screamed as loudly as she could.

The ref blew his whistle and held up his arm to stop play. Even from the sideline, Annie could see Charlotte's face had turned crimson.

The ref marched over and stopped in front of Annie.

"The girls can't hear me," he said. "Even I can't hear me. We can only hear you."

Annie hadn't been the only one cheering. But when she looked around for support everyone else was looking away.

"Consider yourself warned," the ref said. "Next time, I'm carding you."

Annie had no idea what that meant, but it didn't sound good. Still, she nodded as if she understood.

The ref blew his whistle. The game resumed.

A man next to Annie yelled out, "Shoot," but the ref didn't take notice.

"Fourteen is open," Peggy Ann screamed. "Watch behind you. Get around her. Attack."

The ref remained oblivious.

"Go, Charlotte!" Annie yelled. The ref met her eyes and flashed what she understood was a second warning.

A woman walked over to her. "Did he threaten to throw you off the field?"

Miraculously, Annie remembered her name. Mona. "Yes," she said.

"Don't worry about it," Mona said. "He always harasses us. He thinks it makes him seem impartial. Which he isn't. He hates our team."

Several Asteroid parents suddenly cheered. Annie and Mona turned to see a girl running back from the goal, arms in the air, triumphant. It was Charlotte and she had just scored.

"What do you know," Mona said. "You have a kid who can actually play."

"They're all good," Annie said, even though she had no idea.

Another cheer erupted. Again Charlotte raised her arms as she jogged back to the center of the field.

The other team followed up each Asteroid goal with a goal of its own. With only minutes left, the score was tied.

An opponent booted the ball high and hard toward the Asteroids' goal. An Asteroid defender moved into position to block it.

"Okay," Mona said. "We're fine. Nadine is like a brick wall. Nothing gets past her."

But as Nadine's head connected with the ball, an opponent's elbow connected with her rib cage. Nadine careened. The header went wild. The crowd watched in silence as the ball bounced off Nadine's head and soared into the Asteroids' own goal.

Five short whistles signaled the game was over.

"Don't say that again," a voice bellowed.

Annie turned to see Roy, the plumber, standing nose to nose with Chip.

"I didn't say she did it on purpose," Chip said.

The two teams lined up to walk past each other, single file, for their handshakes.

"Hey," a girl called out from the other team. She pointed at Nadine. "She spit on her hand before she touched me. I saw it. She spit on her hand."

"You think that's how you're going to get to move up?" Roy shouted at his daughter when she came off the line. "You think you're going to move up pulling that kind of crap?"

The rest of the parents quickly retrieved their kids and dispersed. Mona and her daughter followed Annie and Charlotte to the parking lot. Roy stormed past them to his truck.

"Bad enough you scored on yourself," he yelled. "Then you go let someone see you spit on your hand?"

Nadine's shoulders slumped so low Annie thought she might actually collapse and fall to the ground.

Roy saw her staring. "You have something you want to say to me?"

"Come on, Roy," Mona said. "These things happen."

"Thank you very much," Roy said. "I didn't know these things happen. Thank you for telling me." He turned to Annie. "You got something you want to add?"

"Yes," Annie said. "Your daughter played with a lot of heart."

Roy clenched his jaw. He looked at Charlotte, and his face changed. "You're the one who played her heart out. You did a great job out there."

"Thanks," Charlotte said. She took a step back and moved so she was hidden behind her mother.

"Get in the truck," Roy told Nadine.

Nadine got in and slammed her door. Roy blasted out of the parking lot.

Annie and Charlotte got in their car. Annie was about to back out when she saw Gerri hustling over. Annie rolled down her window.

"Charlotte," Gerri said. "You are unbelievable."

"Thanks," Charlotte said.

"You're going to bring up the level of play for the whole team," Gerri said. "We are so lucky to have you. But I want to be sure you feel like this is a team where you can grow as a player. So if you want to do some extra technical training, I'll work with you."

"Okay," Charlotte said. "If you want me to."

"Is it okay with Mom?" Gerri asked.

Extra training sounded good to Annie. "Sounds great," Annie said. "Maybe you could give me a few pointers too," she added. "In case Charlotte ever wants to practice with me."

"I think it's better if I stick to practicing with my coach," Charlotte said. "My mom doesn't play sports," she explained to Gerri. "That's why she's wearing a suit."

Annie laughed. "I'm in a suit because I have to go into the city for a meeting."

"If you're interested," Gerri told Annie, "you should come play on my other team. I coach a moms' team too. It's very low key. We just play for fun. You want to play with us?"

"That sounds great," Annie said. "Count me in."

"You can't," Charlotte said. "You have to work. You don't have time."

Annie checked her watch. "Wow. You know what? I'm late. We have to go. But I'll call you," she told Gerri. "I want to talk to you about that team."

"What a bad idea," Charlotte muttered as they drove off. Annie decided to ignore the comment.

When they got to Trissy's house, Trissy came running out to greet them dressed in her usual uniform of starched white shirt, pressed khakis, and fine leather driving shoes.

"How was the game?" she asked.

"Good," Charlotte said. She accepted her aunt's crushing hug and then began scratching the back of her neck.

Trissy sniffed the air around Charlotte's head. "What is that smell? I know that smell."

"Thank you so much for letting Charlotte come over," Annie said.

"Hey, it's a total treat for me. The boys are never here. And that includes Hank." Trissy turned to Charlotte. "Can you do me a favor? Go in the kitchen, look for a big platter of cupcakes and bring it out here so your mom can have one."

"Okay," Charlotte said, and ran inside.

"Thanks but I can't have a cupcake right now," Annie said. "I have to go."

"Before you go," Trissy said, coming closer. "I just spoke to Hank. He said Tim isn't in Atlanta. He's at a conference in the city. I don't know if you want to talk about it or not, but if something's wrong with you and Tim, I'm here for you."

"Nothing's wrong," Annie said. "Except maybe Hank. Could Hank be wrong?"

"Are you kidding?" Trissy laughed. "Wrong is Hank's middle name."

That made Annie feel a little better. "Tim definitely told me he's in Atlanta," she said. "I don't think he would lie to me."

Charlotte came out with the platter of cupcakes.

"Forget I said anything," Trissy told her. "I'm sure Hank doesn't know what he's talking about, as usual. Just go get your work done. Charlotte and I are going to have a cupcake party." She sniffed the air again. "That smell is so familiar."

"Maybe it's the smell of soccer," Annie said.

"Could be," Trissy said, satisfied with the answer.

Annie kissed Charlotte good-bye and walked to her car.

"I think what you smell is lice shampoo," Charlotte said as they stepped inside the house.

Annie quickly drove off before Trissy had a change of heart.

sixteen

POWER POINTERS—*August 15th!!!*
News of the Day

Attention new players: All Power Pointers News of the Day bulletins begin with a review of the previous week's practice and game! Please regard these reviews as the important learning tools they are!!

By today, all new players as well as all old players should have reviewed, and/or learned for the first time, the Winslow West Philosophy Regarding Mistakes.

Mistakes are a welcome and important part of the learning process!! They are not something to be feared or avoided!!

However, since the point of mistakes is to learn from them, there is absolutely no excuse whatsoever for making the same mistake twice.

I suggest everyone memorize this simple yet crucial concept: New mistakes—a sign of aggressive play. Repeated mistakes—not tolerated!!

Scrimmage Review: I'm sure we are all in agreement that

our scrimmage Sunday was not played to our best ability!!
While we did dominate the field, we can take no pride in either
the score or in the aftermath, namely our opponents' crying like
little children!! Had they had any skills at all, the game would
have had a different outcome indeed!!! Especially disappointing was to see some of our players execute crosses and tack-
les in a sloppy fashion.

Remember: Winning comes down to touches on the ball!!
No doubt, someday each of you will meet a competitor who
has touched the ball more often than you have. Indeed, someday you may meet a player who sleeps with the ball. When you
meet that player, will you be ready? Are you ready now?

Complaint Department:

Several players have recently expressed surprise that playing in August means playing in the heat. Let me remind you
that complaints about the heat do not help us play better, nor
do they make the temperature cooler!!

As for the players who complain of stinging because of
sunscreen in their eyes, this is what sweatbands are for!!!

Please note that as of today the Complaint Department is
Officially Closed!!!!

Special Notice for Great Play at last week's Scrimmage
goes to:

Shelby—Congratulations!!! Your eight shots on goal were
mind-blowing!!!

Evelyn—I am pleased to report that our opponents' coach
asked to see your playing card to verify your birth date. This is a
high compliment, indeed!!!!!!!

Bobbi—There are not many goalkeepers who are willing to
play on after sacrificing a tooth for a win, let alone two teeth!

We were all as disappointed as you that the ref insisted you leave the field simply because of a few drops of blood on the ground. We trust your dentist will do a fine repair job and look forward to seeing you at practice on Monday, mouth guard on, please!!!

Jolie—A special thank-you for stepping in as substitute goalkeeper at such short notice. We are all very happy to hear that you have agreed to join Bobbi at the Friday afternoon specialized goalkeeper training class!!!

Dinah—Congratulations on your third yellow card of the summer!

Mud Alert: I have recently noticed that many players seem to have forgotten that muddy cleats are a sign of disrespect! To be sure that all Power players learn good soccer hygiene, as of today I am requiring all cleats to be cleaned immediately after every practice and polished before every game! To ensure that this new practice is strictly observed, I will begin holding Random Soccer Cleat Inspections immediately!! Anyone who does not comply will have ample opportunity to polish her cleats during the next game, which she will be spending on the bench!

Please note: The Winslow West Soccer-Plex Store will soon have a large inventory of soccer cleats, each one personally approved by me! Having a spare pair of cleats will make complying with our hygiene program much easier.

If you have any questions regarding the Winslow West Soccer-Plex Store, please speak to our Store Manager, Vicki West!!!

Tournament Update: Our next tournament is the Twin Oaks Labor Day Tournament! Please have all girls on the field by 6:30 a.m. on game day. Also, please plan on all girls' remaining available at the park all day, on all three days, since additional game opportunities do occasionally arise!

Parents, good news! This one is only a three-hour drive away!

Gwen—On behalf of the entire team, please do not forget to take your Dramamine!!!!

Remember, I am not available for discussion on game weekends or tournament weekends at any time.

Good Luck to One and All from Winslow West!!

seventeen

"Y ou're late," Sondra snapped when the elevator doors opened.

"I'm sorry. Eight minutes. I know," Annie said. "My daughter's soccer game ran late. Traffic was awful. The elevator stopped on every floor. I'm so sorry."

"I just want to make sure we understand each other," Sondra said as she led Annie to the conference room. "My job is on the line here. And I need my job. It is not something I do to keep busy."

"Of course it isn't," Annie said.

"And tomorrow morning, at nine o'clock, I need to stand at the head of this table and present a winning deck or I am gone. Can your brain handle that after a hard day watching soccer?"

Annie closed her eyes for a moment, to focus. Okay, Sondra was both insane and mean-spirited. But she was also Annie's only client. Annie took a deep breath and smiled. "The presentation will be brilliant. Ready to begin?"

"I cannot believe it's come to this," Sondra grumbled. "Working on a Sunday."

"We are a formidable team," Annie said. "Super A. Elite. The best."

"Huh?" Sondra wasn't really listening. She pushed a thick pile of papers across the table. "Here. I made a few notes while I was waiting."

Annie looked at the top page. It was covered with illegible scribble.

"You know what the problem is, don't you?" Sondra asked.

Annie had no idea. She waited to hear.

"The problem is—Who works on Sundays?"

Annie assumed this was a rhetorical question.

"Hello?" Sondra asked. "Are you still here?"

Annie assumed wrong. "Policemen," she said. "Nurses. Doctors. Bus drivers. Athletes. Newscasters." She tried to think of more.

"Wrong," Sondra said. "Losers. Losers work on Sundays. How did I get here? I met with you a full week ago and a week later we still have nothing."

"Let's start out by talking about our mission," Annie said.

"When you got up from this table last week, didn't you notice the folder was empty? I mean one minute it's an inch thick and the next minute it's got nothing in it. You didn't notice that?"

Annie was surprised it had taken this long for the missing papers to become her fault. She pushed on. "I see three major missions. The Corporate Mission, the Upper Management Mission, and the Mission of the Employee."

"You want to know what my mission is?" Sondra asked.

"Your mission is my number one concern."

"My mission," Sondra said, "is to show up at the H-ROC meeting with the best deck anyone has ever created."

"We can do that," Annie said.

"My mission is to bring Ralph to his knees with awe."

"Easily done," Annie promised. "We will awe Ralph."

"But most important of all, my mission is to never ever work on a Sunday again. Do you think we can manage all that?"

"We can satisfy every one of your personal missions," Annie said. "As well as the missions of your core audiences. Let's talk about those audiences."

"It's Sunday," Sondra said.

"Let's start with Upper Management."

"I can't believe I'm here on a Sunday," Sondra said.

"We want to be sure our message is saturating through the entire chain of command," Annie said.

"None of those assholes ever worked a goddamn Sunday in their lives."

Annie needed to shift Sondra's attention. "Okay," she said. "Game time."

"What?"

"We're going to divide the presentation into halves. At halftime, we'll stop and examine our game. We'll look at we've accomplished and what we have left to do."

"What are you talking about?" Sondra asked.

"Who's the decision maker in the room tomorrow?" Annie countered.

Sondra didn't need to think about that one. "Ralph."

"Right," Annie said. "So we're going to construct the presentation for a Ralph brain. I guarantee you, Ralph thinks in halves."

"I don't get it," Sondra said, but at least now she was listening.

"In our first half we'll push hard on the Corporate and Upper Management Missions," Annie said. "In the second half we'll attack the Mission of the Employees. You will win the meeting tomorrow. We just have to get everyone's end visions aligned. Do you have a copy of your organizational chart?"

"Goddamn Sunday," Sondra muttered one last time, but she went and got it.

It was nearly two in the morning when Sondra finally said, "We are done," and, even more surprisingly, "This is good. You know," she admitted, "you're actually better than I thought you'd be."

Annie decided to take that as a compliment. "Thanks," she said. "I guess that means we'll continue with the next project."

Sondra began gathering the material that had sprawled out across the table. "Sure. I'd love to work with you again."

"Great," Annie said.

They headed toward the elevator. Annie pressed the button. The doors opened. Annie got in.

"But I don't make those decisions," Sondra said.

"Pardon me?" The doors began to close. Annie pushed the Open button and held it. "You don't make those decisions?"

Sondra laughed. "Not anymore."

The elevator door began to ding.

"Who does?" Annie asked.

"Ralph. It's all Ralph all the time around here now. If Ralph likes you, you're in. If Ralph doesn't like you . . ."

The buzzer became a siren.

"I have to go get my bag," Sondra said. "You'd better let

go of that door or security is going to come up with their guns drawn."

Annie let go. The doors closed. The elevator began its descent.

Ralph. Her future was in the hands of Ralph, whom she'd never met.

Annie closed her eyes, just for a second, but in that second she drifted off. She woke with a start as the doors closed and the elevator began its climb again.

The doors reopened on Zaxtec's floor. Sondra stepped inside. "Back so soon?"

"I forgot to say how much I enjoyed working with you," Annie said.

"Cool. Thanks. You know," Sondra said, her dimples deepening, "we are very similar. I feel like you're my older sister or my aunt. My really smart aunt."

She stared at Annie's eye. "Oh my God! You have a twitch! I do too! Can you see it?" She pointed to her eye.

Annie shook her head. "No. Sorry."

"It's so frustrating," Sondra said. "No one can ever see it."

They rode the rest of the way to the lobby in silence.

eighteen

Winslow glanced out the window at the rolling hills. "Beautiful, isn't it?"

Vicki stared ahead, her eyes narrowing into an angry squint.

"Come on, now," Winslow said. "It's not my fault Betty's Apple Farm closed down, is it? I couldn't know that, could I?"

Vicki's mouth remained a flat line.

"It is a pity I didn't know Betty Apple was selling her farm. It would have been a perfect location for our second Soccer-Plex, don't you think?" The word *our* didn't come easily from Winslow's lips, but when it did, it always worked.

"Her name isn't Betty Apple," Vicki snapped. "And you should have called to confirm."

"I must say I'm disappointed in Parker," Winslow went on. "He's supposed to be looking for just these opportunities. I don't like missing opportunities simply because I don't know they exist."

"You confirm your soccer games a hundred times a day," Vicki said. "I don't understand why you couldn't make one phone call to confirm that the apple farm was open."

It wasn't easy to tune Vicki out, but he managed. As she droned on, her voice a low hum, he surveyed the landscape. It really was a perfect location for his next Plex. Surely, in a place like this, there would be dozens of salt-of-the-earth people. People like him. People who understood the values of soccer. Commitment. Excellence. Sacrifice.

It might be worth it to pay someone a small stipend to keep his eyes open for the perfect parcel of land here. Winslow wouldn't have to pay much—a token, really.

"Because going on a scouting trip is not my idea of how to spend my birthday," Vicki said. "Dinah and I could have had a very nice day out together. We could have had lunch."

"Lunch?" Winslow said. "Didn't you eat when we stopped at the Burger King?"

"That was a bathroom stop," Vicki said. "Not a birthday stop. You could at least have found out if there was a halfway decent restaurant in Chestnut Heights before you dragged us out here."

"Why did you drag us out here, Daddy?" Dinah piped up from the backseat.

"Good God. I didn't drag anyone anywhere," Winslow protested. "We were supposed to go apple picking. The apple farm was sold. Instead we're going to stop by and visit one of my old friends. Is that really so awful?"

"What's the name of the girl?" Vicki asked.

"Did you get a chance to order the warm-ups yesterday?" Winslow countered. It had been another of his brilliant ideas, giving Vicki the store to manage. She'd be happier this way, even if she didn't know it yet.

"What's the girl's name?" Vicki asked again.

He tightened his grip on the wheel. "If you don't place

the order for the warm-ups by Sunday, we won't have them for the opening. And the photograph will be so much more impressive if the girls are in matching warm-ups, don't you think?"

"Tell me the name of the girl we're going to see or there'll be no warm-ups," Vicki said.

Winslow wondered whether the store might be too much to put on one person's plate. Maybe he should have Parker work in the store too.

"Who is the girl, Daddy?" Dinah asked.

"There is no girl. We're going to stop and say hello to my old friend George. George and I grew up together. He's a gym teacher now." Winslow laughed at that.

"There's nothing funny about being a gym teacher," Vicki snapped. "My father was an amazing influence on all his students."

Winslow made a feeble effort to mask his disdain. "Yes, I know. They all came to his funeral and it was lovely."

"So many people came to pay their respects they couldn't fit in the room. They waited outside," Vicki reminded him.

"Yes, darling," Winslow said. "I know."

"In the rain," Vicki said.

"Don't forget the cold," Winslow added. "It was a cold rain, wasn't it?"

Vicki didn't appreciate the sarcasm. "How old is the girl?"

Winslow motioned with his head toward the backseat. He didn't approve of discussing team business in front of Dinah. "Let's talk about it later, shall we?"

Vicki swung around to face her daughter. "Ask Daddy the name of the girl we're going to see."

Winslow steadied his eyes on the road. What did Vicki want him to do? The new team was not gelling the way he'd hoped. Did she want him to just sit back and watch his destiny unravel?

"What's the girl's name, Daddy?"

"And ask how old she is," Vicki prompted.

"How old is she, Daddy?"

"Just tell us her name and how old she is and we won't say another word about it," Vicki promised.

She was tough, Vicki was. Iron will. Steely mind. He might be an expert at letting the voices of the parents on his team move through him like a breeze, but that didn't work with a force of nature like Vicki.

"Her name is Tia," he said. "And she's turning eleven tomorrow. All right?"

"You're chasing a ten-year-old girl?" Vicki asked.

"I'm not chasing anyone. And she's as good as eleven."

"I don't get it," Vicki said. "You have a brand-new team with a full roster. Why are you thinking about poaching a girl when the season has barely begun?"

"I don't poach."

"Isn't that how I like my eggs?" asked Dinah.

"Right," Vicki said. "I forgot. You don't poach. You flatter. You offer advice. You offer training. And you let Marilyn do the rest." Vicki saw something flicker across Winslow's face. "Is Marilyn going to be here today too?"

"No," Winslow protested, because after all, he couldn't be sure. "Look, the reality is that if the chemistry of the team is wrong, it's up to me to fix it quickly. It's a fact—the best time to replace a weak player is the first moment you notice the player is weak. People don't grasp how quickly one weak player can pull down an entire organization."

"Am I pulling down the organization?" Dinah asked.

Vicki shot Winslow a look.

"Of course not," Winslow said. He hoped he sounded sincere.

"You are one of the very top players on the team, Dinah," Vicki said. "Daddy wouldn't bother coaching your team if you weren't on it. Isn't that right, Winslow?"

"Dinah, you've been working very hard. And you must continue to do just that. You've succeeded at the hardest part. You have figured out what your strength is. And once one has figured out one's strength, the rest is easy."

"What is my strength?" Dinah asked.

"Your aggression on the field," Winslow said, "which, because of your small size, often surprises your opponents."

"Winslow." Vicki's voice held a warning. Dinah's tiny frame worried her even though the doctor promised a growth spurt was imminent.

"I believe your yellow card record will be legendary," Winslow went on.

"But I can't always get the ball to go very far when I kick it," Dinah said. "Do you think I have a bad kick? Is that the problem?"

"There is no problem," Vicki said. "Is there, Winslow?"

"No," Winslow said on automatic pilot.

He went back to thinking about Tia. Could it actually be possible she was as talented as he'd heard?

"If Tia turns out to be half as good as people say," Winslow reasoned out loud, "someone is going to get her. Why shouldn't it be me?" He glanced at Vicki, who was staring at him. "Us," he added quickly.

"The turn is up there," Vicki said, because she never forgot a face, a name, or a road.

They drove down the narrow gutted lane past the elementary school and around back to the field where the game was already under way. As they stepped out of the car, the whistle blew. Halftime.

Vicki took the keys from Winslow. She locked the car and dropped the keys in her purse. "Let's get this over with."

He moved close to whisper in her ear. "Over there, next to George, is the manager's wife, Frances. She's the one with the brother who scouts for the University of North Carolina."

"You didn't say anything about a college scout," Vicki whispered back.

"I'm going to say hello to Tia. Why don't you introduce yourself to Frances."

"You got it," Vicki said. She adjusted her hair. She wished she'd brought a brush. Tia was an irritation. But a college scout—that was something else.

"Wait here, Dinah," Vicki said. "I'll be back."

Dinah sat down on a grassy patch in front of the car. Vicki walked over to the wife with the brother who scouted for North Carolina.

Winslow spotted his friend George on the bleachers. George saw him too, and nodded toward where a small group of girls were sitting. The girls' coach was busy conferring with his team manager.

Winslow, looking as if he owned the field, marched over to where Tia and her friends sat slurping orange slices.

"Excellent job, young ladies," he said. "Very well played." He made eye contact with number eight—that would be Tia—and smiled. Tia smiled back, even though she had no idea who he was, or that he hadn't even seen a second of her game.

"That was quite an impressive half. You do know you're very good, don't you?" he asked Tia. "Or has no one ever mentioned that before."

She blushed. The girls giggled.

"Have I embarrassed you?" Winslow asked. "I'm so sorry. I didn't mean to."

"Winslow?"

He turned toward the voice, his smile broadening. It never failed to surprise him, how far his reputation had traveled. Even here, in Chestnut Heights, he was known.

"Winslow?"

His eyes connected with the voice and his smile flattened. It was only Marilyn.

"I'm here," she said. "It took some doing but I actually got rid of all my kids for the day. Which one is she?"

Winslow stepped farther away from the girls. "Number eight," he said quietly, tilting his head to show where Tia was sitting. "I was just talking to her now."

"Great. I'll find the parents." Marilyn scanned the crowd. "Oh no." She lowered her voice. "Don't look now but Maura is here."

"Who?"

"The plumber's wife. Maura."

Maura turned when she heard her name. "Marilyn? What on earth are you doing here?"

Winslow kept perfectly still, hoping she wouldn't notice he was there too.

"And Winslow," Maura said.

Damn. Winslow turned around to face her. "Hello."

"I'm Nadine's mother, in case you forgot."

He gave her a mild smile. "I know who you are."

"What are you two doing all the way out here in Chestnut Heights?" Maura asked.

"That's what I was going to ask you," Marilyn said.

Maura turned to Winslow. "I'm not going to lie. I'm here because Nadine is miserable. She's been working so hard to move up but she keeps getting disappointed. Frankly, I couldn't stand watching her mope anymore. I decided it was time for us to start looking around to see what our options were. You know—for teams more on her level."

"Good idea," Winslow said. "Forward thinking. Very smart. If you'll excuse me."

"Roy doesn't think it's smart. He says you promised you'd put Nadine on your team next year for sure. He said one more year on the Asteroids could be good for her growth. But I think he's wrong."

"I don't disagree with you," Winslow said. "No point waiting if you can find something better now."

"Would it be just a year?" Maura asked. "She can wait one more year. But if it's more than a year, forget it. It's too frustrating. For a kid like Nadine, who has a passion, being on the Asteroids—well, you can just imagine."

Marilyn, who had managed to slip off, penetrated the group of Chestnut Heights parents. "So you're Tia's mom," she said, her voice carrying too far.

Maura stiffened. "Who's Tia?"

"No idea. Will you excuse me?"

Maura's eyes were fixed on Marilyn now. Who the hell was Tia? She went to see what she could find out.

The ref blew his whistle. Halftime was over.

"Okay," Vicki said, meeting up with Winslow. "Let's go."

"I haven't had a chance to say hello to George yet. I haven't even seen the girl play."

"You didn't talk to George? What have you been doing all this time?"

"Marilyn showed up," Winslow explained. "And then Maura found us."

"Mrs. Plumber?"

Winslow nodded.

He expected sympathy, but all Vicki said was "Okay. Let's go."

"Can't you find a coffee shop or something somewhere. You can get Dinah a hot cocoa and a little something for yourself for your birthday. You can have lunch. You said you wanted lunch, didn't you?" He reached into his pocket and took out a twenty. "Half an hour?" He offered her the bill.

Vicki stared at it like it was puke. "We're going home."

"That's ridiculous. We've come all this way, and I haven't even met the wife with the brother who's the scout."

"I don't know who told you that one," Vicki said. "But her brother is no scout. I asked her straight out." She took the car keys out of her purse and started toward the car.

"I need to talk to George," Winslow said. "I want to watch the girl."

"Fine. Marilyn can give you a lift home."

"Marilyn isn't going home."

"She isn't? How about Maura? I bet she'd love to have you alone for an hour."

"Very nice, Vicki," he muttered as he followed her to the car.

nineteen

Who told you Winslow was scouting in Chestnut Heights?" Roy asked. "And why do you believe everything you hear?"

"I saw him. I was there," Maura said. "Marilyn was there too. You know what? I'm beginning to think Marilyn has blackballed Nadine from the team. Do you think she can do that?"

They both heard the creak and turned. Nadine stood at the bottom of the stairs.

"I'm sorry," she said.

A huge wave of sympathy washed over Roy. "Sorry for what? You got nothing to be sorry for."

"Sorry for heading the ball into my own goal," Nadine said. "And for spitting on my hand."

"What?" Maura asked.

More than anything, Roy wished he hadn't yelled at Nadine for spitting. She had only done it because someone had said something to her. It made him so mad he wanted to spit too.

"Leave her alone, Maura," Roy said.

"I don't want to be on that team anymore, Daddy." Nadine bit her lip, working to hold back tears.

"It's not going to be for too much longer," Roy said.

Nadine came over and laid her damp cheek on his chest.

"Daddy will take care of it, honey," Maura said. But there was no warmth in her words.

"How?" Nadine asked.

Roy couldn't wait to hear the answer.

"He's going to have a talk with Winslow," Maura said. "And after that, either you'll be on the Power, or we'll move."

"We're moving?" Nadine asked.

"I've taken a few drives around Chestnut Heights," Maura said. "You'd love it there. They have farms and ponds with ducks and brand-new houses with no sidewalks to worry about, and plenty of parking. And they have good soccer. You know what else?"

Nadine shook her head. She didn't know anything.

"I happen to know they are about to lose one of the best players on their top team. So they're going to be looking for new talent."

"How do you know that?" Roy asked.

"And guess what position she plays?" Maura went on. "She's the sweeper, like you."

"I don't want to move," Nadine said. "I just want Winslow West to be my coach." Nadine stared up at her father. "Can you fix it so he's my coach, Daddy?"

"Daddy's going to try," Maura said. "But if Daddy can't fix this tonight, I'm going with Aunt Patty to meet with a Realtor in Chestnut Heights tomorrow. You will love it there. The houses are huge, and new, and some even have elevators."

"Don't worry," Roy said to Nadine. "I'll talk to Winslow. I'm not making any promises, but I'll talk to him."

"Now?" Nadine asked.

"I have to go over to the Soccer-Plex anyway," Roy said. "If he's there, I'll talk to him now. If not, I'll call him when I get back."

"Get him to sign something this time," Maura said. "Whatever he agrees to, get him to put it in writing."

Roy got in his truck and wondered how long he could stretch out his work tonight. He tried to calculate what time Maura usually went to bed and how long it took from when she zoned out in front of the TV to when she actually fell asleep.

Twenty minutes later Roy was driving on the outskirts of town. Then, there it was, the Soccer-Plex, rising like a half-moon from the middle of an enormous field.

He pulled into the large lot, where half a dozen vehicles were clustered around Winslow's truck, as if it needed protection.

Roy found him in the lobby, cackling with a trainer about the Power's most recent win.

"Roy," Winslow said when he saw him, "you can help us out here. Were you at Nadine's last game?"

Here we go, Roy thought. Winslow heard about the spit. "Yes," he said quietly.

"What are your thoughts about it?" Winslow asked.

This was a first, Winslow asking for his opinion. Roy took his time answering.

"There are a lot of tough girls on that Center Lovell team," he said for openers. "I think they targeted Nadine from the get-go. Because of how good she is. And also because of her size."

Winslow got that look in his eyes, like Roy wasn't getting the point.

"What exactly is it that you heard?" Roy asked.

"I heard the new girl, Charlotte, is absolutely amazing on the field."

"That's it?" Roy said.

"Why? Was there something else?"

"No," Roy said. "That was the main thing. The girl is good. For a new kid, she's a pretty good player."

"Very interesting," Winslow said. He started to walk away.

"Winslow," Roy said. "About winter training."

"Right. Yes. I've got to go prepare for a staff meeting right now, but let's discuss it later, shall we?"

"I really need to talk to you now. And it's not just about winter training. I need to talk to you about Nadine. About her future."

"Absolutely. Will do. No problem." Winslow touched his watch. "I've just got a couple of calls to return first. Can you give me a few minutes?" He walked backward toward his office. "We'll do it in a bit. I promise."

Roy started to protest but Winslow was too quick. He ducked into his office, closed the door, and turned the lock.

Roy picked up his crowbar, walked into the girls' bathroom, and smashed the center of the concrete floor. It buckled into several large chunks that would take him hours to repair. But even that did nothing to make his rage recede.

twenty

Annie didn't sleep long, but she slept enough to function. She picked Charlotte up at eight and was relieved to hear that the night with her cousins had been fun, her scalp no longer burned, and the forecast for the rest of the week was cloudy with rain, meaning day camp was back on the schedule.

"I spoke to Daddy last night," Charlotte added.

"You did?" Annie had missed two of Tim's calls. She'd called back each time, but both times Tim hadn't been there.

"He said to tell you he'll be in meetings all day but he'll see you later."

"Did he say where he was calling from?" Annie asked.

"No," Charlotte said. "Why? Where is he?"

"Atlanta," Annie said and hoped she sounded more convincing than she felt.

They picked up Charlotte's swimsuit and towel at home and drove to camp, where Nurse Pike examined Charlotte's head under a bright light and cleared her to stay.

On the way back home, Annie stopped off and got coffee. She figured three extra-large cups should help offset her all-nighter with Sondra. She finished one in the car, drank the second on her commute up the stairs to her office, and drank the third as she wrote her Plan for the Day.

Today she would write the brochure. Of course, Sondra still had to get the approval from Ralph. But Annie knew that wouldn't be a problem. After all, at that very moment Ralph was in the meeting, finding out for himself that Annie did great work.

She read through all the papers Sondra had given her to take home, memos about Zaxtec's corporate culture, the time line of its history, and copies of all previously produced pamphlets of now-out-of-date corporate goals.

When she finished reading, Annie checked her watch. It was eleven thirty. Sondra should have called by now. The meeting should be over. They had timed the presentation to the minute.

At twelve thirty Annie wondered if it was possible that a meeting she'd organized had actually turned out to be a disaster.

At one o'clock she concluded Sondra must have forgotten to call. So Annie called her.

"This is Lois," said the woman who picked up the phone. "How can I help you?"

"This is Annie Fleming. I was wondering if the meeting was over yet."

"What?" said Lois.

"The H-ROC meeting that was scheduled from nine to eleven this morning. Is it over?"

"I wouldn't know anything about that," Lois said.

"May I please speak to Sondra?" Annie asked.

"She's out of the office," Lois said. "Who shall I say called?"

"Annie Fleming. I helped put together the presentation deck for this morning's meeting. Is Sondra somewhere I can reach her?"

"And you are with?"

"Could you put me through to Sondra's voice mail, please?"

"And your company is?"

Annie hung up and called Sondra's cell. She left a message and sent an email. She left a message on Tim's cell too. Where was Tim? She pushed the thought out of her mind and tried Sondra again.

"This is Annie," she told Lois. "Can you tell me when you expect Sondra to be back?"

"Are you Annie Fleming?" Lois asked.

"Yes."

"Oh, good. Sondra told me to give you a message. She said don't call her. She'll call you."

"I don't understand. Does she want me to wait until she calls me before I start working on the next presentation deck? Or does she want me to move forward without waiting to talk to her?"

"I have no idea," Lois said.

"Is she going to call me this afternoon?" Annie asked.

"I don't know anything about that," Lois said.

"Would you please ask Sondra to call me as soon as she gets in?" Annie asked.

"She's in," Lois said. "I'll tell her I gave you the message."

Annie heard a click and then a dial tone. She tried Tim again.

"Where are you?" she said into the phone. She knew, but couldn't help, that she sounded forlorn.

She pushed on. By the time she left to get Charlotte from camp, Annie had what she felt was a good rough draft of the brochure. But still no call back from Sondra or Tim.

When Annie and Charlotte got back home, Gerri was on their front step, waiting for them.

"Did I remember wrong?" Gerri asked. "I thought today was our first training session."

"I apologize," Annie said. "I completely forgot."

"That's okay," Gerri said. "Charlotte's here. I'm here. If you still want to have some socca-rific fun, I'm ready. What do you say, Charlotte?"

"Good," Charlotte said.

Annie left them to their soccer and went back to work revising the brochure. An hour later, she heard the sound of the back door opening. Charlotte and Gerri walked inside, laughing. Annie joined them in the kitchen.

"That was a blast," Gerri said. "Wasn't it, Char?"

Charlotte nodded. Her face was flushed, her hair curled in the damp summer heat, her shirt sweaty. Annie could see right away she was happy.

"Lord, I wish I could concentrate more on coaching," Gerri said. "Coaching is what I love. You know, most teams have a coach and a manager. I'm one of the few who does both. Boy, would I love to give up managing."

"You should do it, then," Annie said. "It's just a matter of

restructuring your responsibilities. You have to identify someone from your core audience who has the skills to be the manager. You have to sell the opportunity and sweeten it with an
offer to train the person. Then you can realign your time to
concentrate on what you like. Coaching."

"Realign my time. That sounds so good. That's what I need
to do. Realign my time. Except who am I realigning with? No
one wants to manage the team. At least no one I trust." Gerri
stopped. "Wait a socca-minute. What about you?"

"She can't," Charlotte piped up. "She doesn't know anything about soccer."

There was that defeatist attitude again. It made Annie's
entire body go rigid. "I can learn," Annie said. "I can watch
and learn."

"We can teach her together," Gerri told Charlotte. "And
if she's anything like you, she'll pick it up in a minute and
a half."

"She can't," Charlotte said. "She doesn't have time."

"Actually," Annie said glancing at the phone, which still
wasn't ringing. "I don't have a lot of work right now. It's kind
of perfect timing."

In fact, it was amazing timing. She'd spent so many years
at PC&B, patiently waiting to make partner, and nothing had
come of it. Now, after just a couple of weeks, she was being
offered the plum job of manager of a soccer team. Tim wasn't
going to believe it.

Where was Tim?

"Would you do it?" Gerri asked.

"Absolutely," Annie said. The more she let it sink in, the
better it felt.

"Let me go to my office and get you all the paperwork you'll need," Gerri said. She winked. "My office is the front seat of my car." She ran to her car and returned a moment later with a large cardboard box. She slid its contents out onto Annie's kitchen table.

"You'll probably want to organize this a little better," she said. "I'm not good at sorting. Also, there are a couple of forms missing from some of the girls. You'll have to follow up on that. And I started a log that needs to be input on a spread-sheet. Wins, losses, strikes, assists—like that."

"That's no problem," Annie said. "I'm very organized."

"Oh—and this weekend I convinced Winslow to invite us to a scrimmage at his Soccer-Plex. It's not officially opened yet but he did put together a small tournament. Only now I have a conflict. I can get to the Soccer-Plex, but I'll be late. You think you could get there a little early to get everyone started?"

"She doesn't know anything about tournaments," Charlotte said.

Gerri smiled. "Well then, you've got five days to teach her."

After Gerri left, Annie asked Charlotte to tell her about tournaments.

Charlotte said she didn't know anything either and went up to her room.

Charlotte had a right to be skeptical. Annie would have to prove herself. And she could do that. She could show her daughter that she had the ability to be a great team manager. All it would take was work. And work was something Annie knew how to do.

She took one of the empty file boxes from the dining room and put all the team paperwork in it. She made a master list of all the missing forms—most players were short at least one. When that was done she went online to find a soccer rule book. That was easy too.

This was great. She printed out a manual and started studying it.

She was on the final chapter, "How to Be a Winner and a Good Sport Too," when she heard the front door open.

"Daddy," Charlotte called out.

"How's my favorite girl?" Tim boomed back.

"Good," Charlotte said.

"Just good?" Tim asked.

"Super good," Charlotte said.

Annie went into the living room, where they were sitting close together on the sofa.

"I was just hearing about Charlotte's training session with Gerri," Tim said.

"It's nice to have you home," Annie said. She knew Tim could hear the edge in her voice. "I'll be in the kitchen," she added. "But I'd love to hear about your trip when you get a chance."

"Last night I played poker at Aunt Trissy's," Charlotte told her father as Annie walked out of the room.

"Did you win?" Tim asked.

Annie returned to the kitchen, and the soccer manual. She reread the chapter on offsides for the second time, but still didn't understand a word of it.

Tim walked in a few minutes later. He sat down across from her.

"Go ahead," he said. "Say what's on your mind. You're mad. I can tell."

"I'm not mad," Annie said. "I'm worried. You didn't leave me an itinerary. You didn't answer my calls."

"I answered every one of your calls."

"But you never picked up when I called."

"I was in meetings," Tim explained.

Annie thought Tim looked nervous. She had to say what was on her mind.

"Trissy told me you weren't in Atlanta," Annie said. "Hank told her you were at a conference in the city. They think we're having problems."

Tim shifted over to the chair next to Annie. He covered her hand with his long fingers. "It has nothing to do with you."

"Oh no," Annie said.

"It's not what you think," Tim said. "It has nothing to do with us."

"Who does it have to do with, then?" Annie asked.

"I'm going through a tough time at work. That's all. Scout's honor."

"You were never a scout," Annie said.

"I was hoping you wouldn't remember that."

Annie felt herself soften. It was hard to stay mad at Tim for long. "Were you in Atlanta?"

"Yes," Tim said.

"Why does Hank think you weren't?" Annie asked.

Tim took a deep breath and sighed out the world. "Because I told him I wasn't."

"You lied to your brother?"

"Not exactly," Tim said. "I did go to Atlanta. But I didn't go to the Atlanta office."

"I don't understand."

"I don't want you to worry," Tim said.

Annie took a hard look at her husband and suddenly she saw it. He didn't look right. Tim, whose hair was always perfectly in place, who never gained weight or caught the family colds, who slept like a rock, ate heartily, drank moderately, and could have coffee at eleven and still sleep through the night, did not look good at all.

"What's wrong?" she asked. Diagnoses presented themselves in her mind. Liver disease, blood disease, kidney failure, stroke. Brain disease, diabetes, cancer of the throat.

She thought of all the infirmities of their combined ancestors. The ones with mysterious undiagnosable symptoms—numb feet, neck pain, blurry vision, rash. And the others—celiacs, heart attacks, maniacs.

She took a breath. Tim was her partner for life. There was nothing they couldn't handle together. She braced herself. "What's wrong with you?"

Tim let out a deep breath and told her. "I've got fire-aphobia."

"Pardon me?"

"I'm a fire-aphobe. I'm fire-aphobic. It's a thing. I saw a doctor."

"What kind of thing? What kind of doctor?"

"I've got a phobia about firing people. It's not that uncommon."

Annie was so relieved she almost laughed. But she quickly realized that would not be an appropriate response.

"No one likes to fire people," she said. "Who would? It's not fun."

"I'm not talking about not having fun," Tim said. "I'm talking about going to Atlanta three times in the past two weeks and not being able to do my job. I'm talking about not leaving the airport hotel."

"But you're so good at firing people," Annie said. "You've got that great mix of kindness with a little bit of mean thrown in. I mean you're tough, not mean. I mean, I don't really have a job right now," she reminded him, in case he forgot.

"I know," he said quietly.

"Okay," Annie said. "You know what? You need a vacation. That's all. Why don't you tell Hank you're going to take two weeks off and that he's got to close down the Atlanta office himself. Then you can go away to some beach or someplace, and when you come back you'll feel refreshed and ready to fire again."

Tim smiled. Annie was relieved. At least he hadn't lost his sense of humor.

"What did the doctor say?" she wanted to know.

"He said I should try relaxation techniques. Practice deep breathing. Make some lifestyle changes. Eat well. Sleep more. Exercise."

"Is that the reason for the sudden treadmill use?" Annie asked.

Tim nodded. "So, I'm doing all that. But I still haven't been able to close down the office. I told Hank I was going to a conference because I thought this time I might not be able to get on the plane. But I did. I got on the plane. I went to Atlanta. I ordered the doughnuts. I had them delivered to my room, and I ate them."

"All of them?"

Tim nodded.

"You have to tell Hank. He's your brother. He'll want to help you."

"It's complicated," Tim said. "Hank's been away a lot lately. He's basically never around."

"Why is that?" Annie asked.

Tim shrugged. "I'm not sure."

"What can I do?" Annie asked. "How can I help you?"

"There's nothing you can do," Tim said. Then he thought of something. "Except maybe to lay off asking about Hot Holidays for a while. I have nothing good to report. And when I'm at home I'd rather not think about it. Can you understand that?"

"Of course," Annie said. "What do you want to talk about instead?"

"Anything," Tim said. "Anything good. Let's talk about you. How did things go with your presentation?"

"Next topic."

"Oh," Tim said. "It didn't go well?"

"It's fine," she said, because Tim didn't really need to hear about her work problems right now. "How about if neither of us talks about work."

"Just for now," Tim said.

"Right," Annie agreed. "Hey, I just thought of some good news. I got a promotion."

"Congratulations," Tim said. "I thought we weren't going to talk about work."

"It has nothing to do with work. It's about soccer. Charlotte's coach promoted me. I'm the team manager. Can you believe it? A month ago all I knew about soccer was that some guy from somewhere hit another guy from somewhere else in the chest with his head. Now I'm managing a team."

"That's amazing," Tim said. "That's great. That's the best news I've heard all month."

"I know," Annie said. "And I'm going to do a great job. I'm going to be the best soccer manager ever. I want to make Charlotte proud."

"Now, that's something I look forward to seeing," Tim said, and he meant it.

twenty-one

By the morning of the tournament, Annie had everything organized. She dragged the big cooler of Gatorade to the car, then lugged out two large shopping bags filled with snacks.

"Are you ready?" she called to Charlotte when she came back in the house to get her purse.

Charlotte ran over with the phone. "It's for you."

Annie covered the receiver with her hand. "Get your soccer stuff together and I'll meet you in the car." She put the phone to her ear. "Hello?"

"I don't like to be left on hold," Sondra said. "When are you going to be here?"

"Be where?" Annie asked.

"Are you on drugs?" Sondra asked. "Here. My office. I'm ready. Let's go."

"I'm confused," Annie said. "I assumed—"

"Stop," Sondra said. "Don't assume."

"But your secretary, Lois—"

"Stop," Sondra said again. "I no longer have a secretary

named Lois. Look, you and I are now officially behind. Ralph called three times looking for the video script, which I'm thinking you haven't even started. Am I right? Did you start it yet?"

"You never called me back," Annie said. "I left you over a dozen messages. I thought you didn't want to proceed."

"I thought we had an understanding," said Sondra. "I've got Ralph totally hot for the brochure and leadership script, drooling for the video, and you haven't even started, have you? Didn't you beg me for more projects? There's a big one coming up and I was just about to give it to you. My mistake."

"I thought you weren't in charge of assigning projects anymore. I thought Ralph was the assigner."

"I worked that out. I work everything out. That's what I'm about. I thought that's what you were about too."

For a second Annie let herself think about what it would be like if she lived alone, with few financial responsibilities, or if she were independently wealthy, with no financial worries at all, or if Tim made a lot of money or if Tim had a job that was, at least for now, secure. But none of those were the case.

"I'm sorry for the miscommunication," she said. "But it's not a problem. I can draft a script very quickly."

She could do that. As soon as she got home from the tournament she could chug a pot of coffee and get to work. She could stay up all night if she needed to. If she got tired, she could take a power nap and chug a second pot. There were plenty of things she could do to keep up the energy she'd need for an all-nighter. She could run on the treadmill, take breaks to stretch, eat dark chocolate, eat light chocolate.

"All right," Sondra gave in. "I guess I'll feel better once we get started. When does the next bus or train or plane or whatever it is you take get in?"

Annie thought about Hank not talking to Tim, Tim not firing anyone in Atlanta, the cost of travel soccer, the cost of food. "I can come in first thing tomorrow morning, as early as you like."

"Are you completely nuts?" Sondra asked. "Tomorrow is Sunday. I am not working another Sunday. I've got a lot of people hot for this, Annie. I'm beginning to think we're not on the same planet, let alone the same screen of the deck."

Annie heard the thump of the soccer ball hitting the garage door, a rhythmic reminder of her life, utility bills, tax bills, medical bills, food. Sondra was insane and Annie couldn't afford to lose her.

"This is all good," Annie said. "Keeping Ralph waiting is good. You want him to be hungry for it. You know, when I worked at Proxo we had a name for people who tried to please everyone, making deadlines early, doing more than was asked."

"What do you mean, a name? What kind of name?"

Annie searched her mind for something that would get her out of this.

"One of my clients came up with it. He called people like that sea cucumbers."

"Sea cucumbers? What does that even mean?"

Annie could do this. Charlotte had written a fifteen-page picture book about sea cucumbers as a science project. She could make this work.

"Have you ever seen a sea cucumber?" she asked.

"No," Sondra said. "Why?"

"If you saw one you'd understand. Sea cucumbers make slugs look like cocker spaniels. But it isn't about how ugly they are. The point is they're spineless, they're soft, and they're useless. If they became extinct tomorrow no one would care. I'm not saying Ralph is trying to lower your stock by positioning you as a sea cucumber. But you did tell me there's a political situation."

"Useless?" Sondra said. "That prick. I had no idea."

"You need to show him strength. Having him wait a day or two is a great way to accomplish that."

"Can you come in Monday morning, then? Say, six o'clock? I'm usually here at six because we're goddamn global now and England calls every day at six thirty. France calls at five thirty, but screw them."

"Six on Monday is great," Annie said.

Sondra wasn't quite ready to get off the phone yet. "Are you excited about this?"

The side door opened. "Mom," Charlotte called. "We're going to be late."

"Because you don't sound it," Sondra said.

"You are so perceptive," Annie told her. "What you're hearing in my voice is that I'm on my way out the door to get my fax fixed, and to pick up a new wireless system because my old one doesn't reach everywhere in the house. To be honest, I need one that will reach the third-floor bathroom."

"The bathroom," Sondra said, relaxing at the thought. "Cool."

Annie hung up the phone and ran out of the house. "Let's go."

Charlotte got in the car and closed the door. "We're going to be late," she said.

Annie checked her watch. "Don't worry. Twenty minutes late is the new early."

The Soccer-Plex had a parking lot optimistically built to accommodate enormous crowds. Today's visitors barely filled a corner of it. Annie, like everyone else, parked in a cluster near the entrance.

"I have good snacks, so no one will notice that we're late," she said as she took several bags filled with chips out of her trunk.

"It's supposed to be fruit," Charlotte said.

"They'll like this better," Annie told her as they rushed inside.

Charlotte led Annie through the sawdust-coated lobby, past a raw wood structure that would soon be a snack bar, and two large signs announcing that the bathrooms were closed until further notice.

They pushed their way through a heavy, slow revolving door and stepped out onto a new field of artificial turf.

Annie's ears popped with the change in air pressure. A whistle blew.

"Fury and Power," a voice called out. "Please go to Field One, which is on my left. Comets and Avengers, you are on Field Two, to my right. All other teams, kindly sit with your coaches on the bleachers." The tall, thin man who was speaking stood on a small platform at the back of the field. "Coaches, please be sure your parents stay either on the other side of the glass wall or upstairs in our viewing lounge." He blew his whistle, picked up his portable stage, and walked off the field.

Charlotte showed Annie where her teammates were sitting. Their parents hovered nearby.

"I think you're supposed to wait on the other side of that glass," Annie told the parents. "Or you can watch from upstairs," she added, in case they hadn't heard.

"Where's Gerri?" Chip asked.

"She'll be here soon," Annie said. "Girls, do you want some snacks?"

"Are we eating or are we playing?" Chip asked.

"Does anyone even know how many games we're playing?" asked Peggy Ann. "Where the hell is Gerri?"

"We'll play at least three games," Annie said. "Gerri will be here soon but she asked me to get everyone started. She emailed me some notes about the other teams." She pulled a piece of paper out of her bag.

Annie read from the notes. "We might be able to tie against the Fury. We'll lose to the Force. The Power, as usual, will be a slaughter. Unfortunately, the Holder Crush will probably be an even bigger slaughter. This season they've added two amazing players and their coach thinks—"

"We know about the Holder Crush," Peggy Ann cut her off. "And by the way, who put you in charge?"

"I'm the new team manager," Annie explained. "I volunteered because Gerri told me no one else wanted to do it."

Peggy Ann let out a loud laugh.

Suddenly, Annie remembered what Gerri had actually said was no one she trusted wanted to do it.

"Maura," Peggy Ann called to a late arrival. "Have you met our new team manager, Annie Fleming?"

Maura's face wasn't friendly on a good day.

"Annie asked us if we would mind stepping out into the hall," Peggy Ann added. "Apparently we're not allowed to stay in here, but she is."

"That's not what I said," Annie defended herself. "Once Gerri gets here, I won't stay here, either."

"Oh, that makes me feel much better," Peggy Ann said. "Come on, everyone. Let's let our manager do her job." Peggy Ann led the parents out through the revolving door to the other side of the glass wall, where they stood in a gossipy clump.

Annie sat with the girls. They greedily stuffed their mouths with chips, hurrying to finish before anyone remembered to remind them that this was not allowed.

Gerri raced in just as the buzzer sounded for the start of the second game. "Okay, girls," she called to the team. "Are we going to win today or are we going to have fun?"

"Both," the girls yelled back in practiced unison.

"I'm going to go," Annie said, excusing herself. She glanced at the parents on the other side of the glass wall, and decided to try the view from the second-floor balcony instead.

She stood at the railing watching from above as the Asteroids ran onto the field. Moments after the game began Charlotte scored a goal, quickly followed by a second one, and then a third.

Annie was so engaged, watching the players go berserk with cheers at Charlotte's fourth goal, that she didn't even notice two people had come up the stairs and joined her. Then one of them spoke.

"Hello." It was the man who'd stood on the portable stage. "I'm Winslow West."

"I'm Marilyn," said the woman beside him, "Winslow's special assistant."

"Is that your daughter?" Winslow asked, pointing at the girl getting high fives from her teammates.

"Yes," Annie said.

"You must be very proud," he said.

"I am," Annie said.

Winslow looked back at the field. "She has a wonderful natural confidence, doesn't she? See now? She is completely unintimidated by that girl coming toward her, who's really nearly twice her size."

Charlotte stole the ball from the big girl and booted it.

Winslow laughed with delight. "She's got perfect aim with both feet. My God, where has she been playing?"

"This is her first year on travel," Annie told him. "Before that she played on the town team."

"Ah, yes," Winslow said. "I remember now." He whistled. "All that talent for the town team. That is incredible." He watched as Charlotte stole the ball again, kicked it, and scored.

"Wow!" he exclaimed. "You know what she has, don't you? She has passion."

"She does?" Annie was so happy.

"Now, that is something that cannot be taught," Winslow added. "Skills can be taught. Endurance can be improved upon. But passion is a gift. I hope you have someone very, very good working with her."

"Gerri Picker's working with her."

"Gerri," Marilyn said. She looked at Winslow but his expression remained unreadable.

"Charlotte likes her a lot," Annie said. "She likes the whole team."

"Yes," Winslow said. "They are lovely girls, aren't they?"

"Very nice girls," Marilyn said.

"I do wish I'd known about Charlotte at tryouts," Winslow said. "Well, no use looking back. I have to go get the Power ready for the next game. Great to meet you." He raced down the stairs to the field.

"I know you don't know me from a hole in the wall," Marilyn said once he was gone. "But you have to get your daughter off that team."

"What?"

"A kid like Charlotte on a team like that—it makes no sense."

Marilyn, thick all around, with stubby hands, a wide neck, and full cheeks, stood too close to Annie. She moved her imposing body even closer. "Anyone can see in a second how good your kid is. A kid like that needs real competition. I'm not trying to insult her team or anything. They're really nice girls. But letting her play on a team like that, you're taking a chance. A really big chance. You know what I mean?"

"Not really," Annie admitted. She took a step away.

"I've seen it again and again." Marilyn inched closer. "First the girls get bored. Then they lose their interest. Then they lose their skills. Next thing you know, they're putting on makeup, going to the mall, looking for a date and d-r-i-n-k-i-n-g."

"Charlotte's not bored," Annie said. But suddenly she wasn't sure. Did she know that? Would Charlotte even tell her if she was?

"Face it," Marilyn said. "Your daughter doesn't fit in on that team. Anyone who knows anything can see."

"She likes the girls," Annie said.

"Of course she does. That's because she's a real team player," Marilyn said. "Which is why she deserves more." She dropped her voice even though no one else was around to hear. "Winslow has authorized me to invite your daughter to train with our team. Which means he thinks your daughter is a major talent."

"That's very nice of you to say," Annie said.

"It's not about nice. It's about she could practice with the Power and there would be no charge. She could play as Winslow's personal guest, which is a rare thing for him to offer, I promise you."

"Really?"

Marilyn nodded. "We're talking about the best training available, and for free." She moved so close Annie could smell the coffee on her breath. "Will you talk to her? Will you see if she's interested?"

"I'll talk to her," Annie said. "But I can't promise what she'll say."

"She'll be thrilled," Marilyn said. "Anyone would be thrilled. You know"—her voice dropped even lower—"when my Shelby saw your Charlotte play, she came right over to me and said, 'Mom, you have to get that girl on our team.' It was like a chemical reaction. Shelby could practically smell that Charlotte belongs on the Power."

"That's very sweet."

"With those girls, it's all about the team, which is an important life skill, in my opinion. Don't you agree?"

"Yes," Annie said.

"Tell Charlotte she doesn't need to make any long-term commitments. She can try us out and then decide." On the field below, the Power players were moving into place.

"I got to go watch the game," Marilyn said. "Can I tell Winslow you're going to talk to your daughter? I don't want to tell him if you're not going to do it."

"I will," Annie said. "I'll talk to Charlotte this afternoon."

She watched Marilyn go down the stairs and make a bee-line for Winslow, who was standing on the sidelines waiting for the whistle. Marilyn, close enough to kiss him, spoke with an urgency apparent even at a distance. Winslow looked up and smiled.

When the last game of the tournament was over, Annie went down to the field and found Charlotte in the middle of a group of girls grabbing gym bags and water bottles. Gerri was calling out last-minute observations and instructions. When she noticed Annie she stopped midsentence. "Okay, girls, see you at practice on Tuesday."

She hurried over to where Annie was standing. "What did he say?"

"Who?"

"You just spent an entire game talking to Winslow West," Gerri said. "What did he want?"

"We just spoke for a few minutes, that's all."

"Listen, I don't really care what he said. But in about two seconds there's going to be a mob in here and they're not going to be as nice about this as I am. They all saw you talk to him."

The herd of Asteroid parents was already rushing over to debrief her.

"What did he tell you?" Peggy Ann said. "Did he mention anything about Laurel?"

"We spoke very briefly."

"About what?" asked Pat. "Did he mention Winnie?"

"He said the girls all looked very good today."

Peggy Ann counted on her fingers as she echoed the words. "That took six seconds. What else did he say?"

"We talked a little bit about how Charlotte was doing."

"Uh-huh," Chip said.

"Because Charlotte is the one girl he doesn't know."

Half a dozen pairs of eyes were on Annie now, and none of them were friendly.

Annie decided there was no point in keeping secrets. They'd find out sooner or later. "Marilyn invited Charlotte to train with the Power this winter as a guest."

"Marilyn invited Charlotte to train with the Power?" Maura repeated.

"It probably wouldn't be every week," Annie said.

"Marilyn invited her?" Maura said again.

"It's not for sure," Annie said. "I didn't even talk to Charlotte about it yet. I assume she won't want to. But if she does, it won't be a problem for the team, because she'll still practice with the Asteroids. The Power practice would be extra."

"What a relief," Peggy Ann said. "Don't you think that's a relief, Maura?"

Maura said nothing.

The mob dispersed to collect their kids. Annie found Charlotte sitting alone on the bleachers.

"Guess what?" Annie said. "Winslow West came to talk to me. He said you're really talented and he's invited you to train with him on his team."

"Is that why the parents are all mad at you?" Charlotte asked.

"They're not mad at me."

"Yes they are. I saw how they looked."

"You can't worry about it if people get mad for silly reasons," Annie said.

"I don't want to practice with the Power," Charlotte said. "I like my team."

"Isn't Winslow's team supposed to be really good?"

"They're awesome."

"Don't you think if you practiced with them you'd get to be awesome too?" They were back to this again.

"Maybe. But I like my team better."

Annie decided to try a different approach. "Do you know a girl on the Power named Shelby?"

"Everybody knows Shelby. She's going to be a famous soccer player someday."

"Well, after watching you play today, Shelby begged her mother to invite you to play on the Power."

"Really?" Charlotte seemed intrigued.

"Winslow sees your potential. Shelby sees your potential. You've got some real talent, you know?"

"What I know is, if I practice with the Power everyone on my team will hate me," Charlotte said. "And I won't have any friends."

"That's not true," Annie said. "If you practice with two teams you'll have twice as many friends."

"It doesn't work like that," Charlotte said.

"Winslow really thinks you're a gifted player," Annie said. "It would be a waste if you didn't develop your gift. You have nothing to lose. Go to one practice. If you don't like it, you never have to go again. Will you do that? For me?"

"Just one time?"

Annie nodded.

"Okay," Charlotte agreed. She picked up her bag. "I'll try it once. Can we go home now?"

As they walked out to the car, Annie smiled. Things might be going poorly at Hot Holidays and even worse than that in the land of Sondra, but today, at just twelve years old, Charlotte Fleming had been discovered.

twenty-two

POWER POINTERS—*September 1st!!!*
News of the Day

Congratulations to one and all on winning our first-ever Winslow West Soccer-Plex Tournament!

Please note: After the Winslow West Soccer-Plex's official opening, tournaments will be scheduled every weekend! I am working very, very hard to make sure the level of competition is high!!! Stay tuned for our revised practice, scrimmage, game, and tournament schedule!!!!!

Blister Update: Several girls have come to me complaining about blisters! Remember, today's blister is tomorrow's callus! Wear them as the badges of hard work that they are!!!

Tournament Update: Several of you have not confirmed your reservations for the upcoming Labor Day Tournament! Please call Ken immediately to discuss your attendance! Please note: I am expecting one hundred percent participation!! Alert me immediately in the case of a death in the family!!!

Swimming Update: Several parents have inquired as to

whether the motel has a pool. While the answer is yes, this does not mean players may swim in it. After careful consideration, Ken and I have decided there is to be no swimming permitted until after the tournament is over!

Departure Update: All families are to leave immediately after the tournament ends!! Players must be rested for the highly competitive scrimmage I have scheduled for Tuesday's training session!!!

Training Update: To help our team improve focus, discipline, and unity, I am now requiring all players to purchase training uniforms, which will be available at the Winslow West Soccer-Plex store! See Vicki for size recommendations!

Special Notice For Great Play Goes to:

Evelyn—Your goal-scoring header in Game Three of the tournament caused gasps among the Winslow West Soccer-Plex trainers. At least we know someone has been busy practicing!! Good work, and bravo!!!

Shelby—I enjoyed watching your sharp back passes to Evelyn during the first and second games. As for the corner kick calamity, these things happen to even the best of players. I have no doubt you are already working hard to ensure that this embarrassing bumble does not occur again!!

Bobbi—Your save in game four was amazing to watch. As for the large bruise on your leg, please see Vicki as soon as possible. Bandages in team colors are now available in the Winslow West Soccer-Plex store!

Parent Update: Due to the intense planning necessary before each game, I am reminding all new, as well as all old, parents that I am unavailable for discussions on game day or any part of a game or tournament weekend or the two days directly preceding game days or tournament weekend, whether in town or away.

Furthermore, because I value open communication, I will be contacting you shortly to schedule a conference about your daughters' progress and future!!

Good Luck to One and All from Winslow West!!!

twenty-three

er bad day started with a call to the Executive Health Services, the twenty-four-hour medical center Annie had been using for nearly twenty years.

She told the triage receptionist her problem—a twitch that had spread from one eye to the next and had this morning started up on her lip. "Did you ever hear of anyone having a lip twitch?" Annie asked.

The woman took down all of Annie's information and then put her on hold for what felt like forever. Finally she came back.

"I'm sorry," she said. "You're not in our system. Are you a new patient?"

"No, I'm an old patient," Annie said. "Is it possible I'm listed in a different place?"

"There is only one place," the woman said. "Why don't you call back at nine o'clock and speak to one of our new-patient nurses. I'm sure they'll—"

"You're not listening to me," Annie said. "I'm not a new patient."

"Either way," the woman snapped back, "I can't help you.

This is an emergency line for existing patients. You have a non-emergency situation, and as far as our records show, you don't exist."

The phone went dead. The woman had hung up.

Annie started to dial the number again but stopped herself. The woman was right. Her twitch was not an emergency. Getting to work late would be an emergency.

She crept out of the house without waking anyone, and made good time into the city. She got to the Zaxtec office just before six. Sondra came in at seven, agitated and unapologetic.

"I have really bad news," she told Annie as they walked together to her office. "Ralph has been sea-cucumbered."

"What do you mean?"

"It's an expression," Sondra explained. "It means he's useless to us."

Annie wanted to tell Sondra that she knew what the expression meant because she had made it up. But she also knew that wouldn't be helpful, so instead she asked, "What happened?"

"I don't have the details yet," Sondra said. "All I know is Scott is the new Ralph. But don't ask me who Scott is. No one has a clue. Obviously, I can't meet with you. Sorry." She started scanning her BlackBerry emails. She noticed Annie hadn't moved. "Did you need something?"

Annie handed over a folder of papers. "Here's the draft of the outline for the video. It will only take a minute to read, and then I can get started on it."

"I don't have time to think about videos," Sondra said. She offered Annie her hand. "Thank you very much."

Annie did not like the sound of this thank-you. "For what?" she asked, keeping her tone light. "You mean for coming in this morning? Because I don't mind. I understand. Stuff happens."

Sondra smiled. "Yes. It does. That's true. So long." She gave Annie a little wave and left the room.

Annie used the train ride home to make lists of people to call to ask for work. She dredged up every name in her brain, filling up two pages in her notebook. She even added Roxanne, Crawford, and Biblow, because you never knew. She was going to write down Pederson, but then she decided the only kind of consulting he would consider would be from a caddy.

When she got home she was surprised to find Tim was there, working at the dining room table.

"Hi. What's going on?" she asked.

"I'm going over to meet with Hank," Tim said. "I've been making some notes." He studied Annie's face, like he was trying to figure something out. "We need to talk."

"I'm here." She sat down and braced herself.

"I'm bringing Hank a proposal," Tim said. "I've been thinking about this for a while. Part of my problem with closing Atlanta is that I don't think it needs to be closed. I've worked up a new business plan for Hot Holidays—one that doesn't require shutting anything down."

"That's great," Annie said. "Would you like me write up a Context for Change outline for you?"

Tim held up a piece of paper. "Done." Then he sighed. "The thing is, I don't know if Hank is going to go for it. It's so hard to tell with him, especially now. And in case you never noticed, he's not a fire-aphobe. If Hank gets really pissed off, he'll fire me."

"I know," Annie said.

"I'm aware that things aren't going very well with your work right now," Tim said. "But I feel like I have to do this."

"Then do it," Annie said. "Don't worry about it. We'll deal with whatever happens. Anyway, what's the worst it could be?"

"I lose my job, you have no work, we lose our house, we use up our savings. We end up on the street," Tim said.

"Right. Not the worst thing in the world."

They gave each other weak smiles.

"We'll get through this," Annie told him.

"I know," Tim said.

As soon as he left, Annie, nauseous and twitching, hurried to her desk to begin her cold calls.

twenty-four

ould you please say Annie Fleming called," Annie asked the first half dozen assistants.

"We worked together a bunch of years ago," she told the next half dozen.

"The message is I need work," she snapped to number thirteen on the list.

When the doorbell rang she leaped up as if she'd been rescued. Even a crowd of Jehovah's Witnesses looking for converts would be a relief from her reject-athon of calls.

She opened the door to the confusing sight of Charlotte, just home from school, and Linda, her friend from work.

"Here I am," Linda said. "Where are the trumpeters? Did you forget I was coming?" She saw Annie's confusion. "You did. You forgot I was coming."

"No," Annie said. "Of course I didn't."

"Your mother has no idea how to lie," Linda told Charlotte.

"Did you forget today is my first practice with the Power?" Charlotte asked.

"Yes," Annie admitted, because Linda was right: She was no good at lying.

Charlotte ran upstairs to get her soccer gear. Linda circled the first floor of the house.

"So this is the suburbs. What do we do first? Take a tour? Drink a bottle of wine?"

Charlotte came zipping back down. "We have to go," she told her mother. "I can't be late."

"We have to hurry," Annie told Linda. "Charlotte is practicing with a very high level team. I don't want to wreck the one thing that's going right."

"What does high level mean when you're eleven?" Linda asked.

"I'm twelve," Charlotte said as they climbed into the car.

"Which is old in soccer," Annie added.

"Thank God I'm not in soccer," Linda said.

Annie sped out of the driveway, backed up over the high spot on the curb and hit a tree. She hopped out, checked the car, saw there was no damage done, and got back in.

"Did you always drive like this?" Linda asked.

"No," Annie admitted. "This is the new me."

"I'm afraid of the new you," Linda said, buckling herself in.

When they got to the Soccer-Plex, Charlotte hopped out of the car, slammed the door, and ran across the grass to the building.

"What is that thing?" Linda asked, eyeing the mammoth structure. "A space station? I can't wait to see what it looks like from the inside."

"We're not going inside," Annie said. "Parents aren't allowed to watch."

"What do you mean, not allowed?" Linda asked.

"I made the mistake of watching during tryouts, and I can't afford to make that mistake again."

"Why? What would happen?" Linda asked. "Never mind. I don't care. Let's go. You can tell me on the way back to your house."

Annie didn't move.

"Why aren't you driving?" Linda asked.

"There's not enough time," Annie explained. "We'd just have to turn right around and come back."

"So what are we going to do instead?"

"We'll sit in the car," Annie said. "So, what's new?"

There was a knock on Annie's window. She lowered the glass and saw Marilyn.

"Hi," Marilyn said. "Charlotte told me you were still in the car. Aren't you going to come in?"

Linda leaned over Annie and explained to Marilyn that they were not allowed to watch.

"Of course you're allowed," Marilyn explained. "Winslow loves his parents to watch. He just doesn't want them to talk."

"Oh goody," Linda said as she got out of the car. "I've never been inside a space station before."

"Linda," Annie called.

But it was too late. Linda was rushing to the Soccer-Plex alongside Marilyn, giddily describing the details of her bus ride from the city.

When Annie caught up with them they had just gotten to the bleachers. Marilyn pointed Annie to the best seats and then left to attend to a disgruntled parent.

Linda surveyed the scene. "Why didn't you tell me your life was filled with men in shorts?"

Annie glanced over to the field where Linda was staring at a group of the trainers. "Those aren't men. They're boys," she said.

"Who's he?" Linda asked, pointing to Winslow. "He's not a boy."

"That's Winslow West," Annie answered.

"The Winslow West?" Linda asked.

"You've heard of him?"

"I can read," Linda said, gesturing toward the signs on the walls around the field.

Annie hadn't noticed them before. The Winslow West Soccer-Plex. The Winslow West Soccer University. The Winslow West Summer Soccer School. The Winslow West Soccer Store offering a Wide Selection of Winslow West–Approved Apparel.

"He's very cute," Linda said.

"He's also married," Annie told her. "With a kid," she added, for insurance.

"What about the one who's talking right now?" Linda asked.

"That's Parker, the head trainer."

"Parker. Like the pen. That's so cute. Is he married?" Linda asked.

"I have no idea," Annie said.

Linda stood up, gave her tight skirt a quick tug, ran her fingers through her highlighted hair, and started the tricky business of negotiating the metal bleachers in high heels.

"Where are you going?" Annie asked.

"I'm going to ask Parker to show me where the ladies' room is."

"The bathrooms are out of order," Annie told her, remembering the sign. She stood up. "I can take you home."

"I don't really have to go to the bathroom," Linda said. "I just want to know where it is."

Annie watched as Linda, looking lost, wandered over, as if by accident, to Parker. He stopped in the middle of a sentence to listen to her question. Linda gave him the full blast of her charm.

Winslow blew his whistle to signal the start of the scrimmage.

"So," Marilyn said, taking a seat beside Annie. "I am really happy you convinced Charlotte to come to practice. Shelby is thrilled."

Charlotte booted a ball from midfield for a first-minute goal.

"What a foot!" Marilyn said. "Does she ever pass?"

As if she'd heard the question, Charlotte got the ball again and delivered it, like a present, to Shelby, who accepted the gift and kicked it hard into the corner of the goal.

Marilyn jumped up and gave a silent cheer. She sat back down. "Second goal in the second minute. Well done, Shelby," she said under her breath. She turned to Annie. "Why is Charlotte not on this team?"

"Hopefully she will be next year," Annie said.

Marilyn shook her head. "No. We cannot afford to wait." She scribbled something on a small piece of paper and pressed it into Annie's hand. "This is Winslow West's private number. Up to now, I've been the only parent who's had it. But Winslow asked me to give it to you. All you have to do is call that number and you can get Charlotte on the Power this season, no waiting."

Charlotte won the ball and again delivered it to Shelby. Score.

Marilyn leaped into the air and mouthed, "Beautiful, Shelby." She sat back down. "A word of advice. Don't tell anyone about this conversation. Not everyone understands what's involved in building a really great team."

"Get the ball, Rose," a man called out. He stood as close as he could to the sidelines, with his face pressed up against the netting that kept the balls on, and the parents off, the field.

"For example, Freddy," Marilyn said quietly. "He wouldn't understand one bit."

"Get the ball before he takes you out of the game," Freddy screamed.

"Will you excuse me?" Marilyn said. "Now that Vicki is in charge of the store, I'm in charge of the parents."

"Freddy," Marilyn called as she raced down the stairs. "I have something for you." She pulled a lollipop out of her pocket. "Put this in your mouth, Freddy, so you don't yell."

When the scrimmage was over, and the girls were doing their cooling down stretches, Winslow walked over and sat beside Annie. He didn't turn his head when he spoke. Anyone watching couldn't be certain he was even speaking.

"Did Marilyn have a word with you?" he asked.

"Yes," Annie said. She kept her eyes straight ahead too.

"Did she give you my private number?"

Annie opened the palm of her hand to reveal the slip of paper. "Yes."

"Great! It will take some work to iron out the details. But I can do this if Charlotte wants it."

"I'll speak to her. And to my husband."

"Of course," Winslow said. "It should be a family decision."

The girls were done. Charlotte raced over, sweaty and smiling.

"Hello, young Miss Fleming," Winslow said. "That was quite an impressive job you did out there today. Did you manage to have any fun? Any fun at all?"

"Yes," Charlotte said. "I had a lot of fun."

"You're not just saying that to be polite?"

"No," Charlotte said.

"You mean you're not polite?"

"I am polite," Charlotte said.

"Of course you are. I'm just having fun with you. But you knew that, didn't you?" Winslow gave her a huge warm smile and a quick tap on the top of her head. "Keep up the good work." He hustled down the bleachers to join the large group of parents who had assembled, waiting for their turn with him.

Charlotte talked the whole ride home. The girls were awesome. They had such good skills. She had learned so much. Every kid was nice.

"I've got some great news," Annie said as she turned into their driveway. "Winslow wants you on his team. What do you think about that?"

"You mean for next year?" Charlotte asked. She looked around, confused. "What happened to your friend Linda?"

Annie had forgotten all about Linda. She zoomed out of the driveway, hit the tree, checked the car, got back in, and twenty minutes later pulled into the Soccer-Plex lot.

As they walked inside, Roy, the plumber, looked up from

unpacking his toolbox. His eyes went right to Charlotte's shin guards and cleats.

"Are the Asteroids practicing here today?" he asked. "Because I don't think Nadine knows about it."

"No," Annie said. She peered through the small window into the office where Winslow was talking on the phone.

Winslow met her eyes and gestured that he'd be out in one moment.

"She sure looks like she's got practice," Roy said.

"She practiced with the Power earlier today," Annie explained.

Winslow joined them in the hall. "Everything all right here?"

"Everything's fine," Annie said. "Except I've misplaced my friend."

"Oh, dear," Winslow said. "That won't do. She's not with me. Have you got her, Roy?"

"The new girl practiced with you today?" Roy asked, pointing at Charlotte.

"Maybe she's in the bathroom," Charlotte said.

"The bathrooms are out of order," Roy said. "No one's in the bathrooms. Winslow, I need to talk to you."

"Where exactly did you lose her?" Winslow asked Annie, hoping Roy would give up and go away.

"She went to talk to Parker," Annie said.

"Ah," Winslow said. "Now everything becomes more clear. I've been trying to reach Parker for the past half hour but he's not answering his cell. I suppose that gives us both our answer. My guess is your friend is with my friend."

"Where are they?" Charlotte asked her mother as they headed back to the car.

"They went on a date," Annie said. "So did you think about it? Don't you think it would be great to switch onto Winslow's team?"

"Switching isn't allowed."

"Normally, that's true," Annie said. "But Winslow explained he was going to make an exception for you."

"I don't think there should be exceptions," Charlotte said. "I think there should be one team, and all the girls could play on it together, and both coaches could coach us."

"That's a really good idea," Annie said. "But that might take some time to work out. In the meantime, what do you think about switching?"

"Everyone on my team would be mad at me if I did that."

"Believe me, anyone on your team who got a chance to do this would do it in a blink," Annie said.

"I'm not that good," Charlotte said.

Annie studied her daughter. As a little girl she had possessed such confidence. What had happened?

"Charlotte, the Power is the best team around. You should shoot for the best. If you want my opinion—"

"I know what your opinion is," Charlotte interrupted.

But it wasn't just an opinion. Annie had made up her mind. She was not going to let her daughter pass up an opportunity for success. Like it or not, Charlotte was going to move up.

twenty-five

When did you invite the new girl to start practicing with you?" Roy asked.

What a nuisance, Winslow thought. "How is the plumbing coming, Roy? Are we on schedule?"

Roy was not going to let him weasel out of this again. "Did you forget our conversation about Nadine training with you? It's okay if you did. She can start tomorrow. What time are you planning on practicing tomorrow?"

"You know, Roy, you and I have something in common," Winslow said. "We both have one-track minds. Right now my mind is on the bathrooms."

"Really? Well, my mind is on my daughter. Because yesterday I looked her in the eye and said you told me she could start practicing with your team. So when do you want her to start? Tomorrow? Next week? You tell me."

Winslow studied his shoes. "You shouldn't have told her that, Roy." He met Roy's eyes. Roy looked away. "You and I both know I never said anything of the kind." He needed to make Roy disappear. "Let's be honest with each other, shall we?"

"That's all I'm asking," Roy said.

"The Power is like..." Winslow searched for an example Roy could understand. "A heating system. When you install a heating system, you have to make sure all the pipes are the best pipes for the job. But you also have to make sure that the pipes are going to fit together. If they don't fit together the system doesn't work. You get leaks. Insufficient heat. The system breaks down. Do you see?"

"Nadine is no leaky pipe."

"Of course not. Your daughter is a very good player. A very, very good player."

"That's all I've been trying to tell you."

"I'm just not sure she fits on this team at this time."

"Is it because she's a little heavy? Because I don't think having a lot of muscle mass is such a bad thing for a player in her position."

It was time for a different approach. "Here's my problem, Roy. Nadine is a top-notch player. And for that reason I cannot pull her off the Asteroids right now. She is the key to their future success. The soccer board would have my head if I stole her away from her team. Now next year, that's a different story."

"That's what you said last year. That's what you say every year." His wife was right. It was a hundred percent bullshit. Winslow wasn't even trying to look like he meant it.

"You told me Nadine could train with you this winter," Roy said. "Those were your words. Are you going to do the right thing or not?"

"The problem is I have to do the right thing for all the girls on all the teams. Otherwise my team wouldn't be a team worth Nadine's time." Winslow liked that one. He'd have to use it more often.

He put an arm around Roy's shoulder. "Next year is the critical year in terms of player development. When a girl turns thirteen, everything changes. I promise you, next year I'll be losing several players. It's practically guaranteed. The middle schools are all starting soccer programs now. And they're working hard to convince top players like ours that their programs will better help them get ready for the high school teams."

"I've heard that," Roy admitted.

"Of course the girls are already brainwashed about high school soccer," Winslow went on, happy to move the subject in another direction. "Every year I hear more and more parents sing the same little ditty about how everyone tells them the high school girls love playing soccer for their school team. But don't believe a word of it. Those teams are like nursery schools. They might as well just give the players teddy bears to kick around. They shouldn't be allowed to call it soccer. Which is why my players will stay with me throughout their entire soccer careers. But you already knew that, Roy, didn't you?"

"Yes," Roy said.

"Now, the bigger question is, will the bathrooms be ready by the time Nadine turns thirteen?" Winslow laughed at his cleverness.

The first thing Roy saw when he walked into the rubble of the girls' bathroom was a woman's high-heeled shoe, dark brown, looked like suede. Then he saw the legs.

It took a minute for the woman to notice him, but once she did, she started pounding the guy who was on top of her with her fist. It took the guy a little while to realize they weren't punches of passion.

"Someone's here," she said and hit him harder. "Hey. Someone's watching us."

The guy turned around.

It was Parker. "Would you mind running along now?" he said, like he was talking to a two-year-old. He turned to the woman. "Don't mind him. He's just the plumber." He turned back to Roy. "Are you still here? Do you enjoy hanging around in toilets watching other people? We've got a name for people like you. Does the word *pervert* ring a bell?"

The woman laughed.

Roy headed for the door, making sure to step on both of the brown suede shoes on his way out.

"Hey, Lurch," the woman called after him, "watch where you're walking."

"Probably has a thing for shoes as well," Parker said.

"Are the toilets ready?" Winslow called after Roy as Roy stomped down the hall.

"Roy? Where are you going? Is there a problem?"

Roy just kept walking.

Winslow shrugged, happy to be done with him.

twenty-six

Winslow lay in bed, strategizing. The problem was they were at the maximum number of players now. The only way the soccer board would give approval for taking on the Fleming girl was to get another girl to go.

He quickly corrected his thought: He'd have to allow another girl to go. A girl would have to request to be released. But who?

Vicki came out of the bathroom. "What's the matter?" she asked.

"Do you think Dinah's enjoying the team?"

"Never, ever ask me that question again." Vicki got into bed, turned off the lamp, gave Winslow her back, and fell right to sleep.

Winslow got up, lumbered down the stairs, and paced from room to room. It was a puzzle. That was all. And puzzles had solutions, didn't they? All he had to do was find it.

He went into his study, turned on the computer, and logged onto the soccer forum. It had been almost six hours since the last time he'd checked the posts. For him, that was something of a record.

He lectured the parents about this all the time. He'd made announcements on the subject at several team meetings. This was something they all must avoid. Reading the posts, he told them again and again, was bad for team morale. The idiotic threads were crude and angry and often about them. He did not want his parents goaded into sending back their own churlish replies.

Yet he couldn't help but look himself. When he was home he checked at least a dozen times a day. He would have checked more frequently if Vicki hadn't become his shadow, standing beside, behind him, around him all the time.

He clicked to the comments and read. It took nearly an hour to skim the most recent threads. When he heard the creak of the floorboard—Vicki creeping down the stairs to find him—he quickly tapped a key and turned the computer screen black.

"Why are you up?" Vicki asked.

"I couldn't sleep. Thinking about the team. You know."

"You can't expect to win every game," Vicki said. "No team can win every game."

"Do you think that's what's keeping me awake? Worrying about winning?"

"No," Vicki said. "I know. It's the parents."

"Exactly," he hissed. "The parents."

"You know, if you think about it—"

"Because the girls work very hard," Winslow said. "The girls respect what I'm trying to do."

"Sometimes I think—"

"But the parents just complain. You do know what the real problem is, don't you?"

"The parents," Vicki recited by rote.

"The bottom," he said.

"The bottom of—"

"Exactly," Winslow said. "The parents of the girls at the bottom pull us down with their picky little needs. She can't be there Sunday," he said in his high-pitched imitation of a mother. "Little Gwen needs to see her poppy. He's ill, you know. We don't know how much longer we'll have our poppy."

"It's—"

"Or the tournament is too far. Or the game time is too early. Or there's too much weather. Too hot, too cold, a sprinkling of snow, a drizzle of rain."

"People are—"

"I'm not playing someone enough. I'm playing someone too much. I'm telling you, Vicki, they're pulling us down."

"And you work so hard."

"I do. I work so hard."

"Maybe there's a way Dinah can help with—"

He held up his hand, to quiet her. Her advice was not what he needed now.

"We have to look at this thing dead on. If I don't do something soon, I'm going to start losing my top."

"You're not going to lose your mind," Vicki said.

"I am not talking about losing my mind," he snapped. "I'm talking about losing my top players."

"Oh."

"You know when this started, don't you? It was exactly

two years ago, the day I allowed Elisabeth and Isabelle to leave the team."

"Their family moved away, Win. What could you do?"

"We should have offered to let them live with us. They wanted to, you know."

"They were ten years old," Vicki reminded him. "Ten-year-old kids have to live with their parents."

"They were twins," Winslow said. "They would have had each other." He sighed. "It doesn't matter now. What matters now is that if Shelby leaves, it's over. It's like dominoes. Shelby leaves, then Evelyn leaves, and before you know it, all the talent is gone. And what are we left with? A team of empty pants."

"I don't think Shelby's going anywhere. And even if she did, you've got a lot of good players. I was just telling Dinah—"

"Please. Do not try to change the subject. I fully grasp the situation. And I can fix it. I have a plan. I've found the player."

"You mean Tia?"

"God, no. Tia, it turns out, is not the real deal. I'm talking about the real deal."

"But with Tia you're at your limit. You have a full squad. You're not allowed any more players," Vicki said.

"That's true," Winslow admitted. "However—what if a family decided they wanted to withdraw their daughter from the Power?"

"That would never happen," Vicki said.

"But what if?"

"Well, if a girl wants to be released from the team there's no way we can stop her."

"Exactly," Winslow whispered. "If a player leaves us we have no choice. We are compelled to fill the void."

"But who would voluntarily leave the team?" Vicki asked.

"I haven't figured that part out yet."

She studied him for a moment. "Were you just online reading the soccer posts?"

It was frightening, how well she knew him.

"Winslow," Vicki said. She walked behind him and dug her fingers into the walnuts of tension in his shoulders. "What did you read?"

"I read a very nice compliment about me. A very, very nice compliment."

"Really?" She dug her thumbs even deeper. "Who was it from?"

"It was signed 'Rival Coach,' but I know who that is."

"You do? Who?"

"I'm fairly certain it's that fellow Vincent, from Brookvale. Vincent has been very impressed with me lately."

"Wow. A compliment from Vinnie. That doesn't happen every day," Vicki said.

"I hope it never happens again."

"Why? You shouldn't be so modest."

"It has nothing to do with modesty," Winslow said. "It's envy I'm concerned about. I get one small compliment and suddenly dozens of jealous, small-minded people crawl out of their holes to write posts that are insults, smears, slurs."

"That's horrible." When Vicki had written the anonymous post she had never considered that it might inspire insults and slurs. "You have to write the next Power Pointers bulletin about this. You have to forbid everybody on the team from ever looking at that Web site again. You have to threaten them, Winslow. It's the only way."

"It wasn't someone on the team who wrote those awful things," Winslow said. He narrowed his eyes. "At least I don't think so."

"Forbid it. Come right out and forbid it. They listen to you."

"Do you think it could be Doug?" Winslow asked. "Doug's been quite the loose cannon lately, carrying on about Gwen not getting enough playing time. Or could it be Freddy? Freddy is just the type to do something like this, isn't he?"

"Threaten immediate expulsion. No second chances. Tell them, if you post something on the soccer forum site your child is off the team. End of story."

"That's a very good idea."

"You write it," Vicki said. "I'll type it and give it out at practice tomorrow."

"All right. I will."

Vicki yawned. "Come on up, Winslow. I'm exhausted. Let's go to bed."

"Not now, darling. I'm not tired."

He'd hadn't been tired for nearly a year now. Vicki was keeping track. "Come anyway." She pulled at his hand.

"I'll be up in a bit. I want to work on the bulletin while my thoughts are still fresh. And I have to finish planning how to get Charlotte Fleming on our team. You do remember her, don't you?"

"Yes," Vicki said. "She's the one I told you about at tryouts."

"I should have listened to you," Winslow said. "You are always right. I don't know why I don't always listen to you."

"Listen now. Come to bed."

"I will. In a bit. I just need some time to think, all right? I'm so close to figuring this out. So very, very close." He closed his eyes and wished her away.

Vicki went up alone, again.

twenty-seven

POWER POINTERS—Special Edition
News of the Day!!!

SEPTEMBER 9TH
Special Notice!
Please Note: THIS NOTICE WILL NOT
BE REPEATED!

It has come to my attention that parents have been logging onto the *Soccer News* Web site forum, against my explicit advice.

Anyone who has visited this forum knows how dangerous it is to engage in online discussion with those whom you cannot see.

Today, I have registered complaints with the Mountain Ridge Travel Soccer Board, the New Jersey Soccer Board of Regents, and the United Youth Soccer Coaches of the Northeastern League of Central New Jersey Section IA, requesting their help in shutting this site down.

I feel quite strongly that this site is bad for all of youth soccer.

But I am sorry to report that my contacts at the Soccer Board of Regents tell me shutting down the site is not likely to happen anytime soon, due to issues relating to various government-sponsored freedoms of speech, etcetera.

Therefore, it is up to us to set an example for all teams. With this in mind, as of today, Please NOTE:

No Power Parent or Player is permitted to log onto the *Soccer News* Web site forum at any time, for any reason whatsoever!

ALSO NOTE: This is a zero-tolerance situation. Even compliments posted on the forum can provoke responses from people who are too jealous or dull to understand what our team is working so hard to accomplish!

FINAL NOTE: If anyone has a comment or complaint about the prohibited soccer forum postings or about any other subject, please speak to me directly. Conversations among parents on the sidelines are unproductive for all!!

IMPORTANT NOTE: I am not available for conversation on the days before game or tournament weekends or directly before or after practice as I am concentrating on developing player strategy at those times!!!

Good Luck to One and All from Winslow West!!!!

twenty-eight

The plan came to Roy at halftime at the next game.

A Ludlow mother was walking across the field to bring a bag of snacks to the players. Her dog, a Great Dane the size of a horse, followed her.

Halfway there, in the middle of the field, the dog stopped. He lifted his tail. He lowered his butt. The parents went nuts.

The woman did the best she could. She pulled the dog. She yanked the leash. But the dog was big, and he wasn't about to budge.

When he finished his business, the woman took a yellow newspaper wrapper out of her back pocket and cleaned up the mess. Even from where he stood, Roy could see she was cleaning it well, even pulling up some grass and clumps of dirt to make sure she got every last bit.

The way the Asteroid parents exploded, you'd think she'd smeared crap all over their kids' mouths. There was cursing and yelling and barking. The ref started showing yellow cards like he was dealing poker. It took a while to calm everyone down. Then the game started up again.

Roy was amazed. The Asteroids played like it was the

first game of their lives, like they had no idea what they were doing. Then he realized it was because they were so busy watching where they stepped.

And he thought, hold on—hold on a minute. That's all it takes to get their heads out of the game? A little dog crap? That's how he got the idea.

It didn't take him long to prepare. If there was a travel team for dog crapping, Nadine's dog would be the star player. Roy saved a bunch of bags of crap in a corner of the garbage shed, where no one ever went, except for him. Then he went to the Web site to find the location and time of the next Power home game.

Rain would have screwed up the plan, but for once he was in luck. The night before the game was clear and warm. He told Maura he was going to the Soccer-Plex to work. Instead he drove over to the field. He'd already decided where to empty the bags. He'd watched the Power games enough times to know that the weakest players on the field, the ones who were taking up Nadine's spot on the roster, often left their positions, migrating as far away as they could from where Winslow stood, as if maybe then they wouldn't hear him yelling.

The Asteroids had a game the next morning too, but he simply told Maura there was a problem at the Plex—something about a pipe in the third stall of the boys room.

"I don't need to know which stall," Maura said. "Just try to get to the game before the end."

As soon as Maura and Nadine left, Roy shoved a baseball cap on his head and drove to the field where the Power game was already under way. By his calculation, it was sometime late in the first half.

The dog's deposits had done their job. The Power looked tentative on the field. He watched as a girl with red hair ran like a marionette with uneven strings, afraid of where her feet would land her next.

The red-haired girl had one and then another collision. Her eyes were locked on her feet. Wham—she rammed into a player for the third time.

The ref pulled out a card. Roy hadn't been there to see her get the yellow, but this time the card the ref pulled out of his pocket was red. The girl with the red braids stopped. She put her arms out, the universal sign for "What did I do?" The ref motioned for her to get off the field.

"What was that?" Winslow yelled at her as she stormed to the sidelines. His arms flapped in the air as he yelled, like some big bird of prey not quite ready to land. "What is wrong with you?"

He turned toward the ref. "That was a stumble, not a foul." The ref reached into his jacket and showed Winslow a yellow card. Winslow let his arms fall to his side and gave the ref his back.

By halftime the Power were down three, and the girls that weren't crying were poking sticks in the valleys between the cleats of their shoes to clean out the mess.

Shoe-wise, the Hillcrest Bombers were doing no better, but the Bombers thought it was funny. The Bombers laughed as they scraped away the crud.

The ref agreed to extend the halftime break so Winslow and the Mountain Ridge parents could clean up the field. Winslow walked quickly, pointing out piles to his manager, Ken. Barbie, Ken's wife, followed behind with rolls of paper towels, ripping off bunches of sheets and stooping to pick up the squashed pats of dung as quickly as she could.

The Bomber parents near Roy argued amiably about whether this field, spoiled by dog crap, was worse than the one in West Rumsford, where last month one of the players nearly sprained her ankle in a gopher hole.

Which was how Roy got the idea for the holes.

He was in luck. The next game was a home game too. But this time his work was harder. The digging went slowly. Camouflaging the holes went even more slowly. He needed to do it, though. The last thing he wanted was for Winslow to spot half a dozen grass plugs on the field right before the game got under way.

The truth was, Roy thought, Winslow should be thanking him. Because it wasn't the good players who were going to be affected by these annoyances. The good players wouldn't let something as stupid as stepping into a pile of crap mess up their game. No. The players who were going to find dog crap and gopher holes too much to cope with were the players who didn't belong on the team in the first place. And if those players left, there would be more room for the ones who really did belong on the team. Players like Nadine. Nadine deserved a chance.

This time he couldn't watch at all. The Asteroids had a game at the exact same time, and no way was Maura going to let him miss two in a row. Afterward, he read about it on the Power Web site.

"Look at this," he said to Maura. "One of the Power players got hurt at the game today."

"Who?" Maura asked. "If it's their goalie, that's not news. Their goalie gets hurt all the time."

She turned her attention back to a stack of real estate print-outs. "Don't you think this center-hall colonial looks exactly like ours? It's much cheaper, though." She studied the tear sheet. "No basement," she said, when she figured it out.

"Is their goalie named Dinah?" Roy asked.

"What?" Maura stood up and came to read over his shoulder. "Winslow's daughter got hurt?"

"Dinah is Winslow's daughter?"

"You're kidding me right? You don't know who Dinah is? The little girl with the red hair who looks like a miniature clone of her mother?"

"Sure. I know who she is. I hope she's okay." Roy felt a little sick to his stomach.

Nadine came in and joined them, the whole family gathered around the computer screen, like it was a campfire.

"Uh-oh," Nadine said after reading the news. "That's bad. The Power have a big tournament coming up. Winslow is going to be mad if Dinah's not better by then."

"Knock, knock," Roy said.

"Who's there?" Nadine answered.

"Opportunity," Roy said. "Opportunity for you."

Maura said, "What the hell are you talking about, Roy?"

"I'm talking about maybe Nadine can guest at the next Power tournament. If they're short an important player, they could use someone like Nadine to step in."

"Oh," Maura said. "Roy, you are so smart."

"Winslow won't let me guest," Nadine said. "He doesn't think I'm that good."

"Don't be negative," Maura snapped. "You are much better than you think. You just don't know it because you're spending too much time with loser players." She turned to Roy. "Can you get Winslow to invite Nadine to guest?"

"I can try," Roy said.

"I don't want to guest," Nadine said, but the only one who heard was the dog, and he showed no sign at all that he cared.

twenty-nine

Annie laid out her new clothes on the bed. She hadn't had time to try them on in the soccer store, but the woman said years of dressing customers who were on the go had made her an expert at eyeballing sizes. She absolutely guaranteed everything would fit perfectly, like a dream.

She neglected to say what kind of dream, but it was obvious now. The shorts and jersey Annie had bought were nightmarishly small. And what had she been thinking when she let herself be talked into pumpkin-colored socks?

She yanked at the plastic sales tag on the tiny shorts. When it wouldn't come off, she tried pulling it with her teeth. Finally, she grabbed a pair of scissors. As she cut off the tag, she cut the shorts as well.

Why was she so nervous? Sure, she had never played a sport before. Okay, she had no idea if she would be any good. But Gerri had promised it wouldn't be a problem. No one on the team had great soccer skills, she'd said. Everyone played to have fun.

"I swear on the socca-Bible," Gerri said. "If Winslow West

decided tomorrow he wanted to have an elite team of soccer moms to compete in a tournament with the greatest soccer players ever, we'd all tell him no."

Annie slipped on the shorts, which pinched at her waist. She put on the soccer jersey—weren't the jerseys supposed to be loose?—and tugged so it would cover the hole that she'd made in the shorts. She was as ready as she was ever going to be.

The truth was, telling Gerri that Charlotte was about to leave the Asteroids was going to be awkward no matter what. But putting off calling Winslow was not going to make the conversation with Gerri any easier. In fact, if Annie didn't call him soon, she could end up jeopardizing Charlotte's entire soccer career. Because what if Winslow changed his mind? Annie had to call him now.

She took a deep breath and picked up the phone. She'd make the call, deal with Gerri, and it would be done. She waited for a dial tone. Why was there no dial tone?

"Hello?" came a voice. "Annie?" It was Hank.

"Did the phone ring?" Annie asked. "I didn't hear it."

"I don't know," Hank said. "All I know is you picked up. So how are you, stranger?"

"I'm fine," Annie said. They were not exactly phone buddies. "Is everything okay?"

"Everything is good. Really good. Listen, I'm calling about my brother."

"Is Tim okay?"

"That's what I want to ask you."

"Why?" Annie wanted to know. "Did something happen?"

"No. Well, yes. Timmy stopped over the house when I was out of town. And Trissy said he didn't look very good. She said he seemed kind of weird. So I figured I'd call and ask. Is everything okay?"

"Tim's fine," Annie said. "But he does want to talk to you. Are you around today?"

"I'm still out of town. Do you know what Timmy wants to talk to me about? Trissy has pretty good radar about this kind of stuff, and she thinks something's going on."

"Tim is fine," Annie said. "But you should give him a call. When are you going to be back?"

"How about on the home front?" Hank persisted. "Are things okay at home? You can tell me anything, Annie. I'm not Trissy. I don't judge. Unlike my wife, I know that none of us is perfect."

Annie felt a rare wave of sympathy for her sister-in-law. "We're fine," she said.

"What about Charlotte? Is everything okay with her?"

"Charlotte is great," Annie said. "She just started playing travel soccer and it's going extremely well. Why do you ask?"

"Trissy told me about the soccer. She also mentioned that Timmy's missed a lot of the games. She said you've had to drop Charlotte at the house a few times."

"I left her there once," Annie said.

"I'm not trying to put you on the spot," Hank said. "It's just Trissy and I are worried that something's wrong."

"Nothing is wrong," Annie insisted. "Everything is great." To seal the deal she added, "In fact Charlotte just got offered a chance to move up to the Power."

"No kidding," Hank said. "Wow. Trissy didn't tell me that."

"It's not official," Annie said. "I probably shouldn't have mentioned it yet."

"Whatever you tell me goes right in the vault," Hank said. "You can tell me anything. I mean it. Anything."

"I give up, Hank. What is it you're fishing to find out?"

"Hey," Hank said, sounding hurt. "All I'm trying to do is to get a handle on what's going on with my baby brother, that's all. Like, today for example. Where is he today?"

"Atlanta," Annie said.

"See, that's what I'm talking about. What's with all the trips to Atlanta? Does Timmy have another family down there or something?"

"That's an awful thing to say."

"I'm kidding," Hank said. "We both know my brother's too boring to have a second family."

"That isn't funny."

"Okay, Annie. When you talk to Tim, tell him I tried to reach him in Atlanta and that I'm not funny. I don't think the second part is going to be any big news to him. And by the way, contrary to popular opinion, I am not completely self-absorbed. Okay? I notice what's going on around me. And I worry about Timmy."

"Well, you don't have to. Tim's fine. We're all fine."

"Okay. Whatever you say. And congratulations about Charlotte. That's one hell of an accomplishment, getting on Winslow West's team. Maybe my brother is doing better than I thought."

Annie hung up the phone. A car honked. She looked out the window. It was Gerri, waiting for her.

She picked up the phone to call Winslow. Gerri honked again. She'd have to call as soon as she got back.

"You don't look happy," Gerri said as Annie slid into the car. "Anything wrong?"

She sounded so sympathetic. Annie wondered if she would still be sympathetic after she heard Charlotte was going to quit her team. And what about managing the team? Was Annie supposed to stay on as team manager after Charlotte left?

"You want to talk about it?" Gerri asked. "We're like family now, you know? I'm here for you. You're here for me."

Annie decided to send out a probe. "What would you think if Charlotte had an opportunity to move up to Winslow's team?"

"Not you too," Gerri said. "Look. I'm sorry. It's just that people have the oddest ideas about how this works. But I understand. You're new. So let me explain it to you. Once in a blue moon, after the soccer season's started, there's some movement from team to team. But right now, the move date is past and, more important, the Power are at their maximum number of players. Which means the team is frozen. Totally. No more players allowed. End of story."

"I'm sure that's normally true."

"Believe me, everyone thinks their kid is going to be the one exception. But I'm telling you. I've been doing this for a long time. It's never happened. And it's never going to happen. Once a team roster is at the max it's set in stone."

Gerri glanced over at Annie. "Look, it's not as bad as you think. Not to toot my own horn, but I'm not such a bad coach. I can teach Charlotte a lot. I know she's a really socca-rific player. But it won't be the worst thing for her to spend a sea-son with me. Next year is another story. Next year I'm sure she'll have the opportunity to move up. If she wants that life. And I'm not so sure she will."

"But what if an offer did come?" Annie asked. "Would you be really upset if Charlotte moved up to Winslow's team? Of course, if Charlotte left the team it wouldn't make sense for me to continue as manager, would it?"

"Ha!" Gerri laughed. "Imagine what a socca-nightmare that would be, managing a team where the parents literally wish you dead. You'd have to have done something really bad in a past last life to deserve that."

"So if Charlotte moved up now, you'd be fine if I resigned as manager?"

"Yes. If Charlotte moved up now, you'd have to resign as manager. But you'd also be able to sprout wings and fly whenever you wanted, and you could pick money off of trees. Which is to say, it isn't happening. But if it did, I would say, great news. If she wants it, go for it." Gerri pulled into a spot at the park.

"Really?" Annie said. "That's really generous of you. I know it wouldn't be very good news for you if Charlotte left the team."

"Charlotte is a great kid," Gerri said. "She should do what she wants. Now talking about good news, you want to know what's good news for you?"

"Sure. What?"

"You are about to experience the world of socca-magic firsthand."

"What do you mean?" Annie asked.

"Socca-magic is what happens when you start running after a ball," Gerri explained. "All of a sudden, all the crazy thoughts cluttering your head fall away, like magic."

That sounded good to Annie. And as soon as the practice started, she discovered Gerri was right.

thirty

Vicki read the revised schedule. "We've got a game on Halloween?"

Her schoolmarm tone made Winslow cringe. "Have I ever penalized someone for missing a game for religious reasons?" he asked.

"Who are you?" Vicki said. "Who said Halloween is a religious holiday? It's a regular holiday. An important holiday that everybody celebrates."

Winslow laughed. "Please. If it were up to you every day would be an important holiday. What is the problem here? I promise you, we'll buy a pumpkin, which you can put on the front step so a teenager can have something to smash. All right? Feel better? Problem solved?"

"The problem is the kids should get the day off so they can go trick-or-treating."

Dinah poked her head into the bedroom. "I can't go trick-or-treating?"

It was dirty tricks, Vicki bringing this up with Dinah lurking about, especially when she was on her crutches, looking like a little injured bird.

"We'll just celebrate it another day, all right?" Winslow asked.

"That's a good one," Vicki said. "What's she supposed to do? Ring doorbells the day after Halloween? What do you want her to say? 'Trick or treat, and by the way do you have any candy left?' You can go with her. You walk up and down the block ringing doorbells on November first and see what happens."

"All right. So she'll go the day before."

"Even better," Vicki said. "Ding-dong. 'Did you get your Halloween candy yet?' I don't think so."

"Is that the problem?" Winslow asked. "Candy? All right. Tell you what. Dinah, I'll buy you all the candy you want. Whatever you want. You can have the best Halloween stomachache in town."

"You have to change the game," Vicki said. "The girls will be totally bummed if they can't go trick-or-treating. And the parents will be totally pissed."

"How can you expect me to support a holiday that completely revolves around the overconsumption of sugar? I have spent years teaching the girls about proper nutrition and fitness. Halloween could undo everything."

"I can't go trick-or-treating on Halloween?" Dinah asked again.

"Dinah," Winslow said. "How can you even think about going trick-or-treating with those crutches?"

"I'm going as a car crash victim," Dinah explained. "With gauze around my body. And fake blood on my face."

"You have to admit," Vicki said, "it's a hell of a great idea."

"It's ridiculous," Winslow muttered.

"I already got the fake blood and the gauze," Dinah said. "And I have the crutches. Mom said maybe we could all dress up like car crash victims. Like it was a family accident."

"You are both out of your minds," Winslow said. He put on his shoes and stomped downstairs.

"Why is he mad at me?" Dinah asked.

Vicki stroked her daughter's fine hair, and began to redo her braids to make them tighter. "He's not mad at you."

"Is it because I got a red card?"

"No. That wasn't your fault. He's not mad about that."

Dinah lowered her voice. "Maybe I shouldn't be on the team anymore."

"Dinah, you stop that. There wouldn't be a team if you weren't on it. You think Daddy would want to coach a bunch of strangers?"

"If they were talented strangers he would."

Vicki shook her head. "No way. If you leave the team, Daddy leaves the team. That's the way it is. He's just cranky because he's tired, that's all."

Vicki pulled the second braid too tight. Dinah put her hand to her ear but didn't say a word.

"Don't worry about this," Vicki said. "I promise you, you're going trick-or-treating."

"I won't worry," Dinah said, and she hobbled off to bed.

Vicki went to the kitchen and put up a pot of water. When the tea was perfectly steeped, she called Winslow from his study.

He came in and sat at the table, waiting to be served.

Vicki filled the teacup and put it before him. Then she walked back to the sink.

Winslow stared at his tea. "Where's the sugar?" he finally asked. Vicki knew he couldn't drink his tea without sugar.

"I'm so sorry," Vicki said. "I threw the sugar away. Good thing, right? I would have thrown it away years ago if I had known how bad it is for you. I mean, from what you told me tonight I realize I've been practically poisoning you. Are you sure you feel okay?"

The phone rang. They stared each other down.

Vicki got up. She checked caller ID. It was the plumber. "What's up, Roy?"

Winslow shook his head and mouthed that he wasn't home.

"I need to speak to Winslow," Roy said.

"Is there a problem at the Plex?" Vicki asked.

"No. It's nothing about that."

"What can I do for you then, Roy?" Vicki asked.

"Is Winslow there? I need to talk to him."

"If you tell me what it's about, maybe I can help you," Vicki said.

"I think Winslow will want to talk to me himself."

"He might," Vicki said. "But he'll never know you called unless you tell me what it's about."

There was silence on the line, Roy trying to decide if he should bother telling Winslow's wife, or just try back another time.

"He's hard to get, Roy," Vicki said. "Believe it or not, I'm your best shot."

Winslow pantomimed slitting his throat. Vicki had given Roy too much time already.

"Okay, Roy," Vicki said. "I got to go."

"Wait. Tell Winslow I want to make him an offer."

"What kind of offer?" Vicki asked.

There was another long silence. Then Roy went on. "Maura told me there's been some problems on the Power."

"What kind of problems do you mean?" Vicki asked.

"I heard about the player injuries. Me and Maura, we were so sorry to hear about Dinah. Is she going to be okay?"

"Dinah is just fine," Vicki said. "Thanks."

Winslow looked up, alerted by Vicki's icy tone.

Roy spilled the rest out fast. "The thing is, Maura told me you've got a big tournament coming up. And you might end up short a player. And Nadine, she's really good. The only reason she wasn't put on the Power in the first place is she didn't start playing soccer till she was eight, so she kind of missed the boat there."

"You know what, Roy? You were right. Your best bet is to talk to Winslow at the Soccer-Plex. He is so busy he's practically never home anymore. So why don't you call him at work. The phones are in. You can leave a message. Tell him exactly what you told me. How good your daughter is and all."

"I want to offer Nadine to him," Roy said. "Because I know he needs someone to guest in the tournament. Because of what happened to your daughter."

"Because of Dinah. Thank you, Roy. You should definitely tell Winslow that on the message too." Vicki stared at Winslow and shook her head.

"Okay," Roy said. "That's what I'll do. Believe me, as soon as Winslow puts Nadine on the field he'll see what I've been talking about. Plus she has the same number."

"Pardon me?"

"As your daughter. Maura told me Nadine has the same number as Dinah. So it's almost like it was meant to be, you know?"

"The other phone is ringing, Roy," Vicki said. "I got to go."

She hung up. "That was frigging unbelievable. Roy called to say he knows we're short a player for the tournament. And he wants to offer you the opportunity to put Nadine on the team in Dinah's place. The best part? Nadine and Dinah have the same number. So it's meant to be."

"What a fool," Winslow said.

"What a jerk." Vicki reached into the cabinet and pulled out the sugar bowl.

"What complete and utter nerve." Winslow helped himself to three heaping teaspoons.

Vicki licked her finger, dipped it in the bowl, sucked the sugar off, and said, "People have no idea."

thirty-one

FIELD BEHAVIOR ALERT!!!!!!!!!!!!!!!!!!!

Because of several isolated incidents at our recent home games, I am sorry to report that some of our players are displaying an acute lack of confidence on the field!! This Tentative Field Behavior cannot be tolerated! Tentative Field Behavior can spread like a disease, from player to player within seconds!! I am therefore putting in place a new program that will ensure this behavior will not recur!

Beginning immediately, all players are to arrive at the field one and one-half hours before game and/or practice time for a Team Field Check! Team Field Checking is a wonderful way to help players gain confidence on the turf!!

Full participation is mandatory! Latecomers will find themselves plucking splinters out of their bottoms because of time spent as benchwarmers. No exceptions!!!

Note: Special Field Check vests are on order at the Winslow West Soccer-Plex Store. Details on sizes and price to follow!!!

Challenge of the Week Update: The girls tell me they are enjoying my latest good idea, the Winslow West Weekly Challenge. The Winslow West Weekly Challenge will continue to be held at the end of all Monday practices.

Congratulations to our first ever Winslow West Weekly Challenge Winner, Evelyn Murphy!!

For those who were unable to stay to the end to watch, Evelyn successfully juggled the ball two hundred and sixty-four times! Evelyn told her teammates that she has been practicing juggling a minimum of two hours each day! Sometimes more! Sometimes in the house!!

While I do not recommend juggling in the house (any soft ball will work well for this purpose), it is a reminder that soccer is nothing more than a sport where hard work is its own reward!!

Congratulations also go to Shelby, who juggled the ball seventy-five times, and most surely would have done more had we not run out of daylight!

Game Update: As you know, we have a game scheduled for the 31st of October, otherwise known as Halloween!

To make sure we all get to enjoy this very important holiday, Barbie and Ken have generously volunteered their home for a postgame Halloween Celebration! Please make sure all girls pack a costume in their soccer bags, as a costume contest will be held at the end of the day!!

Prizes for best costume will be: First Place—a one-hour private training session with yours truly! Second Place—a half-hour private training session with yours truly! And so on!

Note: On Halloween we will be facing the Holder Crush, a

team that has managed quite an impressive record this season. Remember: Our Halloween festivities will be better enjoyed if we are coming off a well-played (that is winning) game!!!!

Special Notice for Great Play in the East Meadow Tournament:

Evelyn—Passing to yourself! A brilliant idea! Bravo for an incredible combination of precision ball handling, speed on the field, aggression in tackle, and excellence under pressure!!!

Jolie—We are so happy you agreed to take your new position as starting goalkeeper. Please do not get discouraged by the occasional loss. Goalkeepers cannot make up for sloppy defense or inefficient offense. We hope you continue your excellent record of no injuries, as it is always quite dispiriting to see a goalkeeper carried off the field, particularly in the first quarter.

Bobbi—We look forward to your return. Please send regards to Xavier, your physical therapist, whom I know quite well indeed.

Conference Update: As of now, only one family has confirmed their conference appointment with me! A Special Thank-You for Prompt Response goes to the Evelyn Murphy Family!!

Note: I am unfortunately no longer available by phone at home, as some people have been taking advantage of my easy accessibility. From this point on, I must ask everyone to hold all questions until your child's upcoming conference! Therefore it is imperative that all parents call the Soccer-Plex immediately to confirm the reservation of your conference spot!!!!!

Good Luck to One and All from Winslow West!!!

thirty-two

Winslow couldn't understand it. Why hadn't the mother called?

He walked up to the small office at the back of the viewing lounge and picked up the phone.

Marilyn answered on the first ring.

"Do you think there's a problem with the girl?" Winslow asked. He noticed how hard he was gripping the phone and forced himself to ease up.

"Don't worry," Marilyn said. "The mother is going to call. I promise."

"Did you give her an end date? A specific call by time frame?" Winslow asked.

"No. My gut told me not to," Marilyn defended herself. "My gut told me if I pushed her too hard it wouldn't work out."

Winslow closed his eyes. "How long does your gut tell you I need to wait? Because, frankly, if they're not interested in me, I'm not interested in them."

"We need this girl, Winslow. Evelyn has turned out to be a big disappointment."

"I think Evelyn is quite good," Winslow said.

"She's not a team player. If she can't take the ball the whole way, she doesn't bother trying. What's that about?"

Ahh, Winslow thought. She's jealous. "Let's give Evelyn some time, shall we? There's always a period of adjustment when one takes on a new player."

"By the way," Marilyn said, "what position are you thinking of for the new girl?"

The jealousy was more serious than he'd imagined. He could use that. "Possibly midfield. We could do with another strong player in midfield." He knew Marilyn would like that answer. Midfield was Evelyn's position.

"That is a great idea," Marilyn said. "I love that idea."

Winslow smiled. "All right then. If I don't hear from the Flemings tonight, will you follow up tomorrow?"

"Just give me the word and I'm on it," Marilyn said.

Winslow hung up the phone and laughed at how easy it was to get people to do what he wanted.

"Hello?" a voice called. "Winslow? It's me. Freddy."

Damn, Winslow thought. The last people he wanted to talk to were Rose's father, Freddy, and his silent appendage of a wife.

He checked his watch. They were early. Why were people like Freddy always early? Why must he waste his time talking to Freddy at all, when what he wanted to do was to think about Charlotte Fleming? Was that too much to ask? That he have a moment, one single moment, to sit and think about Charlotte's possibilities?

"Winslow?" Freddy bleated. "Are you up there?"

This was not how he'd organized it. He'd organized it so the parents of the top players would get the first conferences. After he pumped up those parents, they would go home and pump up their daughters, who would come to practice and pump up the weak players, who would then maybe, if he was lucky, go home and practice for five minutes for once in their lives.

It wasn't to be. First Evelyn Murphy's mother called and said Evelyn had a doctor's appointment. Then Marilyn canceled because of car trouble. Disappointing Tia had a reading tutor. And he was left with this, Freddy and his wife, a woman so quiet that for all he knew she didn't even have a tongue.

Why couldn't he be having a conference with the Fleming parents? He'd love to discuss Charlotte's footwork, her instinct, her joy on the field. He yearned to talk about her raw, uncorrupted talent.

He laughed out loud at the wonder of it. Even Shelby, whom he'd gotten when she was seven, played as if she'd passed through someone else's hands first.

He closed his eyes to regain his calm. With a player like Charlotte it was only a matter of fine-tuning. Some softening around the edges. He glanced at his hands and was not a little surprised to see them trembling.

"Winslow?" Freddy called out.

Winslow checked his watch again. They'd been waiting five minutes. All right—eight. Eight minutes and already Freddy had a chip on his shoulder you could see a mile away.

Winslow slowly climbed down the stairs.

"We've been waiting ten minutes," Freddy said.

"Well, the good news is you don't have to wait any longer." Rose stood behind her mother.

"Hello, there," Winslow said. The written instructions had been very clear: *Do not bring your daughter to the conference.*

Why did he bother spending his time writing those damn things when people didn't bother to read them?

"Rose," he said, "tell Parker I'd like him to practice with you while I talk to your parents."

"Okay," Rose said.

She always did what he asked her, right away, without question. Fact was, he wished she didn't. He wished she'd challenge him, curse at other players, throw a shoe, spit. Something that would give him cause to put her off the team.

"Tell him I'd like you to practice your headers," Winslow said.

"Okay," Rose said, and she skipped off to find Parker.

"Headers," the mother said. It was the first time Winslow had ever heard her speak. "I hate headers."

Winslow glanced at her, thinking she was joking. Then he remembered with whom he was dealing.

Freddy and his appendage trailed after him up the stairs, like a pair of potatoes with feet. No wonder Rose was so lacking in luster. The thing that irked him most of all was that he'd expected more from them. He knew Rose wasn't going to be anything special, but he thought what she lacked in talent she'd make up for in family commitment.

There was no commitment. There was no interest. There wasn't even a fleece. They were the only family on the team who refused to purchase it. It galled him to no end, seeing a squad of fifteen girls in green fleece and one in a sweatshirt the color of pink bubble gum, or whatever she happened to pull out of her drawer that day.

Not to mention the financial issue. The man drove a Jaguar, but he still hadn't paid the second half of the yearly fee.

Yet here they were, snapped out of their coma, first in line for a conference. He despised them and all people like them. Selfish, slow, dull, dim.

When they got to his small gallery office, Winslow slid behind his desk and motioned for Freddy and the wife to sit down.

"You played Rose exactly nine minutes in the last game," Freddy said, snapping Winslow to attention.

"Have a seat. Please," Winslow said. That was another thing he despised. People lacking manners.

"I prefer to stand," Freddy said.

His appendage looked unsure of what to do. Winslow motioned again to a seat. She sat down.

"I don't remember seeing you at the last game," Winslow said. He didn't usually bother himself with who was or wasn't at the games. His attention stayed where it belonged, on the field. But he had people who let him know.

"I was there. I don't have to advertise when I'm there, do I? I can come and go when I please, right?"

"Of course, Freddy," Winslow said. "Please. Sit down."

Freddy sat. "Nine minutes at the last game and the game before"—he took a small piece of paper out of his pants pocket—"seven."

"May I see that?"

Freddy handed over the crumpled paper. It had dates and times scribbled all over it. Winslow noted they were written by several different hands. Freddy had help.

"I don't have my notes with me," Winslow said, patting down his shirt, which had no pockets at all. "But I can assure you, the league rules are very specific on this matter. I am required to play each girl a certain percentage of the time that she's present at the game, and that is exactly what I do."

"Nine minutes, and then seven minutes," Freddy said like a broken record. "Is that the required percentage? Because that's what she played. I timed it."

"I'm afraid I have to challenge your numbers."

"How can you challenge a watch?" the appendage asked, meeting his eyes for the first time in her life. "What time is it now, Freddy?"

Freddy checked his watch. "Six thirty-five."

The appendage pointed to the large electronic clock on the back wall of the Soccer-Plex. "Six thirty-five. Same as yours."

Winslow noticed that the appendage's cheeks were red. She was angry. Freddy was angry too. Some might even describe him as being in a rage.

Winslow wanted to smile but willed himself to keep a serious expression on his face. This was exactly what he'd been looking for. This might work out quite well.

For the next twenty minutes, he sat perfectly still as first Freddy and then the appendage spewed out their bilious rage. Of course, he only knew they were complaining by their tone. He'd stopped listening to their words almost at once.

He let the music of their anger wash over him as he thought about where to best position the new girl for her first game. He'd told Marilyn midfield, but Charlotte actually might be better suited as a forward.

There was a pause, and he realized they were done. He forced himself to remain seated as they stormed out of his office. He even tried to look a little shaken. This was going to work out just fine.

But why hadn't the Fleming mother called? He picked up the phone. Why did nothing get done unless he did it himself?

thirty-three

Rose carried the envelope into the small kitchen. "Mommy. What's this?"

Lenore glanced up at the envelope in Rose's hand. She turned back to Nicky and tried to force in another spoonful of spinach and rice. "I don't know. Where did you find it?"

"It was on the floor near the front door," Rose said. "Someone put it through the mail slot."

Lenore tried to push the spoon into the baby's mouth, but he clamped his mouth shut. "Leave it on the counter," she said. She had no time to read every flyer someone stuck through the door.

It was still on the counter when Freddy came back from the car wash.

Rose had just toasted herself a set of frozen miniwaffles. Her father took one off her plate.

"Dad!" Rose complained, but she didn't mean it.

It was when he went to get a paper towel to wipe his greasy fingers that Freddy saw the envelope. He opened it out of boredom more than anything else.

Halfway through reading it he stopped. "Where did this come from?"

"What?" Lenore looked up. "That's junk mail Rose found. Where did you find it, Rose?"

"On the floor, by the front door," Rose said.

"This is how he tells us?" Freddy said. "He slips a letter through the door slot in the middle of the night, for anyone to find?"

"Who did?" asked Lenore. "What kind of letter?"

Freddy shook his head quickly. He wasn't going to discuss it. Not here, in front of the children.

"Rose," Lenore said. "Watch Nicky for me." She sat Nicky on the floor next to Rose and went off with Freddy to the living room.

She sat down next to him. "What is it?"

He handed her the letter. "Read it."

Lenore glanced at the signature, then kept her voice low as she read the letter out loud. "*Dear Freddy...*" She looked up at her husband. "After all these years, he doesn't even know my name."

"Read it," Freddy urged her.

"At our recent conference I was quite surprised to discover how dissatisfied you and your family are with Rose's experience on the Power."

"See?" Lenore said. "He doesn't know my name."

"Keep going," Freddy told her.

"After giving this careful consideration, I have come to the conclusion that it is to no one's benefit for Rose or your family to remain this unhappy. It is only because I have the utmost

respect for your family's strong feelings—" Lenore's eyes skimmed ahead. "What?"

Freddy grabbed the letter back and read the rest, his voice dull and flat: *"It is only because I have the utmost respect for your family's strong feelings that I am willing to release Rose from her obligation to play on the Power, even though the season has not yet come to an end. Enclosed please find her player's card."* Freddy turned the envelope upside down. A small laminated card with his daughter's smiling face on it fell into his lap. *"Gerri Picker, who coaches the Asteroids, will contact you shortly to see if Rose would be interested in joining her team. However, at this time, Rose is under no obligation to play for that or any other Mountain Ridge Travel Soccer Team this year. If you choose to move to an out-of-town team, please contact the Mountain Ridge Soccer Board for instructions regarding their policy about the refund of your travel team fee."*

Lenore started fanning herself with the empty envelope. "This can't be."

"It is with great regret that I bid good-bye to Rose. I have very much enjoyed working with Rose over the past three years, but I feel confident that this solution is best for all involved. Good Luck to One and All from Winslow West!!"

Freddy dropped the letter. He picked up his daughter's player's card and stared at her smiling face.

"Did you know," Freddy said, "that the Power is the only team in New Jersey that has laminated cards?"

"Can he do this?" Lenore whispered.

Freddy picked up the letter and pointed to the bottom.

"He sent a copy to Geoff MacGregor, the Mountain Ridge soccer commissioner. It's a done deal."

"Call the commissioner, then. Tell the commissioner what happened, because this is not right."

"What do you mean, 'call the commissioner'?" Freddy asked. "Don't you think Winslow West and the commissioner are good friends? And what do you think the commissioner is going to say to me?"

"It's not right," Lenore said. "It's not fair. You have to call."

"You don't understand how this works," said Freddy.

"How it works is you call the commissioner and he'll do what's right. He'll make Winslow keep Rose on the team for the rest of the year. In the spring, she'll try out for next year. If she's not good enough, she won't make it. That's fair. The commissioner will make sure it's fair."

"Is Rose suddenly your only child?" Freddy asked.

"What do you mean?" Lenore said.

"I mean, think about the boys. You know how much they love soccer."

"Of course they love soccer. Little Freddy is the best on his team. All the parents say so. And how many kids Christopher's age are already playing up an age group? I think Nicky is probably going to be the best of them all, once he learns to walk." She was proud of every one of her kids.

"So think for a minute," Freddy said. "If I complain, what do you think will happen? Next year, Little Freddy will be the best player on his team, but he'll be on the worst team in his age group. Christopher—he'll stay on the team where he is, but he'll sit on the bench the whole season. As for Nicky, by the time Nicky is old enough to play with the big boys, you'll be so sick of it all you'll be begging me to let him play baseball."

"Baseball? Have you lost your mind?"

"It's politics. It's how it is."

"That's not true," Lenore insisted. "Winslow has to treat our children fair. It's not right."

"It's how it is," Freddy said again. And he went to the kitchen to break the bad news to his daughter.

thirty-four

thought you were kidding," Gerri said.

Annie took her sweaty hand off the phone and wiped it on her pants. "I wasn't. I'm sorry."

"How the heck did Winslow get this through the soccer board?" Gerri asked.

"I have no idea," Annie said. "You do know that Charlotte really likes you, right? She likes all the girls on the team too."

"Don't worry about it," Gerri said. "Like I told you before, I wish the best for Charlotte. She's a sweet kid. She deserves to move up. Tell her I said congratulations. And don't worry. I'm not taking this personally. Believe me, all I'm thinking about right now is what I'm going to do to pacify the army of parents who will go into attack mode as soon as they hear this news."

"Do you think it's going to be hard to find someone to volunteer to manage the team?" Annie asked.

"That is the least of my worries," Gerri said.

"I really am sorry."

"Forget it," Gerri told her. "There's no one on the team who wouldn't do the same thing if they got the chance."

When Annie got off the phone, she saw Charlotte standing across the room watching her. She didn't look happy.

"It's fine," Annie said. "Gerri was lovely. It's totally fine."

"She's mad at me, isn't she?"

"The furthest thing from it," Annie said. "In fact Gerri asked me to tell you congratulations. She thinks you totally deserve this. She's happy for you."

"She's a good coach," Charlotte said. "I don't think I should change teams."

"Gerri said anyone on the team who got this chance would do the very same thing."

"I don't think I'm going to like it on the new team," Charlotte said.

Annie didn't want to admit it, but she wasn't sure of this either. Still, they'd agreed to go for it. "Winslow's worked very hard to arrange this," Annie reminded her. "You said you'd give it a chance. How about it?"

"Can he unarrange it?" Charlotte asked. "I don't think it's a good idea."

"You won't know though, unless you give it a try," Annie said, because that was the truth. She checked her watch. "Are you ready? You don't want to be late for practice."

"Okay," Charlotte said. She retied her shoelaces and picked up her water bottle. "I'll give it a try. But just so you know, if it doesn't work out I won't ever be able to go back to my old team. I'll have to quit soccer."

They rode to the park in silence. Charlotte walked to the field like a soldier conscripted to play. Annie reminded herself of all the reasons this was a good decision. Charlotte had a lot of talent. Talent shouldn't be wasted. Gerri didn't know what to do with a kid like Charlotte. Winslow would.

Winslow, spotting them, rushed right over. He smiled widely. "It's the Flemings," he cheered. "Welcome to the Power."

"Thanks," Charlotte said, staring at her shoes.

"I imagine you're quite eager to get on the field so you can show the girls exactly why you belong on this team," Winslow said. "Am I right?"

Charlotte nodded but didn't look up.

"Great. Now, there are several options for positions today. But first let me ask you this. What position do you most enjoy playing?

Charlotte shrugged. "I don't know."

"What position did you play for Gerri, then? Midfield? Forward? Some secret combination I've never heard of?"

"She's very flexible," Annie said. "I'm sure wherever you put her is fine. Right, Charlotte?"

Charlotte nodded unconvincingly.

"All right. I do like what I've seen of you in midfield," Winslow said. "Shall we try that today? Does midfield sound all right to you?"

"Yes," Charlotte said.

"Good," Winslow said. "All right. The girls have finished the field check, which I will explain to you later. They are about to start their stretches. Would you care to join them? I'll be there in a moment."

Charlotte ran as fast as she could to where the girls were lying on the grass, stretching their legs.

*   *   *

Winslow walked closer to Annie. He narrowed his eyes. "Is there something wrong?"

"No," Annie said. "She's just a little shy."

"Yes. Well. We're all very excited about Charlotte's joining the team. However, if there is something she's unhappy about, it would be better if I knew. I can only help if I know what's wrong."

"I think she just feels a little bad about abandoning her old team," Annie admitted.

Winslow nodded and forced a smile. "Well, that's understandable. However, real competitors can't afford to waste time feeling bad, can they? Is this going to be an ongoing problem?"

"No. Absolutely not," Annie said.

"Because if Charlotte doesn't really want to play with us, if she doesn't like the girls or if she doesn't like me, it's fine. I have no ego involved here. But I do need to know, before damage is done to the team."

"She likes the team," Annie said. "And the girls. And you. There's no problem. It's going to be fine."

"Fine," Winslow said. "Well then, all right. Thank you.

"Damn," he said under his breath as he strode toward his players. He'd concentrated so hard on how to get the new girl he'd never sufficiently considered the possibility that she might not want to be got.

He glanced over at the Power parents, all of whom immediately looked away, as if then he wouldn't notice they'd been watching his every move.

Damn. He hadn't figured the girl for high maintenance. She had been completely enthusiastic during the training session. He'd have to see, that's all. If it wasn't going to work out, he'd know by the end of the day.

"Problem?" Vicki asked when he joined her.

"No," Winslow said, shaking off the question. He turned his thoughts to a girl he'd seen at a tournament in Fruitvale. Her footwork wasn't polished, but she had powerful legs and attacked the ball with almost frightening intensity. Best of all, her family had made a point of walking over and saying hello. Kinsey was her name.

He'd better have Marilyn get Kinsey's phone number so he could give the parents a friendly call. He wouldn't make any promises, of course. He'd just explore a bit. Find out their thoughts on how she liked her current team, and ask what her dreams were for her future.

He felt better just thinking about it.

"All right," he called out. He clapped his hands and the girls gathered round him, arms crossed, awaiting instruction.

"On the field," he said. "Hustle! Hustle! Hustle!"

All of them, Charlotte included, immediately obeyed.

thirty-five

Twice, Maura came down to ask Roy if he was coming up to bed.

"Soon," he said twice—and didn't move.

He wasn't going to move. Not until he could shut his eyes without seeing Winslow West's face painted on the inside of his eyelids.

He hadn't meant for anyone to get hurt. He had meant to shake them up, sure. But he hadn't meant for them to sprain their ankles and twist their knees. He hadn't wanted them to end up on crutches.

He shouldn't have stopped at the game. It hadn't helped, seeing the three girls on the bench with their ankles and knees wrapped, and Dinah with her crutch. That's not what he'd wanted.

He sat for another half hour in the Barcalounger, spinning the events of the week around and around in his brain. When he couldn't stand it anymore, he moved to the computer.

In the soccer forum it was the usual stuff. People making predictions. People bashing people making predictions. Bellyaching, speculating, interrogating. Pages upon pages of complaints about how bad the linesmen were, how bad the coaches were, how bad the parents were, how bad the trainers were.

He read on.

What are the top ten Under Eight boys' teams? What are the top ten Under Nine girls' teams? Which towns have the worst refs? Which refs have the worst towns? Which towns have the worst fields?

That last one stopped him. He clicked onto the threads and read every word of every comment. He expected complaints about Mountain Ridge, about the dog crap and the gopher holes. Instead he saw a complaint that made him want to kiss the screen.

West Millstone has the worst fields in the state, a parent wrote. *The sidelines are so faded the players are lucky if they can see them at all.*

How perfect was that? Faded or uneven field lines weren't going to hurt anyone, but they might be enough to mess up someone's game.

Saturday night the weather was perfect. Even the moon cooperated, a big, bright gift in the sky. Roy told Maura he was taking Puffy for a walk.

"What? Now?" For three hours Maura had been watching DVDs of *The Sopranos* on their new flat screen TV. For three hours she hadn't moved from her chair.

"Puffy looks like he needs to go. Did you take him out at all today?"

"Okay," Maura said, because she wasn't listening.

Roy loaded up his backpack in the basement, and threw it in the backseat of the car along with the dog. Sunday's game location had just been changed. He didn't know why, but he was happy that he'd bothered to go online and check.

He parked the car, put on his pack, grabbed the dog, and hustled to the field.

He never expected it would be locked. He pulled on the chain, but the chain and the padlock were both brand-new and locked tight.

He stepped back and studied the situation. The fence was only five feet tall. Even with a pack on his back he could hike over a five-foot fence with no problem. Except for the dog.

He drove back to the house.

"I'm home," he called as he let the dog in.

"What?" Maura called, but she wasn't even listening to herself.

He put the leash on the doorknob and closed the door softly behind him. Who was he kidding? He didn't need an excuse like taking the dog for a walk. Not only did Maura not know where he was, she didn't even care.

When he got back to the field, he grabbed his equipment and hitched himself over the fence. He wasn't as spry as he used to be. There was no grace in his movement and he made a fair amount of noise upon landing. But he did it. That was all that mattered.

As soon as his feet hit the ground he hiked up his pants and marched to the far side of the field.

He'd tested the plan in own his backyard. First he used the sprayer to paint a white line on the grass. Then he sprayed over it with green. It wasn't exactly the same color green as the grass but it was damn close. And even Winslow wasn't going to stop to compare two shades of green.

Slow and steady, that's how he worked, carefully covering the white line with the green line until the white line disappeared. Then slow and steady, he made a new line a few feet farther inside.

He had to admit, he'd done a damn good job.

He had just finished—the paint sprayers were back in his bag—when a flashlight sent a figure eight of light dancing across the field, just missing him.

"Sean. How's over here?"

Roy froze.

"Anywhere is fine."

It was two of Winslow's trainers. He recognized their voices. Then came a giggle.

"Now, now," Sean said. "Not yet."

There was another giggle. Two trainers. Two girls.

"I'm thirsty," one said. She sounded young, not much older than Nadine.

"Keith," Sean called to his friend. "Marilee is thirsty. Did you bring the water bottles?"

"Let's see," Keith said. "I've got a bottle here but I'm not sure what's in it. It doesn't smell like water at all. Well, what do you know. It's Jack."

"I thought your name was Keith," the second girl said.

"That's right, Janine. I'm Keith."

"So who's Jack?"

Keith and Sean laughed.

"Jack Daniel's," Keith said. "Jack Daniel's is a very good friend of ours. Would you like to meet him?"

Marilee and Janine giggled.

Roy started moving, slowly, toward the fence.

"Shit," Keith said.

Roy stopped.

"What is it?" Sean asked.

"I just sat down on something wet. Shit," Keith said. "Sean—did Parker say anything to you about repainting the lines tonight?"

"I'm not exactly Parker's confidant."

"Look at this. I've got paint on my pants."

Roy tried to figure out the best escape route. If he made a run for it they might hear him, but if he stayed, they might sweep their light across the field again, and he'd be caught.

"Oh no," Marilee whined. "I've got it on me too. Look. It's on my shirt. Do you think it will come off?"

"I think the shirt might come off," Sean said. "Let's have a look-see."

Another giggle.

"Keith, throw me one of those blankets, will you?"

"Get your own blanket. I'm trying see how much paint I've got on my trousers."

"I can help take them off," Janine said. "Would it make you feel better if I took mine off too?"

The new field lines weren't going to be a problem for the trainers after all.

"How long do you have to stay here tonight?" Marilee asked.

"I'm on watch till dawn," Sean said. "Do you think you could keep me company until dawn?"

"I've got a midnight curfew," Marilee said.

"Then we'd better get started removing the paint from your shirt right away."

At the next burst of laughter, Roy ran alongside the fence, wondering how he was going to climb over without making a racket. But when he got to the gate, he saw it was wide open now. The trainers had come with keys.

He ran, light on his feet, stopping when he got to the sidewalk to make sure no one had heard him. They hadn't. They were all too busy, removing shirts and trousers, and getting friendly with Jack Daniel's.

Roy risked a smile. He felt better than he had in years. Maybe it was time for a career change. To hell with being a plumber. Maybe he should go into the military. Join an elite corps. CIA. Special Forces. Get himself a pair of night vision goggles.

He started the car but didn't put the lights on, didn't even close the door all the way, until he was several blocks from the field.

When he got home Maura was sleeping in front of the TV.

"Maura," he said and gently shook her. "Maura. Come on. Get up. Let's go."

He gave her a kiss and her eyes popped open. She looked surprised as she stood up. She leaned on Roy and snuggled closer. They walked together to bed.

thirty-six

It's good," Sondra said. "I'm not saying it's not good."

Annie took the receiver away from her ear, just for a moment, before responding. "I'm not sure I understand the problem."

"I'm not excited. It's not making my heart race. You did what I asked. It's perfectly good. But I'm not dizzy. I'm not fainting. I want to be dizzy and fainting. You know what I mean, right?"

Annie knew the key here was to ignore Sondra's words and stay focused on figuring out what was really bothering her. Once she knew that, she could fix it.

"Is it the tone?" Annie asked. "Is there content missing? Do you think the message of the mission is off?"

"It's not any of those things," Sondra said. "It's so hard to articulate what it is that's missing. But I guess if I had to say one thing, I'd say it's missing soul."

"Soul?"

"Yup. That's what it is. It's missing your soul."

"My soul?"

"Don't worry. I have an idea how we can go about fixing it. You ready?"

Annie was afraid. "Sure."

"I just hired this absolutely brilliant assistant. Her name is Cyndra. She's ambitious, loyal, hardworking—my totally best, ever. She doesn't need me to hold her hand to explain everything all day long. Actually, she reminds me a lot of you."

"She does?" Annie said.

"Yup. She has an amazing work ethic. No matter how much I throw at her, she does it. She never complains. She just does it. Once it's done, she worries that it's not good enough. Nothing is ever good enough for Cyndra. And forget saying no. It is totally not in her vocabulary. Just like you."

"Wow," Annie said.

"Actually, Cyndra is the one who flagged the problem. She looked at everything you did. She thought it was all very good. But she said it felt like you stopped just before you added your soul to the mix. That's all it needs, really. Some of your soul."

Annie never really thought about her soul. But she could feel it now, shrinking, protectively, as if it knew it was under attack.

"What I'm thinking—what we're thinking," Sondra went on, "is that the three of us should have a retreat. We should hole up somewhere and work straight through for as long as it takes to give this baby a soul. Isn't that a great idea? It was Cyndra's idea, but I love it. What do you think?"

"I think I'm not sure what it is you want to do," Annie said.

"I want us to go on a retreat and hunker down for a couple of days. And here comes best part of the idea. You're going to love this. We're going to do it at your house."

"What?"

"It's a thinking-outside-of-the-box idea, isn't it? You have to admit, the whole office setting thing, the whole city thing, sometimes it can strangle your creativity. We need a change of scenery. If we get that, and we agree we won't stop working until we're all happy, we'll get it done. You have food, right?"

Annie sat down. It was suddenly clear. No amount of work was ever going to make this right.

"How does tomorrow morning look for you?" Sondra asked. "Or do you think it would be better to start our retreat tonight?"

"I'm sorry," Annie said. "I don't do retreats."

"Pardon me?"

"I might have done retreats once, but I don't do them now. They don't work for me. But feel free. If you and Cyndra want to have a retreat you should. Maybe what the project needs is some of Cyndra's soul. Maybe with her young and less jaded eyes she'll be able to see things in such a new way, it will actually make you faint."

"I don't mean I literally want to faint," Sondra said.

"Look," Annie said. "The deck doesn't need to have my soul. It just needs to be good. And it is. It's very good. I've given you my best work. And I stand by it."

"You do?"

"Yes," Annie said, and waited to be fired.

It would be okay. There had to be other jobs out there. She could always be a cashier in the supermarket. That was the perfect job for a change specialist. She was very good at making change.

"I guess you're right," Sondra said. "What you did is pretty damn good. I don't know why I listened to Cyndra. She's only twenty-two years old. Okay. So we're good to go. I'm happy. I'm not fainting, but I'm happy. Are you ready to move on to the Buzz kit? What do you have on that so far? I assume by now you're almost done."

"No."

"What do you have—an outline?"

"No."

"What do you mean, 'no'? I feel like you're not managing this job flow very well, Annie. I thought you planned out all the sections of the deck after our first meeting. That's what you led me to believe. But we're constantly playing catch-up. I need everything planned. Every word. Every thought. I thought I hired a real Plannie-Annie. What happened to her?"

"She's gone. And you're right. You deserve a real Plannie-Annie. You should find one and hire her immediately."

"Wait a minute. You sound like you're giving up. Why don't we go ahead and have that retreat—just you and me. We can be Plannie-Annies together."

"Sorry," Annie said. "But no. I'm done. Good luck. Got to go. Good-bye." She hung up the phone.

She walked up to her office and gathered every Plan for the Day she could find. Her arms full of paper, she came back downstairs, went outside, and deposited it all in the trash.

The phone was ringing when she came back in. It didn't matter anymore if it was Sondra. Annie was immune to her now.

She picked up the receiver. "Yes?"

"Hey there." It was Linda.

Annie heard what sounded like a television in the background. "Where are you?"

"God, you know everything," Linda said. "I'm in New Jersey."

"Where?" Annie asked.

"I don't know. Some town near where you live. I'm at Parker's place. He's got a huge apartment he shares with five trainers. They're not here at the moment. Do you want to come over and hang out? But don't wear open-toed shoes. The floor is gross."

"I can't," Annie said.

"What about lunch tomorrow with Roxanne Lacombe?"

"That's a funny joke. What's the punch line?"

"I'm not joking," Linda said. "That's really why I'm calling. Roxanne wants to take you out to lunch. She asked me to set it up."

"Why?"

"Things have imploded with Blaine Glass. And by 'imploded' I mean he's now in rehab. They want you back. Roxanne said you won't have to live at Proxo anymore. She promises."

"Sure," Annie said. "She'll say anything now. But she'll end up asking me to move again. I know how it goes."

"She won't. Really. She gets it. They want you back. Roxanne will kill me for telling you this, but I'm telling you anyway. They'll take you part-time."

"What do they think part-time is? Sixty hours a week?"

"Annie, just have lunch with Roxanne. Listen to what she

has to say. Unless your consulting business is turning out to be too good to give up. In which case I totally understand."

"That's certainly not true," Annie said.

"I know. So why not see what Roxanne has to offer?"

Annie thought about Sondra and Cyndra and Tim and Hank and Charlotte and Winslow.

"It's just lunch," Linda said. "Really, what do you have to lose?"

"Nothing," Annie had to admit. So she agreed.

thirty-seven

POWER POINTERS—*October 21st!!!*
News of the Day

A Fond Farewell:

It is with a mixture of bittersweet sadness that we must say good-bye to one of my favorite players, Rose Fern.

It has been my great pleasure to coach Rose over the past five years. However, when her parents came to me requesting her release from the team, I felt I had no choice but to respect their wishes and comply. Please join me in wishing Rose the best of luck in all endeavors, both on and off the field!!!

Player Development Update:

Several parents have asked Ken my view about player development. As you know, I am committed to developing each player on our team to her fullest potential. However, when a player, her family, or the management of the Power feels a girl's best potential would be better realized elsewhere, it is our paramount duty to do what is best for her and for all. Remember, what is right is not always what is easy.

Special Welcome Update:

In light of the space made available by Rose's unexpected withdrawal from the team, we are now able to offer a spot to a new player. It is therefore with great pleasure that I welcome Charlotte Fleming to the Power.

As we know from her visits to our training sessions, Charlotte demonstrates a strong combination of excellent foot skills and superior sportsmanship! Please join me in offering Charlotte our warmest hello!!!

Conditioning Update: I have recently noticed that general levels of fitness on the team are not where they should be in order for us to get to the next level. Also, due to incidents beyond our control, team confidence has still been lagging.

To combat these situations, I have arranged a series of scrimmages over the next twelve Saturdays with a boys' team, one year older. The boys think they will have an easy time of it with us. I trust the girls will rise to the occasion, and not be put off by the boys' size (some are quite large) or aggressiveness (some are quite aggressive, both on and off the field).

Challenge of the Week Update: Congratulations to this week's Winslow West Weekly Challenge Competition Winner, Evelyn Murphy. On Monday, Evelyn successfully headed the ball one hundred and forty-two times. Some players are still having trouble with this rudimentary skill. I urge any player who is unsure of how to perform successful successive headers to see Evelyn for tips!

Special Notice for Great Play Goes to: Evelyn! With Dinah now on the bench, Evelyn has picked up the slack in the aggression department. Congratulations, Evelyn, on your very first Yellow Card!

Which brings me to this week's Word of the Week: "Pressure"!

Remember: When we keep up the pressure, we dominate the game.

Field Marshal Update: I am happy to report that our new field monitoring program is now in full swing. I feel confident that no further complications shall arise. Any parent who has not yet signed up as Field Marshal, please see Ken before next Sunday's game. Also, Vicki is waiting to finalize the order for Parent Field Marshal jackets. Those of you who have not given her your measurements and checks, please do so at once!!!

Game Update: I understand some parents have concerns about facing the Holder Crush on the 31st of October. Yes, they are good, and yes, they have been boasting about wanting to put us in our place. Do not be intimidated! Our place is first place!! Domination Will be Ours!!!

Good Luck to One and All from Winslow West!!!

thirty-eight

The front door opened, and slammed shut. Annie heard something drop on the floor, then heavy footsteps climbing the stairs. Tim was home.

He walked into her office just as she dumped another stack of papers in the wastebasket.

"Hey," Tim said. "What's going on?"

"I just finished throwing out all my Plans for the Day. Now I've moved on to trashing the To Do lists." She read the heading of the one in her hand—"Five Steps to a Happy Week." She ripped it in half and tossed it in the can.

"What happened?" Tim asked.

Annie scooped up several papers that had drifted to the floor. "I was wrong."

"About what?"

"A lot of things. 'Never say no,' for one thing. That's been my motto, right? Can you believe I have a motto?"

"You don't have a motto."

"Yes, I do. I have a few mottos. 'Work hard, and if that doesn't work, work harder.' I really believed that one," Annie said.

"What's going on, Annie?"

She dumped another pile of papers in the trash. "I have to make a change."

Tim looked at the open, emptied desk drawers, the papers on the floor, the overflowing garbage can, the completely clear and clean surface of Annie's desk.

"What kind of change?" he asked. "You don't want to move to a cabin in the hills of West Virginia and live on clover and worms, do you? Not that I couldn't grow to love West Virginia. I hear it's a beautiful place. And I bet clover is really nutritious. And if I have to, I could learn to eat worms. What I'm trying to say is, whatever your new plan is, it better include me."

"There is no new plan," Annie said.

"Mom?" Charlotte called up the stairs. "It's time to leave for the game."

"We'll be right there," Annie called back.

"If there's no plan," Tim said, "what's the plan?"

Annie smiled. "I don't know. I think we're just going to have to wait and see. Do you think you can do that?"

"I'm not sure," Tim said. "I guess we'll just have to wait and see."

Charlotte was waiting for them in the back of the car, grim faced and silent.

"Is everything okay?" Annie asked her.

Charlotte sighed. "It's against the rules for me to speak while I'm getting focused."

"Who told you that?" Tim asked.

"Winslow. We're not supposed to talk for two hours before every game."

"Well, Winslow isn't here right now," Annie said. "So feel free to talk all you want."

"He'll know," Charlotte said.

"How?" Annie asked.

"By how we play," Charlotte explained. "Winslow said he can see by watching how we play who focused before the game and who didn't. He said even if we're on the bench he can see just by looking in our eyes."

"I think you were right," Annie said as they turned into the parking lot at the field. "I think joining the Power wasn't a good idea."

"It is a good idea," Charlotte said. "A very good idea."

She slid down a little in her seat so she could talk without being seen by anyone passing by outside.

"I should be on the best team I can be on. The girls on the Asteroids aren't serious about anything. They're afraid of working hard and I'm not. And if working hard doesn't work, I'm not afraid to work harder. I have to go," she whispered.

She got out the car and ran to join her team.

"What have I done?" Annie asked.

thirty-nine

The girls walked across the field, checking the ground for irregularities.

"Thank you, ladies," Winslow called out when they were done. "Let's warm up. Miss Fleming, I'd like you in midfield, please, left side."

Charlotte took her place.

The girls looked good, Winslow thought. And once they loosened up, they'd look even better.

The refs arrived, checked the players' cards, and called in the captains for a handshake. The whistle blew, and play began.

Winslow's feet moved a phantom ball as he watched. Good aggressive opening by Evelyn. Nice—very nice—pass by Charlotte to Shelby. But, wait. Something was off. Something was wrong. His eyes scanned the field, searching for—what? He couldn't quite tell.

Vicki got off the bench and joined him. "What's the matter?"

"I don't know." He scanned the field.

"The girls are looking at you, Win. You're not acting like yourself."

"Settle," he yelled out to the girls as he scanned the field again.

The girls looked over to Vicki. The other team was making a substitution. The ball was no longer in play.

"Why are you telling them to settle the ball, Win?" Vicki asked. "The ref just called a time-out."

Ken walked over. "What's up?"

"I'm not sure." Winslow scanned the grass for holes. They'd done their field check. The field was fine. "Did you talk to the pest control people today?" he asked Ken.

"Yes," Ken said.

"What did they say?"

"We can talk about it later," Ken said.

"Why later?"

"You're busy now," Ken said.

"Kenneth." Winslow turned to face him. "What exactly did they say?"

"They said it was a gopher, didn't they?" Vicki interrupted. "Or was it a mole. Alice, who lives behind us, had problems with moles. Winslow thinks it was a groundhog, but groundhogs are definitely too big to dig holes that size."

"Actually, what I said was it might be a badger," Winslow corrected her. "Badgers are devious creatures. Very clever. Smarter than you think." His eyes scanned the field again. Something was not right—what?

"It wasn't a gopher or a mole or a groundhog or a badger," Ken said.

Winslow stepped to the side where there was a small rise in the grass. He moved to the top of the rise and looked down at Ken. "What was it, then?"

"The holes were dug by a human."

The ref blew the whistle. "Offsides."

Winslow turned to the ref and threw up his hands. "What?"

"Winslow," Vicki whispered and tugged his arm. "You weren't watching."

Winslow took three steps back and nodded, coach code for apology.

He kept his eyes on the game now. "What exactly do you mean by *human*?" he asked Ken.

"The guy said there was no way those holes were dug by an animal. He said he was a hundred percent sure they were dug by a person using a small shovel."

The ref blew his whistle, and pointed toward the other team's goal to show who got the throw-in.

"What is wrong with the girls today?" Winslow hissed.

Vicki couldn't help herself. "They're waiting for you to tell them what to do, Win. You're not talking to them."

Winslow continued sweeping the field with his eyes. "My God," he said. "Look at that."

Vicki turned. "What?" She didn't see anything.

"The sideline. See how it bows out slightly, and then curves back in. Don't you see?" He walked onto the field.

The Power stopped their play. The Crush played on, and scored a goal.

When the whistle blew the Power didn't move. They watched as Winslow walked the field.

Shelby sat down first, as if she were hurt. The rest of her teammates followed. The ref yelled at Winslow to step off the field. He reached in his pocket for a card.

Winslow ignored him. He stopped in front of the Power parents.

"May I ask everyone to please stand up and move your chairs a foot back from the sideline."

They stood up as one and did what he asked.

Slowly Winslow walked the line. It was obvious now to everyone. The sideline bowed out in an arc at the middle, and then in again at a sharp angle. Someone was playing games with them.

How had he missed it? How had everyone missed it?

"Ref," Winslow called.

The ref came over. The Crush coach joined them. They walked, single file, up and down the sidelines. When they were done, they huddled together to discuss what to do.

The ref blew his whistle, and called out, "Play on."

The Power lost the game.

Winslow called the police.

forty

They stopped at a drugstore for a costume on their way to the Halloween party, but there wasn't much of a selection left. Charlotte settled for a clown. Annie bought a bag of candy corn.

When they got back in the car Charlotte's face was a snapshot of misery.

"Why don't we skip the party?" Annie suggested.

"I'm fine with not going," Tim added.

"We have to go," Charlotte said. "The only one who's allowed to miss the party is Bobbi, and that's because her grandmother just died."

"What do you think would happen if you didn't show up?" Annie asked.

"I'm going," Charlotte said. "You don't have to come if you don't want to."

Barbie and Ken's house was easy to spot. A smoke machine blew clouds from behind the bushes. Stone grave markers were set into the lawn. Two headless bodies, made of old clothes, swung from a crabapple tree. Skulls swayed from branches. Heads hung out of windows. Every ghoul clutched a soccer ball.

A green-faced witch answered the door. She smiled, showing off yellow teeth. She scratched her nose with her long black nail, and her wart fell off.

"I told Ken it wouldn't stay on," Barbie cackled. "Come on in. Winslow is meeting with the team now. And while the girls bob for balls in the basement," she told Annie and Tim, "we can bob for olives in the living room."

"We can only stay for a little while," Annie said.

"That's fine." Barbie didn't seem to care either way. "Come on, Charlotte. I'll take you back to Winslow."

Annie and Tim joined the parents in the living room.

"I didn't realize we were supposed to wear costumes too," Annie said as she scanned the zombies, bunnies, ghouls, and ghosts.

"You should have known," said the bride of Frankenstein, sitting beside a vampire who was Parker. "You never wear a pink suit to a navy meeting."

"Linda?" Annie asked the bride. "What are you doing here?"

"Parker invited me. Annie is how we met," Linda explained to everyone.

Ken, the grim reaper, came in with a tray of Bloody Marys. He handed one to everyone, whether they wanted it or not. When he got to Annie he leaned closer.

"Winslow would like to speak with you. Would you mind coming with me?"

All eyes locked onto Annie as she followed Ken out of the room.

"Right in here," Ken said, stopping in front of a pair of French doors.

Annie could hear Winslow lecturing someone. Her eye began to twitch.

"It's your left eye, isn't it?" Tim asked, coming up beside her. "I can see it."

"You can?" Annie asked. "For real?"

"Yup. There it goes again. I hope it's not because of that guy." Tim pointed to Winslow. "Come on. Let's go find out what he wants."

"Thank you," Annie said.

"Hey—we're on the same team, right?"

"I'm quite sure you will," Winslow was saying to someone they couldn't see. "Because you're a team player, aren't you? Ah," he interrupted himself. "Here come your parents now. Why don't you run along and join the other girls?"

Charlotte got up from an oversized chair. Annie saw that she was fighting back tears. As she squeezed by her mother she quietly said, "I'm fine," before Annie could even ask the question.

"The girls are all in the basement," Winslow called to Charlotte.

"We'll be leaving in about five minutes," Annie added.

Charlotte nodded and Annie took note that she made no attempt to negotiate more time.

"We just had the most delightful chat," Winslow said, leading Annie and Tim farther into the room. "I was a bit concerned that Charlotte was demoralized by today's disgraceful game. But she has a wonderful attitude. She's a very hard worker. Did you know she has a plan for how to improve some of her weaker skills? She has a plan for every day of the week. Very impressive."

He gestured to the sofa. "Please. Sit."

Parker, Marilyn, Barbie, and Vicki appeared as if on cue, and joined them. Ken closed the door.

"Before I begin," Winslow said. "I just want to remind everyone that nothing said in this room is to be repeated. Is that understood?"

Parker, Marilyn, Ken, Barbie, and Vicki nodded vigorously.

Winslow turned to Annie and Tim. "I assume you are both aware that our team has had some problems over the past month."

"Oh my God," Barbie said. "The worst was the dog poop all over the field. I'm still nauseous thinking about it."

Winslow shot Ken a look, which Ken then shot over to Barbie.

"There have been several incidents," Winslow continued. "The incident that was just referred to, as well as the incident with the holes."

"You mean the gopher holes?" Annie asked. Vicki had told her about that.

"We had the field checked by an expert," Winslow said. "And they weren't gopher holes. They were traps."

"Can you believe it?" Vicki said. "Because of that, Dinah can't play for a month."

"Dinah is not who I'm worried about," Winslow said.

"Winslow," Vicki warned.

"Don't misunderstand," Winslow went on. "Dinah is a very fine player. A very, very fine player. But there are other players who—" He was talking himself into a hole. He started again. "We need to protect all our players."

"All of them," Vicki echoed.

"As you know," Winslow continued, "we had a bit of a problem with the field lines this morning."

"They were repainted," Vicki interrupted. "By someone who was not authorized to do so."

"The police took a report," Winslow said. "But I do not feel they were appropriately concerned. So I am going to begin my own investigation—which is why I wanted to speak to you."

He turned to Annie. "I have reason to believe that these acts may have been committed by someone on your former team. Vicki, would you please pass around the roster."

Vicki handed everyone a roster of the Asteroids.

"I offered to give this to the police, but they were not keen on the idea of interviewing these suspects, because they claim they have no proof that any of these people have committed a crime."

"It's because you cut Heather King," Vicki snapped. "If Brian King were still a parent on this team, he'd have the whole Asteroids roster locked up in jail by now."

"Be that as it may," Winslow said. "The police may claim their hands are tied. Mine, thankfully, are not. It is my firm belief that the name or names of the person or persons responsible for these acts of terror are on the list you now hold in your hands. So, Annie, would you please look over the list, and tell us what you can about each member of your former team."

"Acts of terror?" Annie said.

"What would you call it?" Winslow said. "Did you see how the girls played today? They were paralyzed with fear."

"What exactly are you asking me to do?"

"I want you to go through the list, one family at a time, and tell us everything you know. For example, have any of these people ever expressed any feelings—jealousy, curiosity, admiration—any feelings at all, about either the Power or about me?"

A soft knock on the door stopped the conversation.

Ken got up and opened the door a crack. Annie heard a small voice. It was Charlotte.

Annie came over.

"Can we go home?" Charlotte whispered.

"Of course," Annie said. "Give me a minute."

"Why don't we start with the unhappy people first," Winslow said.

Annie walked over to Tim.

"Or, if you'd prefer, we can start at the top of the list and go down the alphabet one family at a time. What can you tell me about the Andersons?"

"Charlotte wants to go home," Annie told Tim.

Winslow stiffened. "This won't take long."

"We have to leave now," Annie said.

"We're all members of the Power family," Winslow reminded her. "We all want the same thing. Now, I have my suspicions as to who might be responsible. What I'm looking for is some proof. A comment. A question. Anything you remember overhearing."

Tim stood up. "Let's go."

Annie and Tim started toward the door.

"Excuse me," Winslow said, his voice rising. "I need a few

minutes of your time so we can figure out which of the pathetic parents on your former team is behind these awful acts."

Annie stopped. "They are not pathetic parents. They are decent people. All of them."

"You do realize you're not on that team anymore," Winslow said. "You're on my team."

"I'm afraid I can't help you," Annie said.

"Leaving this way looks very bad," Winslow said.

Tim put his arm around his wife. "We have to go."

Annie and Tim headed for the door. Vicki walked over and yanked the list of Asteroid families out of Annie's hands.

Winslow turned toward the window that faced the backyard.

"Well," he said as he stared at his own reflection in the dark of the night. "It appears as if we're done."

forty-one

POWER POINTERS—*November 1st!!!*
News of the Day

IMPORTANT! READ IMMEDIATELY!

Bad Patch Update: All teams have bad patches! But bad patches are really opportunities in disguise!! What one does with one's bad patch is what determines one's future success!!!

Team Strategy Update: Beginning today, all players are to view each game as if it were their first game ever! All players are to put all thoughts of all previous games, indeed all thoughts of all games they've ever played, behind them once and for all!!

Focus Update: To improve our focus, we will continue my new policy of having a Winslow West Word of the Week every week. This week's Winslow West Word of the Week is *Focus!* And the lack thereof!!!

I am well aware that not all players adhered to our new focus-boosting Pre-Game Silence Period before our last competition. I hope the debacle of that game has convinced all players that this new policy is worth the effort!!!

Safety Update: As you know, Safety is my Paramount Concern. Therefore, beginning today, no player or player's family member is to speak about team business with any player or family member of any player on any team in our league or any league or anywhere at any time!

Envy Update: Envy is the unavoidable result of the hard efforts of a team such as ours. This is always true on teams where a high level of play has been consistently attained! Therefore, if you suspect someone of envy and are unsure whether or not it is appropriate to speak to that person, please check with me at once! My door is always open!!!

Winter Training Update: Winter training will commence the day our fall season ends! We will continue our Saturday scrimmages with the boys, and because we no longer have Sunday games, we will have Sunday scrimmages as well! All players must continue to be vigilant about attendance at all practices and scrimmages!!

Reminder: Outdoor training will only be canceled when there is snowfall greater than one inch!

Details regarding Specialty Clinics, which will be available Monday through Fridays for all players—No Exceptions!!!!!!!—will be coming shortly.

Exciting Update: The Winslow West Soccer-Plex Opening Exhibition Game is finally here! Local celebrities will be on hand!!! Game time is 10 a.m. this Saturday. All team members are to report to the Winslow West Soccer-Plex no later than 8 a.m. in full uniform, hair tied neatly back (Bailey!!!).

Good Luck to One and All from Winslow West!!!

forty-two

The rain was coming down like a scrim, turning the afternoon sky dark gray. Annie checked the weather forecast. The chance of thunderstorms over the next two hours was high.

She called Marilyn to find out if practice would be canceled.

"Canceled?" Marilyn said. "No. But don't worry. The girls will have a great time. They love playing in the rain."

Annie turned on the news. A weather warning scrolled across the bottom of the screen.

"Maybe you should skip practice today," Annie told Charlotte.

Charlotte shook her head. "I can't. Winslow gets really mad when someone misses practice. He makes everyone else work twice as hard and then he tells everyone who's to blame."

"I'm sure he wouldn't do that if you just missed one practice," Annie said. "Besides, I thought you weren't even sure you wanted to stay on the team."

"I'm giving it a chance," Charlotte said. "Like you asked

me to. Come on. We have to go. The only thing worse than missing practice is if you're late."

They found Winslow in his normal spot, at the top of the rise. It was raining even harder now, but the players were doing their stretches, backs pressed flat into the muddy grass.

Charlotte ran over and took her place. Winslow made a show of checking his watch, taking a small pad out of the pocket of his anorak, and scribbling a note.

Annie's spine stiffened. She walked over. "Can we talk for a minute?"

Winslow peered out from his hood. "I am coaching. I do not talk to parents while I'm coaching." He took a step away, clapped his hands, and called the girls in.

"Thank you for leading our stretches, Shelby," he said. "Evelyn, please lead the team once around the field. Charlotte, I'll need two additional laps from you."

Annie walked over to a group of parents who were watching, huddled under an oak tree to keep dry.

"Is it safe to run on the field when it's this wet?" Annie asked.

"They love it," Marilyn said. "Shelby keeps falling down on purpose so she can roll in the mud like a puppy. Last time they played in the rain she came home—I swear to God—with muddy teeth."

The other parents laughed.

Annie heard a distant rumble. "What was that?"

"Probably thunder," said Marilyn. "Can you believe it's warm enough to thunder in November? Is this global warming or what?"

"Aren't they going to get off the field?" Annie asked.

"Because of one thunder?" Marilyn said. "That's funny."

It wasn't funny to Annie. She walked toward the girls.

"Where are you going?" Marilyn called.

By the time Annie reached the perimeter of the field the girls were glancing at the sky as they ran.

"We're leaving," Annie told Charlotte as she passed her. "This isn't safe."

Charlotte nodded. She wanted to go.

"We're leaving," Annie called over to Winslow. "It's not safe to be here when it's thundering."

"The storm is miles away," Winslow called back. "It's probably in Pennsylvania."

"We're going home," Annie said. She had to yell now, to be heard above the wind and rain.

Winslow yelled something back, but Annie couldn't hear it. She took Charlotte's hand as they ran to their car.

"Thanks, Mom," Charlotte said as they drove home.

Annie smiled. "Anytime."

forty-three

POWER POINTERS—*November 2nd!!!*
News of the Day

EXTREMELY IMPORTANT!!!! READ AT ONCE!!!!

It Has Come To My Attention That A Small Number Of Parents Have Been Voicing Concerns About My Safety Policy As Regards Lightning!

Please Note: All parents with concerns about this or any other matters should share their concerns with me and not jabber among themselves on the sidelines. Sideline jabbering does not solve problems! It causes them! As of today, all sideline jabbering is prohibited!!!!!!

League Lightning Policy:

The Mountain Ridge Travel Soccer Board Policy on Lightning is as follows:

During a storm, all fields are to be cleared immediately upon the second strike of lightning. To determine a storm's potential for danger, the club uses the following well-known formula:

To figure out the distance of the approaching thunder-storm, divide the seconds from the second flash to the second crash by six. Due to the fact that an approaching thunderstorm is at its most dangerous when one mile away, and that a storm travels one half-mile per minute, a storm five miles away will arrive in roughly ten minutes, giving plenty of time for even the slowest runner to evacuate the field. This conservative formula does not include all the storms that travel at the above speed but then stall and never, in point of fact, arrive at all.

Note: The Mountain Ridge Travel Soccer Board Policy on Field Evacuation says No Player is ever to be left on the field during a Board Certified Evacuation.

Anyone wondering if I follow the above policy need only look inside my vehicle, which was the site of yesterday's field evacuation for four of our players.

The girls enjoyed the evacuation, particularly the part where they painted the tan upholstery in my vehicle brown with mud taken from their cleats and hair. A mud bath was also applied to all windows. Anyone wishing to see the mud in my vehicle must do so immediately as I have asked the girls responsible (Jolie, Bobbi, Gwen, and Dinah!) to clean the upholstery and windows directly following this afternoon's makeup practice drills.

Good Luck to One and All from Winslow West!!!

forty-four

Gerri offered everyone a drink.

"Forget the drinks," Peggy Ann said. "It's late. I have three kids who need to get to bed waiting for me at home. You said this was an emergency. Why don't you just get to the point."

"We all have somewhere we'd rather be," Gerri said. "I'm going to turn the meeting over to Brian King. In addition to being a new parent on the Asteroids—and let me say how fortunate we are that Heather has decided to join our team— Brian is also a Mountain Ridge police officer. Brian?"

Officer King stood up, cleared his throat, and crossed his arms. "Gerri asked me to talk to you tonight because there are some problems going on with the Power right now. I don't know how many of you are aware of the situation. The reason I wanted to talk to you all is that Winslow West has been saying some things I think you need to know."

"What kind of things?" asked Peggy Ann.

Even the parents who didn't like to waste their time discussing the Power's business leaned forward in their seats to hear the answer. Most of the parents knew Brian from around. He was a genial guy. But he was dead serious now.

He cleared his throat again. "Winslow called the Mountain Ridge Police Department two days ago to report several incidents of what he called terrorism on the soccer field. At that time, he told a police officer that he believes the perpetrator of these so-called terrorist acts is a disgruntled member of the Asteroids."

"He's accusing our kids?" Chip said. A vein on his neck began to bulge.

"Actually," Gerri said, "he's accusing us."

"Of what?" Mona asked.

"Vandalism and terrorism," Brian said. "The first incident, as some of you know, was dog excrement on the field. The second incident was holes in the field. This last time, the sidelines were reconfigured in the middle of the night."

"That's just plain weird," Chip said.

"I wanted everyone to be aware of this," Brian continued, "because Winslow has requested that the Mountain Ridge Police Department bring the Asteroids in for questioning."

Peggy Ann stood up. "I'm calling my brother. He's a lawyer. Maybe I can get him to come over here. Where's the phone?"

"Hold on," Brian said. "There's no need to panic. No one is coming over to arrest you. If Winslow was even a little bit smarter, we might be in a pretty ugly situation right now. But luckily that's not a problem."

"What do you mean?" Peggy Ann asked as she sat back down.

"For one thing," Gerri said, "if Winslow were smarter, Brian's daughter would not have been cut from the Power this fall. I want to say again that I think Heather is one hell of a player and we are socca-lucky to have her on our team."

"Do we have a lawyer, Roy?" Maura asked her husband.

Roy didn't answer. He was sitting very still, concentrating on everything that was being said.

"You don't need to call a lawyer," Brian said. "No police officer is going to turn up at your house because of this. Winslow has no basis for his suspicions. And to be honest, he does not have a lot of admirers down at the station house."

"What do you mean?" Mona asked.

"I mean there are one or two young cops with little kids who Winslow thinks are in his pocket. But there are a lot more guys whose kids, over the years, have been treated very badly by him. I'm talking about cops whose kids have been overlooked, kicked off teams, lied to, and just plain treated like crap. And these are people with long memories."

There was a long silence.

"So who do you think is vandalizing the fields?" Mona finally asked. "Teenagers?"

"That's probably who it is," Roy said. "Drunk teenagers."

"Could be," Brian said. "But I don't think so. I'll tell you my personal belief—which, I might add, is shared by most of my fellow officers."

Heads nodded vigorously, urging him on.

"There's only one person who has a reason to bother to do these things because there's really only one person who would benefit from it. And that's Winslow himself. Because think about it. The Winslow West Soccer-Plex Opening is coming up and it's perfect advertising. I can just hear him—'I love the fields in this town but I'm sure we can all agree that at the current time they are no longer secure.' Winslow's new indoor facility, however, will be completely secure."

"It's so obvious, he should be embarrassed," said Peggy Ann.

"It's sick is what it is," Chip said. "Hey, I have an idea. Roy—can you fix up the toilets in the Soccer-Plex, so that the next time Winslow flushes, one of them explodes in his face?"

Everyone laughed, except for Roy and Brian.

"Listen, folks," Brian said. "We can't make jokes like that anymore. We need to conduct ourselves above and beyond reproach. You know what we really have to concentrate on doing?"

"What?" asked Peggy Ann.

"Nothing," Brian said. "Absolutely nothing. I've seen people like Winslow before. I know what makes them tick and I know what makes them crack. I promise you, if we do nothing, it will drive him out of his mind. And there is no more satisfying punishment than that."

When the meeting was over, everyone left energized, hyped up, and smiling.

Except for Roy.

forty-five

The windshield wipers were on high but did little to improve visibility.

"Can you see the road?" Charlotte asked from the backseat.

"Yes," Tim said.

"How can we have a barbecue in the rain?" Charlotte asked, after a moment.

Tim turned up the defroster. "You know how Uncle Hank is. He probably hired half a dozen workers this morning to install special awnings over a brand-new rainproof barbecue pit he had built just for the occasion."

"What is the occasion, anyway?" Annie asked.

Tim shrugged. "All Hank said was that he has news, and it's big and good and he wants to tell us in person over a rack of ribs."

As they pulled into Hank and Trissy's driveway, the radio weatherman announced it was a record-breaking seventy-one degrees with a ninety-percent chance of severe thunderstorms.

"Did you hear that?" Annie asked Charlotte. "The thunderstorms are going to be severe. Your practice will be canceled today for sure."

"Winslow won't cancel because of a weather report," Charlotte said. "He told us the rule is he has to wait for a flash and then count to the crash, remember?"

They got out of the car. Trissy welcomed them into the house.

"Your cousins are downstairs watching a movie," she told Charlotte.

Charlotte ran to the lower-level media room. Tim and Annie followed Trissy into the Adirondack-camp-style family room.

Despite the unusually warm temperature, several carefully arranged logs were burning in the fireplace. Soft jazz played from hidden speakers. Thermoses of tea, coffee, and cocoa were set out on a mission-style buffet table, along with trays of small sandwiches, skewered shrimp, chicken satay, and cheese. On a second table were bottles of cream soda, root beer, tonic water, wine, vodka, scotch, gin, cognac, small ramekins of pudding, and two large platters of doughnuts.

Thunder rumbled.

"That's good," Annie said. "Charlotte is definitely off the hook for practice now."

"You probably should call Winslow and check," Trissy advised. "In case one thunder isn't enough."

"I have to pull her off that team," Annie said. "She seems so unhappy."

"Who isn't?" Trissy asked.

Something in Trissy's voice struck Annie as odd.

Tim didn't seem to notice. "Where's my brother?"

"Liquor store," Trissy said.

Annie eyed the drink table, which was stocked with enough top-shelf choices for a small wedding. "What is he getting?" she asked.

"Away from me," Trissy said. She laughed at her joke, then poured herself a tall glass of tonic water. "He thinks I drink too much, but let me tell you, I am stone cold sober now."

She took a swig of her tonic. "I hate to steal Hank's thunder—and Tim, I'm sure you already know this. But, what the hell. Here's the news flash. Hank asked you two to come over so he could tell you he's leaving. As in moving out. As in abandoning hearth and home."

"What?" was all Tim could manage.

"I thought he asked us over because he wanted to tell us some good news," Annie said.

"Right." Tim nodded, happy for that to be cleared up. "That's what he said. He's got really good news."

"How adorable. That must mean he thinks you'll agree that it's really good news that he's leaving me and the kids to move to Tortola."

"What?" Tim asked. "Where?"

"The beautiful island of Tortola," Trissy said. "To live with a younger and less interesting version of me. Come on, Tim. You must know this already. The whole office knows."

Tim shook his head. "I don't know anything about this." He struggled to jam the information into his brain.

"You know what my favorite part is?" Trissy said. "The new me owns a hotel in Tortola, and Hank wants us to do a partial ownership deal with her. Hanks says her hotel is very wow and now and today." Trissy let out a laugh. "Isn't that great? She has a wow hotel. Wow!" She sat down, kicked off her expensive shoes and put her feet up on the wide leather ottoman.

Annie noticed that both her cashmere socks had holes in the heels.

"I get it," Tim said. "It's a joke, right? An April Fool's joke?"

"It's November," Annie pointed out.

"The joke is Hank thinks I would agree to this," Trissy said. She twirled her large diamond ring so that the stone faced her. She studied it for a moment. "Do you think he forgot that Hot Holidays was my father's business? Or do you think he's just hoping I forgot?"

She didn't wait for an answer. "I haven't worked out all the details with my lawyers yet, but here's the basic idea. I'm going to have Hank removed from the company. He's not going to fight it, because practically speaking he's already living in Tortola with Wow Woman and he doesn't want to give that up."

"Is that why he's been away so much?" Tim asked as random facts began to come together in his mind.

"You got it," Trissy said. "And every time I brought it up he changed the subject to you. It's actually been a very good diversionary tactic. I've spent a lot of time worrying about the two of you."

"We're fine," Annie said.

"I can see that." Trissy got up and poured herself another tonic. "So here's the million-dollar question. I think you are the perfect team to take over Hot Holidays. What do you think?"

Tim didn't need time to mull it over. "No. Absolutely not. I don't particularly like my brother. He's not a nice person. But he's my brother. I can't push him out."

"No pushing necessary. He's going. That's not up for discussion."

"Why don't you run the business?" Annie asked.

"It's not my thing," Trissy said. "Believe me, if it was, I would have stepped in long ago. Besides, I'm too busy. Daddy put Hank in charge of Hot Holidays, but he put me in charge of the rest of his portfolio. I'm not trying to boast, but do you think we'd still be living in this house if we had to live off Hank's mismanagement skills?"

"You're not doing a very good job of selling us your business plan," Annie pointed out.

"My brother's moving where?" Tim was having trouble absorbing the facts.

"Tortola," Trissy said. "And the business is going to be fine. It's been mismanaged, that's true. But I convinced Hank to hire you, Tim, because you have the goods to turn it around. Unfortunately once you got there, Hank wouldn't listen to you."

"That's nothing new," Tim said.

"Well, now that problem has been eliminated. Hank is leaving the scene of the crime." Trissy turned to Annie. "You are the hardest-working person I know. And transition is your thing. This is perfect for you. And, Tim, you are a brilliant numbers guy. If Hank had listened to me, you'd have been running the place for years. Believe me, Hank is out either way. Whether you fire him or I fire him makes no difference."

"I can't fire him," Tim said. "But don't take it personally. I can't fire anyone. It's a problem."

"My father was the same way." Trissy smiled at the memory. "He never fired an employee in his life. That's why they loved him so much. He was incredibly loyal."

"Hey, baby brother and sister-in-law of my dreams," Hank said, barreling into the room with an armload of grocery bags filled with bottles of twenty-five-year-old scotch and fifty-year-old port. "It's a goddamn nightmare out there. Storm of the Century, part two."

He put the bag down on the buffet and took off his drenched leather jacket. Then he noticed the mood.

"Trissy." Hank was peeved. "I wanted to tell them."

Trissy gave him a tough-luck look.

"I don't know what the hell she told you," Hank said. "But I'm sure she managed to make me out to be an asshole."

Trissy laughed. "That part comes across without any help from me at all."

"I didn't mean for this to happen," Hank told Annie, as if she were the conscience of the group. "I'm a very faithful man. But sometimes nature takes over."

"What are you, an orangutan?" Trissy asked. "You don't have a brain? You don't have the ability to choose?"

"How about if we try not to judge me for a change?" Hank said. "How about we try it for just sixty seconds?"

"Poor you," Trissy said. "You want to come out of this with everyone thinking you're a hero just because you finally admitted you've been lying to me for years."

"I'm going to do the right thing," Hank told Tim. "Moving to Tortola is really going to help the business grow. You'll see."

"He won't see," Trissy said. "No one is going to see. You can flush that idea right down the toilet where it and you belong."

"See what I'm up against?" Hank said to Tim. "See what I've been living with? Do you have any idea what it's like? On second thought, maybe you do."

"You're being an idiot, Hank," Tim said.

"I'm being an idiot? Oh, sorry. I forgot. I'm talking to Perfect Boy. But wait a minute—I hear everything is not so perfect anymore. I hear you're having a little work problem."

"Don't bring me into this," Tim said.

"Why not? What's wrong? Is it because Annie doesn't know? Hey, Annie? Did you know Perfect Boy here is having a little work problem? My sources tell me Timmy gets a little freaked out whenever he tries to fire people. Why is that, Timmy? Huh? Are you worried people won't like you? That must be hard. Because you're supposed to be the one everyone likes, right?"

"You should stop talking now," Annie said.

"Awh, Annie. You don't like what I'm saying, either? Well, guess what? I don't give a crap. Because at the end of the day, you're just like Trissy. I mean, who are you to judge? Really, what the hell is your problem anyway? What's the rush? Where's the fire? I never saw anyone running so fast to nowhere in my life."

Tim sighed, stood up and walked over to the buffet, to the large platter of doughnuts. They were chocolate with vanilla frosting, his brother's favorite.

"Hank," Tim said. "Why don't we grab some doughnuts and go sit down somewhere."

"Great idea," Hank said. "The air in here is getting unbearably self-righteous."

Tim put three doughnuts on a plate. "Is there somewhere private we can go?"

"Sure, Timmo. Follow me." Hank turned and led his brother to his study.

A clap of thunder exploded directly overhead.

forty-six

Don't feel bad for me," Trissy said. "This really is going to be for the best."

She walked over to the buffet and picked up a platter of sandwiches. "I'm going downstairs to see if the kids want food. They don't know," she added.

Annie nodded. "I'm sorry."

Trissy took a breath and composed herself. Then she plastered a smile on her face and breezed out of the room.

Annie heard something vibrate. It was a phone. It was her phone. She found her purse and fished it out just in time.

"I'm calling to let everyone know practice is on," Winslow said, instead of hello.

"There's a huge thunderstorm going on," Annie said. "You don't want the girls to practice in the middle of a thunderstorm, do you?"

"I haven't heard any thunder," Winslow insisted.

"You might not have heard it," Annie said. "But it's happening."

"Maybe it is thundering where you are. But it is not thundering where I am. And we have no idea if it is thundering where we're going to be, do we? It's always thundering some-where. So all we can really do is to make our decision based on what is actually happening where we are."

"I will not allow Charlotte to practice in a thunderstorm," Annie said.

"Perhaps you didn't get a chance to read my bulletin on this. The league policy is quite clear. All games and practices are canceled immediately at the second flash."

There was another rumble.

"Did you hear that?" Annie asked.

"Perhaps I am not speaking in a language you under-stand. Let me try again. Any player who is not on the field when practice begins will be assumed to have resigned from the team. Is that clear enough?" Winslow hung up the phone.

Annie walked to the top of the stairs that led down to the entertainment wing. "Charlotte?" she called. "Can I talk to you?"

Charlotte came upstairs. "Yes?"

The house turned bright with another flash of lightning. A second later a huge clap of thunder exploded.

"You're off the team," Annie said.

"Winslow dropped me?"

"No," Annie said. "I'm pulling you off."

"But you and Dad don't like quitters. If you pull me off the team, will you think I'm a quitter?"

"No," Annie said. "If you leave the team, I'll think you're a winner."

Charlotte's forehead remained furrowed. "Is it because I'm not good enough?"

"Absolutely not," Annie said. "It has nothing to do with that. You're as good as it gets."

"Because I can work harder. I haven't been practicing that much at home. But I can. I should."

"Charlotte, have you had any fun on the Power?" Annie asked. "Be honest."

Charlotte shrugged. "The girls are really nice. But it's not fun."

"Why do you think that is?"

"Winslow said we aren't playing at our level. He says we need more discipline. And our skills aren't as good as they should be. And our conditioning is terrible. And our attitude isn't right. We don't have enough commitment. And we aren't hungry enough to do the work to win."

"It's not supposed to be like that," Annie said. "You're twelve years old. It's supposed to be fun."

Hank stormed into the room. "I cannot believe this," he said to Annie. "Did you know your nutso husband just tried to fire me? Is he out of his mind? He can't fire me. He works for me."

Trissy was right behind him. "Honey, I'm so sorry. I forgot to tell you. Tim works for me now."

Tim came in last, just as another lightning bolt struck. A clap of thunder followed a second behind. The storm was now directly overhead.

"Daddy, what would you think if I quit my soccer team?" Charlotte asked. She still wasn't sure it was okay.

Tim's face exploded into a smile. "I would think, without question, that is the very best news I've heard all day."

"I get it now," Hank said. "You're all a bunch of losers and you deserve each other."

"Hank, honey," Trissy said. "Would you mind taking the next lightning bolt to hell?"

"Need any help carrying out your things?" Tim asked.

If Hank heard the offer he didn't say. He grabbed his jacket and stormed out of the house. The next flash of lightning illuminated his hunched departure.

forty-seven

Winslow opened the van door. "No, I will not cancel."

Vicki started to speak, but Winslow cut her off.

"Do not say another word. I will not have this discussion with my wife. We practice in the rain."

He slammed the van door. The rain pelted him with hard drops. For a moment he thought it was hail. No. It could not be hail. He would not let it be hail. He pulled up the hood of his slicker, opened the back door of the van, yanked out the large net ball bag, and threw it over his shoulder.

"Dinah," he called. "Get out."

He could hear the muffled noise of Vicki telling Dinah not to go. Then the passenger door glided open. Dinah climbed out, leaving her crutch behind.

Vicki ran after her. She shoved a Winslow West Soccer-Plex baseball cap on Dinah's head. "It's hailing," she yelled at Winslow. "Are you insane?"

"Dinah, get the cones."

Dinah leaned on the van as she made her way to the

back. Keeping her weight on her good foot, she lifted out the tall stack of orange cones.

"This is ridiculous," Vicki screamed.

"We do not cancel practice because of rain," Winslow screamed back.

The wind whipped up, blowing Dinah's cap off. Dinah put down the cones to run after it.

"Forget your hat," Winslow yelled. "Let's go." He lurched forward, toward the field.

Drenched, Dinah hopped behind him.

Shelby was already there. So was Mary Ann Hunter, with her father. She clung close to him, trying to stay beneath his small umbrella.

"It was hailing a minute ago," her father said.

"And there were glaciers in New Jersey in the ice age. But there are no glaciers here now, are there?"

"They're talking about thunderstorms all afternoon," Mary Ann's father told him.

"Thank you. I'll be sure to deal with the future when it arrives."

A figure ran up the hill. Winslow turned to see who it was. "Bailey," he said, cheering up a bit. "Where is your slicker? Saving it for a sunny day?"

"I forgot it," Bailey said.

Winslow smiled. Now there was a little trooper.

They heard a distant rumble

"What was that?" Mary Ann asked.

Winslow walked away and started setting up the cones.

Another rumble followed, distant but distinct.

"Winslow," Mary Ann's father called over. "What do you say we cancel?"

Winslow struggled to ignore the use of the pronoun *we* and continued setting up the cones in perfect lines.

At the third rumble, Dinah hopped over to him to tell him that Mary Ann was crying.

He glanced over at the irritating sight of the whimpering child.

"I'm taking her home," the father said.

"She is not dismissed," Winslow said. "No one is dismissed." He shouted to be heard over the thunder. "No one is to leave until she is officially dismissed."

Winslow glanced up at the sky, rain streaking down his face. There was no flash of lightning. There was no reason practice shouldn't go on.

A bright blue Gortex track suit ran toward him. Barbie waved her arms, calling for Bailey.

"Tell your mother practice is not canceled," Winslow said. "Tell her the thunder is still miles away."

Bailey ran to tell her mother.

Another mother approached, her tan poncho plastered to her body. The poncho waved its arms wildly. The mother inside sounded hysterical as she screamed something half audible about running off the field.

Winslow yelled, to be sure he would be heard. "You idiot! This is a soccer practice, not a picnic. Look up. Do you see any lightning? Or are you so stupid that you don't know where to look?"

. The poncho marched closer, close enough so he could hear the voice. "Dinah, get over here now."

"Vicki. Sorry. I didn't realize it was you."

"Dinah," Vicki yelled. Her cheeks were wet, and red as her hair. "Get in the car now."

"Vicki. Practice is not canceled."

"Yes it is. Dinah!" she shouted, and motioned for her daughter to come.

Dinah made her way as fast as she could. Vicki hustled them to the parking lot. Bailey and Shelby ran alongside. When they caught up to Barbie, she ran with them too.

"Practice is not canceled," Winslow raged into the wind as he watched them all disappear.

The first bolt of lightning struck as he stood alone, at the top of the rise. He had no memory of what happened next.

When he opened his eyes, he was on his back on a gurney listening to a nurse explain to an aide how a bolt of lightning had hit the ground and bounced up through someone's foot.

The nurse noticed he was awake, and asked him to tell her his name.

"Don't you know who I am?" Winslow asked.

"That's good," she said. "At least he can talk."

His left foot was wrapped in a bandage, and even though he was groggy from the painkillers they'd given him, he could still make out a distinct throbbing.

"What happened?" he asked.

"You're very lucky," the nurse said. "All you did was lose a toe. Your little toe. That's all you're missing. Are you a lucky man or what?"

But he was already gone, passed out in a dream, where he remained for the next twenty-seven hours.

forty-eight

As far as Roy knew, his only crime was being late for dinner. He stared at the brick of food on the plate in front of him. He knew it was meat loaf, from the shape. But even though he picked at it from every angle, his fork couldn't penetrate.

He saw the pile of papers on the table. Of course Maura would pretend she'd just forgotten to put them away—a dozen computer print-outs of homes in Chestnut Heights, Sandy Creek, and Grover, and estimates from four different movers.

Maura slammed the cabinet door shut to get his attention. "Gerri Picker called," she snapped. "What the hell does she want?"

Roy shrugged. "Maybe she finally got the call from Winslow saying he was moving Nadine up to his team."

"You are hopeless," Maura said. She turned on the garbage disposal.

Roy didn't know what was in the pipes but it sounded like teeth being ground to dust. He took advantage of the noise and went to the refrigerator. He pulled a piece of cheese off an antipasto plate she'd put together and forgotten to throw at him.

She swung around. "What are you doing?"

He gulped the cheese. "I'm going to call Gerri."

"While you're on the phone, why don't you tell her I said she can go to hell."

Roy escaped to the family room, where the TV was playing to no one. He turned it off and dialed.

"Thanks for getting back to me, Roy," Gerri said.

"No problem. What's up? Did Winslow call you about Nadine?"

"It's not about Nadine. I'm calling because I have a favor to ask."

"What is it?"

"I need to find a new coach for the Asteroids," Gerri said. "I'm stepping down. You'd make a great coach, Roy. I really hope you'll agree to do this."

"Me? I can't. I'm pretty sure Nadine is not going to be on the team that much longer. You should ask someone else. Like Peggy Ann. She would do it. Why are you stepping down anyway?"

"Peggy Ann can't do it, either. Peggy Ann and I are going to be Power parents."

"What?"

"I know. I was surprised too," Gerri said. "Winslow called me as soon as he got home from the hospital. You heard about his toe, right?"

It happened now and then. Roy got a feeling of unreality, like he wasn't really there—like he was high up in the sky, watching a movie about someone who looked exactly liked him, a movie that didn't make any sense.

"Roy?" Gerri said.

He crashed back to earth. "What?"

"Did you hear about Winslow's toe?"

"What did you say about you and Peggy Ann?" Roy asked.

"I know players don't normally move this late in the season. But a couple of kids left the Power unexpectedly." Gerri lowered her voice. "I don't actually know if they left voluntarily, or if they were asked to leave. All I know is Winslow called and asked if Meredith could join the team. And he called Peggy Ann too. I hate to do this to the Asteroids, taking away two of their best players and their coach, but it's an emergency. Winslow's got the Power playing in the big exhibition game at the opening of the Soccer-Plex. And Meredith's wanted to be on his team forever. You can understand, right? I couldn't say no."

Roy could understand. But he couldn't speak.

"I know Nadine wants it too, Roy," Gerri said. "I know she wants it bad. And I want you to know, I spoke to Winslow about it. Because he and I both think she's got a lot of talent. Plus she's been working so hard to move up. And not for nothing, you'll be happy to know. Winslow told me she has an excellent chance of being picked for the team next year. A really excellent chance."

"Next year," Roy said.

"Obviously right now the Asteroids need her more than ever. And they also need a socca-rific coach. Frankly, Roy, I can't think of anyone better than you."

He figured with ten girls left on the team, he must be the tenth person she called.

"I got to go," Roy said.

"Can you do it, Roy? Can you help me out here?"

"I got to go," Roy said again, and he slammed down the phone.

forty-nine

What?" Roy snapped when the phone rang again.

"Roy?" It was Vicki. "Is that you?"

He wondered how she had the nerve. "Yeah, it's me."

"Thank God," Vicki said. "Roy, we've got an emergency at the Soccer-Plex."

"Why don't you call Gerri and see if she can help you out."

Vicki didn't understand. "It's a plumbing problem, Roy." Her tone turned frantic. "Look, I don't know what to do. I told Winslow he should delay the opening. Between his foot and everything else, everyone would understand. I told him the world won't end if we wait another week for the opening. But he won't listen to me. He's not himself, Roy," she added quietly.

That got Roy's attention. Vicki wasn't the type to say a word against her husband. At least not to someone like him.

"He won't listen to the doctor, either. The doctor told him he has to keep off his foot for one more week. But he won't stay in bed. The doctor said I have to make him stay in bed. But what am I supposed to do? Tie him down?"

"What's the problem?" Roy asked.

"You mean besides the fact that Winslow nearly got Dinah killed by lightning? Because it could have been her who got hit, you know. And the doctor said if it had been her, she'd be dead."

"What's the problem with the plumbing?"

"I don't know. Parker called and said half of the toilets aren't flushing. Parker thinks it's not a big deal. He says we should go ahead with the opening anyway. He says half the toilets are enough. But when Winslow heard that, he freaked. Now Parker and Winslow aren't talking, Winslow and I aren't talking. I'm so mad at him," she said. "The toilets, Roy. They're not flushing."

"I can fix them," he said.

"Oh, my God. Thank you."

"It's okay."

"No, it's not. You are so good," Vicki said, and then very quietly she started to cry. "Winslow doesn't deserve you," she said sniffling back her tears. "You know what that bastard had the nerve to say?"

Roy stayed perfectly still. "No."

"He said if you didn't fix the toilets tonight he'd call every paper in town and tell them you are the worst plumber in the state of New Jersey. And possibly in the country."

"He said that?"

"It's not him talking really," Vicki said, sensing that sharing this might have been a mistake. "It's the painkillers talking. And the stress of the Soccer-Plex opening. And the toe. Did you know the toe he lost is on his kicking foot?"

"Yeah."

"So don't pay attention to what he said. He's not himself."

"Okay."

"I can come over right now and bring you the keys to the Soccer-Plex," Vicki offered. "That way you won't even have to see him. Would that be okay?"

"Sure," said Roy.

"Thanks, Roy. You're the best. I'm leaving now."

When Vicki came over, Maura was at the dining room table studying her real estate tear sheets. She didn't even look up. But Vicki didn't notice. She handed over the keys and left.

Maura started in on him again. "If we use this mover," she waved one of the brochures, "they'll pack and unpack everything for us. All we have to do is just show up in the new house and it will all be done. This one is cheaper." She waved a brochure in front of his face. "But we'll have to do all the packing ourselves."

At least at the Soccer-Plex he'd get some peace.

Roy was standing in the middle of the turf, just enjoying the quiet, when the door marked "Authorized Personnel Only" opened, and the two of them walked out.

Given what Vicki had told him, Roy wasn't sure if Parker still counted as authorized. But he knew for sure the woman wasn't.

He recognized her right away, the one whose shoes he'd stomped on in the bathroom a couple of weeks ago. Only this time she wasn't lying down on any floor. This time she was standing up, walking toward him with an odd look on her face.

"Roy," Parker said. "I didn't expect you to get here so fast. Thank you so much for taking care of the toilets."

Parker was polite, nervous, like he'd just been caught.

Roy took another look at the woman. Her cheeks were flushed. She made an effort to fix her hair, but it was in a knot and she couldn't quite shift it back into place.

Roy felt a twinge of pity for her. He couldn't even say why.

"Linda," Parker said, "do you want to go freshen up? I can wait a minute for you if you do."

Linda gave another try at patting down her hair, then turned and hurried toward the bathroom.

"Don't flush the toilet," Roy called after her.

"I have a little favor to ask you," Parker said as soon as she was gone.

Suddenly, everyone wanted a favor. Roy couldn't wait to hear what this one was.

"Could you keep it between the two of us that you saw me here tonight?"

"How come?" Roy asked. "Aren't you allowed to be here anymore?"

Parker smiled. "Here, yes. With her, no. In there with her"—he pointed to the room they'd just exited—"never."

"Why?" Roy asked. "What's in there?"

"Nothing important," Parker said, laughing. "Just the fans. Just the big blowers. Just what keeps the bubble inflated." He laughed again.

Roy laughed too, but as he laughed he thought about Winslow dangling the team in front of him again and again, and then yanking it away every time.

"How big are the fans that keep up the bubble?" Roy asked, as if he were just curious.

"Huge," Parker said. "They are mammoth, massive, noisy machines."

"Can I see?" Roy knew there was no way Parker could say no to him now. "I always wondered what they looked like."

"Certainly," Parker said. "We're friends, right?"

Roy nodded, and tried not to look as excited as he felt.

The alarm box was on the wall next to the steel door. Roy watched carefully as Parker pressed in the five numbers. The alarm beeped, disarmed, and Parker opened the door.

Roy followed him inside, repeating the numbers in his head until they were stuck in his brain.

Parker was filled with nervous energy and was happy to use it up giving Roy a tour.

"These two fans keep the vault inflated. These two back-ups are purely for emergencies. They have their own generator, over there. So if the primary blowers go down for any reason, the backup generator fires up and the backup blowers immediately kick in."

"Mind my asking the appeal of using this place as a bachelor pad?" Roy asked. "It's kind of noisy," he yelled. "Isn't it?"

Parker smiled and came closer to share his little secret. "It's like a giant vibration chamber." He gestured to the floor. "Try it. Lie down, right there, and you'll see what I mean." He winked. "I've got to go have a word with Linda. I think she was a bit upset you discovered us here. Would you mind shutting the lights and the door? When you're done, that is."

"No problem," Roy said.

Parker left and Roy stood perfectly still. The fans pulsed, sending tremors through his body. The blowers were huge, so loud and strong he didn't have to touch the walls or lie on the floor to feel their power. The air vibrated. Or was it just his racing heart?

He took one last look at what he'd noticed right away, the way the blowers were connected to a complicated instrument panel with rows of gauges he knew Parker checked every day. But despite the complex system, it all boiled down to two switches and a couple of plugs in the wall. He was no electrician, but this was something even a plumber could figure out.

The door opened a crack. "All done?" Parker asked.

"Yup."

"Would you mind bringing out my sleeping bag, then?"

Another favor. Roy scooped the sleeping bag off the floor.

"How did Winslow sound when he called about the toilets?" Parker asked.

"I spoke to Vicki," Roy said. "Why?"

"No reason," Parker said. "I was just wondering. He was a bit stressed when I spoke to him. Sounded like it wouldn't take much to send him over the edge, if you know what I mean." Parker winked.

Roy wasn't a religious man, but he knew when he was being given a sign.

fifty

The banners above the entrance to the Soccer-Plex snapped and buckled in the breeze.

One advertised a supermarket. Another touted a bank. Xavier, the physical therapist, had ponied up for one of his own, as had the real estate firm that had found Winslow the land on which he'd built his dream.

Winslow had tried to get a professional soccer team to hang a banner. But none of the blithering idiots he had gotten on the phone had the power to make a decision. Apparently none of them knew who he was.

But that was all right. That was going to change. It wouldn't be long before every one of those idiots, whose names he'd written down and filed away, would regret every word that they'd said.

All that mattered now was that the opening go as planned— as it had been planned for years.

Of course small adjustments were to be expected. Like Parker's role, for example. It had been Parker who was supposed to come tonight, to take the contractors on their final walk-through. But he and Parker weren't speaking now. So here he was, as usual, doing everything himself.

That was all right. This was just a minor irritant. After all, it was best that he found out now about Parker's insubordinate attitude. He didn't need disloyal baggage weighing him down as he made his final ascent to the top.

He assembled the contractors in the lobby: the electrician, the tile man, the plumber, the landscape crew. He even got a fireman to show up, in uniform. Of course that wasn't hard to accomplish. The fireman had been badgering him for months to start up a new team of Under Seven girls next year, when the fireman's daughter would become eligible to play.

Actually, it wasn't a bad idea to start a new team. He'd learned quite a bit from his experiment with the Power. But the girls had reached an age when they just weren't working as hard as they used to. They were getting soft. Full of complaints. It was time to move on. Because imagine what he could accomplish if he took everything he'd learned from the girls on the Power and applied it to two dozen fresh legs.

Once the last of the contractors arrived, he greeted them all. After giving the promised tour, he singled out each workman in turn for praise, ticking off the list in his head as he went.

His limp was quite pronounced, and the pain more than a little intense, but everyone knew better than to mention it.

He checked the lights, the fans, and the toilets, smiling at Roy when they flushed hard and with immediate recovery. He checked the sound system, the scoreboard, the alarm, the heating system, the cooling system, the phones in the office, and the phones in the store. He even dragged his lame foot along the checkerboard café floor, to point out the tiles, the fresh paint on the walls, and the soda machines, which were fully stocked with sports drinks and vitamin water.

Sean, testing the deep fryer, offered the contractors some fries. He knew they had no idea the free food was not a sign of gratitude and generosity, but rather a way to make sure the oil wasn't rancid, the fryer wasn't broken, and the ketchup dispensers didn't stick.

Tomorrow everything would be perfect.

Winslow waited a decent interval, giving the men enough time to sample a few fries, but not enough so that they'd settle comfortably into their seats at the small café tables. Then he called them to attention.

"Before I hand these out"—he waved a stack of checks in the air—"I want to personally thank each and every one of you, and to say that tomorrow's opening doesn't belong to me. It belongs to all of us."

"What time does it start?" the tile guy asked.

"I will arrive at eight o'clock, as will the Power. Vicki will join us later." He didn't know what made him share that piece of wishful thinking. In fact, Vicki's parting words when he left the house had been something to the effect that she'd never step into the Soccer-Plex as long as he was alive.

"I am expecting a good show from the media. I am very optimistic that channels four, seven, nine and eleven will all be here when the exhibition game begins."

The toe that wasn't there began throbbing again. He resisted the temptation to rip off his sock and check to be sure it hadn't grown back. His hands squeezed the top of one of the plastic chairs until the wave of phantom pain had passed.

"Of course the *Mountain Ridge Times* will be here, and it is my intention to ask the photographer to take a group shot of all of you, the best workmen in America."

There were smiles, and handshakes, wishes of good luck, and the handing out of checks. Then he sent them on their happy way. The only one who lingered was—no surprise— the plumber.

"Not now, Roy," Winslow said, waving him off. And then, too quietly to be heard, he muttered, "Not ever."

The cleanup crew arrived on time to give the Plex its pre-opening cleaning. At eleven the cleaners left. Finally, Winslow was alone.

He took one last foot-dragging walk around his creation and smiled, thinking about tomorrow, when he would introduce his empire to the world. Then he turned off the lights, closed the door, limped to the car, and drove himself home. Thankfully, the missing toe was on his left foot. At least he could still drive.

As soon as he walked in the house he saw that Vicki had made up the couch for him to sleep on. The couch—tonight— the night before the biggest day of his life. Damn her.

He started up the stairs to claim his rightful place but his foot began to throb so he changed his mind. He couldn't risk irritating it now.

He was too tired to change, so he climbed under the thin blanket fully dressed and fell asleep while rehearsing the welcome speech he had written for this occasion well over a decade ago.

fifty-one

It wasn't yet dawn when Roy arrived at the Soccer-Plex. He had plenty of time, but still he worked fast, just in case.

It took less than half a minute to disable the alarm. A few minutes more and both blowers were shut down. It took longer than he expected for the backup generator to click on. But as soon as it did, he quickly disconnected that too.

He estimated that with the power cut, and both emergency exit doors open, deflation would still take too long. So to hasten things, he'd brought along insurance—three extension cords, a ladder, and his trusty electric saw.

The white fabric that covered the bubble was like a thick tough skin, but the electric saw sliced through it like it was air. Roy had planned it all beforehand, and he'd worked it out just right. Ten three-foot slits at even intervals did the trick.

At first, the escaping air leaked out in a gentle hiss, but by the time he cut the last slit in the white skin the hiss had turned into a low roar.

He did not rush. Mistakes happened to people who worked too fast. He packed up his tools, took a careful look around to make sure he hadn't left anything behind, and only then, once he was sure that all his belongings were put away, did he finally run as fast as he could to his car.

By the time he pulled into his driveway his damp palms had turned the steering wheel wet. He wiped his hands on his pants as he walked into the house. Then he crept up to his room, got out of his clothes, and slipped into bed.

His alarm went off at seven. He let the radio wake Maura so that she would think she was the one who had gotten up first.

"Clouds with a chance of rain," the weatherman said.

Maura grumbled, rolled over, turned off the alarm, and gave him a shove. "Roy. Get up."

"Huh?" He made sure to sound groggy.

"It's time to get up," Maura said. She checked the clock. "We got to get to the Soccer-Plex soon. Come on, Roy. Get up."

"I'm up. I'm up." He swung his legs around to the floor. "I was just in the middle of a dream." He rubbed his eyes as if they were sticky with sleep.

"What kind of dream?" Maura took dreams very seriously.

"I dreamed we moved to Chestnut Heights."

Maura nodded. "See? It's a sign that it's meant to be. I'm telling you, Roy, we could be very happy in Chestnut Heights."

"I got to admit it," Roy said. "I think you're right."

Maura shot him a loving smile. Roy shuffled off to the shower to get ready for the day.

When they arrived at the Soccer-Plex, a little after nine, there were four police cars, six fire engines, news crews from three major networks, and over a hundred people, craning their necks from behind police tape, for a good look at the ragged remains of Winslow West's deflated dream.

fifty-two

The first hint that it wasn't a casual business lunch was the restaurant Roxanne picked. Like all PC&B muckety-mucks, Roxanne usually ate lunch at the Italian place on the corner, where the owner greeted her by name and gave her the best table.

Today, Roxanne had asked Annie to meet her downtown, at a restaurant in the meatpacking district, where she was treated like any other intruder. She made a minimal amount of small talk and then got to the point: "Did Linda tell you what happened with Blaine?"

"Yes," Annie said. "It sounds awful. Will he be in rehab long?"

"Who knows?" Roxanne said. "Who cares? He's never coming back. I'm trying to forget he ever happened."

She took a big bite of her porterhouse steak and concentrated on chewing, as if that would take away the nasty aftertaste of the memory Blaine had left behind. She pushed the large mound of garlic mashed potatoes into the pool of her steak's bloody drippings and put down her fork.

"The problem isn't that Blaine's gone. Blaine was a bust from the beginning. Proxo couldn't stand him. Luckily I found them someone they love. Of course, they'll never love anyone as much as they loved you. They didn't even love *you* as much as they now think they loved you. You've become a legend over there."

"That won't last forever," Annie said.

"I know," Roxanne agreed.

"So if Proxo's happy, what's the problem?"

"The problem is I'm not happy," Roxanne said. "Since you left I've had the displeasure of personally discovering the staggering number of young people now working at PC&B who have absolutely no idea what they're doing."

"They just need some mentoring," Annie said. "That's all."

"Is that what you call it?" Roxanne asked. "They hound me with questions all day long. Ridiculous, inane questions. At first I didn't understand what was going on. It seemed like the staff got stupid overnight. Finally, someone explained it to me. It was the young guy with the blond hair and the twitch in his eye. Do you know the one I mean?"

"I had a twitch in my eye," Annie said, because suddenly she realized she didn't have it anymore. Her twitch was gone.

"I know," Roxanne said. "So anyway, the guy with the twitch—"

"His name is Jeffrey," Annie said.

"Right. So Jeffrey told me he used to go to you whenever he needed advice. He told me everyone did. Now that you're gone, he asked if he could come to me. Of course I said no. Meanwhile I'm thinking, how was everyone asking you for advice when you were in Connecticut all week?"

"A lot of them called me at night," Annie said. "Once they got home."

"That must have driven you crazy," Roxanne said.

"I didn't really mind it. There wasn't much to do in that hotel room. Actually, it was my favorite part of the day."

"Well, it's not my favorite part. All that carrying on. I feel like I'm in a bad horror movie. I told HR to call a meeting and explain that I am unavailable by phone or email for their stupid questions. So now they're sending me text messages. Do I look even mildly sympathetic to you? Don't they understand they're acting like annoying children and I am not their mommy who loves them no matter what? Did they treat you like you were their mommy, Annie? Is that what was going on?"

"I listened to them. That's all."

"See, that's the difference between us right there. If I'm going to listen to someone, it's going to be someone who pays me. I'll listen to clients. That's my limit. I want you to come back."

"I can't," Annie said.

"Look, we're sorry for how we treated you. How much more plainly can I say it? We made a bad decision. We have a huge signing bonus for you, to show our remorse. We also have a seat at the partners' table. No waiting, Annie. Come back and you're in. Done deal."

"The timing isn't good," Annie said. "I just got an opportunity to go into business with my husband."

"Are you nuts? Do you want to ruin your career and your marriage at the same time? That's the worst idea I've ever heard. Don't do it, Annie. Come back and work with us. Do you want part-time? We can do part-time. You want to come in at nine and leave at four thirty? We can do that."

"That's not part-time," Annie said. "That's just civilized."

"I was kidding. Tell me how many hours a day you want to work and we'll make it happen."

Annie felt a twinge. She knew she was being expertly roped in. Still—while she didn't agree that her marriage was in danger of collapsing if she and Tim worked together, she didn't think it would be the best thing for them either.

"A lot has changed since you left PC&B," Roxanne went on. "You're probably not aware of this, but we have a new mission. Crawford and Biblow have decided they want to be leaders in the flexibility-in-the-workplace movement. They're a hundred percent committed to this. We see you as a role model, Annie. We want you back. What will it take to get you to say yes?"

Annie hadn't come to lunch with a plan, but if she had, it certainly wouldn't have been this. Was it possible she could make the job into something she actually wanted to do?

"Four days a week," Annie said, after a moment. "Nine thirty to two. No travel. No client contact. I do staff development and mentoring. Nothing else."

Roxanne pushed away her plate and sucked the little liquid left in her glass through her straw. "I think we can live with that. Except for the four-day-a-week thing."

"I understand," Annie said. "And if I think of anyone who'd be right for the job I'll let you know."

"Okay," Roxanne said. "We'll try it. Four days a week for six months. Then we revaluate."

"You have to give it a year," Annie said. "Six months is too soon to know."

"Okay," Roxanne said. "I'll commit to a year. Is it a deal?"

Annie wasn't done dreaming. "I'm just not sure you

can make it worth my time financially. I do have that other opportunity."

"Name your number, Annie. I'll take it back to Biblow and Crawford this afternoon and see what they say."

Annie thought of the highest number she could reasonably ask for. She tripled it and said it out loud.

Roxanne winced and asked for the check. While she waited for it to come, she said nothing. When it finally came, she signed it and looked Annie in the eye. "Is that really your number?"

Annie forced herself to sound confident. "Yes."

"Okay. I think I can get Biblow and Crawford to go for it."

And for once Annie knew she hadn't undervalued herself.

As they walked out of the restaurant, Roxanne promised to get back to her by the end of the day.

"But I have to ask you, Annie," she said. "What did you do? You didn't used to be this tough. What's your secret? Did you enroll in some kind of program?"

"No," Annie said. "I just picked up a few things on the sidelines."

fifty-three

THE DEMONS BULLETIN #1
March 15th

Welcome to all players and parents!! It is indeed an honor for me to be coaching my new team, the Winslow West Demons, the Future Finest Team of Soccer Players in the History of Soccer!!!!!!!!!!!!

Let me begin by directly addressing several rumors I understand have arisen on the sidelines:

Rumor Number One: Did I deflate my own Soccer-Plex?

NO! This spurious falsehood is completely erroneous and untrue. While the police have not yet located the culprit of this terrorist act, it is my opinion that the damage to the Winslow West Soccer-Plex was perpetrated by a competitor who wished to hurt both me, and my new and future players.

Rumor Number Two: Have I been ejected from the League?

NO! This groundless falsehood is completely unfounded. The decision to leave the League was solely my own. I did so because of my deep disappointment in the League's complete lack of support and concern for myself and my players in the day and days directly following the collapse of the Winslow West Soccer-Plex.

Rumor Number Three: Have I been banned from participation in all organized leagues this spring?

NO! This rumor could not be further from the truth. I have chosen our orphan status for the simple reason that it affords us the ability to train for several months with no distractions or interference from players, trainers, or team managers who do not share my philosophy of success!

Onward and Upward Update: Beginning next week I will be arranging weekend scrimmages with high-level teams of Under Eight girls, most likely from Pennsylvania, Delaware, or Maryland. While this will mean some travel, it will also mean that when we do join a league in September, the girls will be more prepared than any other team in their age group in the history of time.

Safety Update: As most of you know, Player Safety has always been my Paramount Concern. Anyone who doubts this has only to count my remaining toes. In case anyone has been away, or dead, and has not heard, I lost one of my toes while protecting the players on my former team, the ill-fated Power. While I would most certainly be willing to lose another toe to protect one of my new players, I am well aware that I have thirteen new players and only nine remaining toes.

Therefore, I am happy to report that Fireman Fred, our intrepid team manager, has agreed to be Safety Director for the Fort West Soccer-Plex, my new indoor soccer facility, which will open next spring in nearby Chestnut Heights!!!!

Please see Firemen Fred if you have any suggestions for

lyrics or tunes for the "Fort West Battle Cry," which I am currently developing.

Soccer Trainer Fraud Update: While the Winslow West Soccer-Plex Organization has been disbanded, it has come to my attention that several trainers are still representing themselves as authorized Winslow West Trainers. To avoid confusion with people pretending to be associated with me, I am asking all members of the Winslow West Demons and their families to refrain from interacting in any way at any time with any former trainer previously under my employ.

Also, due to the fact that several members of the team formerly known as the Power have become disgruntled and bitter, I am also asking all Winslow West Demons and their families to refrain from interacting with any former members or family members of the team formerly known as the Power, for as long as we all shall live.

Change of Address Update: Please note my new Mountain Ridge address: 421 Lark Street, Apartment 1B. Also, please be aware that any messages left at my former home phone will not be forwarded to me. Ever.

I look forward to seeing all of you at the Olympic Stadium in roughly thirteen years time!!

Good Luck and See You at the Fort—from Winslow West!!!!!!!

fifty-four

The night was clear, but to be on the safe side, Trissy had rented a tent. With small white lights strung around its perimeter, the large tent gave the backyard the look of a state fair.

The evening was unusually warm. Heaters were arranged on the patio to keep away the spring chill, but they proved unnecessary. A small jazz ensemble played under a tree before a cluster of people sitting in forest green Adirondack chairs. A clown circulated, making balloon animals for young children. There was a line waiting for a session with a fortune-teller, whose table was set up beside the bar.

Tim, Annie, and Trissy watched, smiling. The night was perfect.

It had been Trissy's idea to host the party, a celebration to mark the end of a week of meetings Tim had held with managers from all the surviving satellites. It was Annie's idea to make it an even bigger event, opening it up to friends, neighbors, and the press. After all, she advised, this was a fresh start for Trissy and Tim's reinvented company, the newly dubbed Happy Holidays, and that was something worth celebrating.

Tim had begun the week with an announcement to the managers that he was committed to a no-job-cuts policy. The branch managers met his words with cheers and applause. Staff loyalty had been an issue for Hank, but it was not going to be a problem for Tim.

Trissy had relented, joining the company as codirector and head of marketing, promotion, and publicity. She was a woman on a mission now, determined to do anything to make Happy Holidays succeed, even going so far as to allow Hank to stay on. The Tortola hotel had turned out to be a good business opportunity. For now, Hank was in charge of that project. His contract, renewable month to month, specified that he would report daily to Tim. But all contract negotiations and any termination proceeding would be handled by Trissy.

Annie looked past the rented hot-dog cart and saw Charlotte pushing a soccer ball with the toe of her shoe as she wandered through the crowd. She looked bored.

Annie joined her. "Want to go kick around the ball?" she asked.

"Sure," Charlotte said.

They left the tented area and walked across the side yard to the park that abutted Trissy's property. Annie kicked the ball. It veered off into some bushes. Charlotte didn't mind. She scrambled under the bushes to get it, and then booted it back.

It wasn't long before the sound of the ball and their laughter drew more kids to the field. Tim took a break from mingling and snuck over too, stealing the ball away from Charlotte before she even knew he was there.

More adults wandered over, drawn in by the sound of the

pickup game. Before long there were enough people to make up two teams. Annie started organizing them—and when it was clear it was the will of the majority, she arranged them so that it was children against adults.

When Trissy came upon thirty of her guests enjoying a raucous game of soccer, she asked her sons to put up the goals, which had been lying on their sides at the back of her yard unused for months. Once the goals were set up, her boys ran inside to see if they could find cleats that still fit.

"I don't believe it," Trissy said to Annie, who had stepped out of the game to let another parent in. "My kids haven't wanted to play soccer in years."

"We need a ref," someone called out to the crowd.

"I'll do it," Trissy said. "Anybody have a whistle?"

No one did, but it didn't matter. There were few disputes, none of them serious.

At half past seven, the caterer came over to let Trissy know he was putting out dinner.

"We should do this every week," she said as she broke up the game. "We could organize it for Sundays, before the travel teams take over the fields. Wouldn't that be great? We could have a mother/daughter league, a father/son league, or we could mix it up—have fathers and daughters and mothers and sons. Want to have a meeting to discuss it—the first ever Mountain Ridge Caregiver/Caregetter League? It's a great idea, right?" Trissy herded the players back to the tent.

"Would we need to have previous experience to play?" a mother asked.

"Definitely not," Trissy said. "How about it? Annie? Tim? You guys want to be the first to join?"

Annie, Tim, and Charlotte looked at each other and smiled.

"No thanks," Annie said.

"We're going to pass on that," Tim said.

"We're not all that interested in organized soccer," Charlotte said.

Charlotte walked to the far end of the field where they'd been playing, and placed her foot on top of the ball to steady it. "Is this a regulation-sized field?" she called to her aunt.

"It is," Trissy said.

Charlotte tucked her toe under the ball, ready to kick.

"Oh honey, you're way too far back," Trissy called over. "I don't even think Winslow could have scored from there. And I'm talking about when he had all his toes."

"It doesn't matter," Annie said.

"She's just having fun," Tim explained.

Charlotte stared at the ball, backed up, and kicked. Her foot connected perfectly.

The crowd watched as the soccer ball took off in a high arc. It soared through the twilight sky, and descended.

Goal.

about the author

I was standing on the sidelines, minding my own business, when it hit me. Not a ball, but a thought that eventually grew into this novel.

The catalyst was a mom. Let me be clear: she was a smart, kind, and totally reasonable mom. She just happened to be the "anti-rage rep" for our daughter's team. Yes, our league required every team to have one: an "anti-rage rep," responsible for policing parents so none of us got out of line.

We were a particularly obedient group, not the type to yell out "Get her!" or "Attack!" We cheered politely and clapped briefly at all the appropriate moments. But not every team was as well trained.

The anti-rage rep mom pulled a handful of red lollipops out of her pocket and told me her great idea. Any parent who yelled too loud would be given a lollipop to suck on. What a plan! You might get mad at someone who asked you to zip it, but who could get mad at someone who smiles as she hands you a lollipop? And just try yelling "Kill her" with an all-day sucker in your mouth!

On the field, twenty-two girls who had trained hard, eaten right, and slept well played on like miniprofessionals. Off the field, two dozen parents stood with cherry red lips and sticky fingers, a lollipop stuck in every mouth.

And it struck me—something was wrong with this picture. While coaches barked complex commands at our hardworking eight-year-olds who complied at once, we—the grown-ups—stood with our mouths plugged with lollipops to make sure we behaved. What would be next? Would we get Play-Doh to keep our hands busy? While our daughters ate carefully measured portions of fruit at halftime, would we get a Baggie of animal crackers and be admonished not to eat the heads off first?

What would happen if someone unfamiliar with this world were suddenly plunked down in our midst, given a lollipop, and told not to cheer? Would she think we were all nuts? Were we all nuts?

So the character of Annie was born, a woman surprised to find herself booted out of her demanding job and sidelined to a soccer field rife with customs she did not understand.

Unlike Annie, I have never been a change management specialist. But during my years working as a movie executive, searching for books, plays, treatments, haikus, graffiti—anything that might be nurtured into a good movie—I met more than a few people whose job, like Annie's, threatened to swallow them alive.

I never did figure out why we were such obedient suckers. But I sure did enjoy what grew out of that sticky snack—going on a journey with Annie, who finally understands that the disparate worlds many moms straddle, crazy work and crazy home, are not really different at all. And in the end, all anyone is trying to do is find her way.

Nancy Star

FIVE WARNING SIGNS THAT YOUR KID'S COACH IS CRAZY:

1 Believes getting hit by a little bit of lightning can be a good thing for increasing speed and endurance

2 Instructs all players to count Beckhams jumping over a fence, at bedtime, to increase probability of having soccer dreams

3 Makes any player whose shoelaces become untied during a game attend intensive all-day workshop on knotting techniques, with special sessions on tying for speed, and on the pitfalls of the granny knot

4 Uses a ball pump as a key chain

5 Adapts "The Creed of the United States Marines" as the "Team Creed," requiring all players to recite the creed every day, upon awakening, substituting the word *ball* for the word *rifle* (see below)

This is my ~~rifle~~ ball. There are many like it, but this one is mine. My ~~rifle~~ ball is my best friend. It is my life. I must master it as I must master my life. My ~~rifle~~ ball, without me, is useless. Without my ~~rifle~~ ball, I am useless. I must fire my ~~rifle~~ ball true.